THE EXPLOITS OF
BRIGADIER GERARD

Brigadier Etienne Gerard is a Hussar in the French Army, in Napoleon's service. He's a vain man, believing in his own superiority in many things: being the bravest soldier, the greatest swordsman, and most gallant lover in all France. Perhaps he is. Gerard's missions, on behalf of Napoleon, are numerous and dangerous, and include avoiding capture by marauding Russian and Prussian troops, the threat of certain death by the British and his escape from imprisonment in Dartmoor. For Brigadier Etienne Gerard, wherever his mission takes him — England, Germany, Poland or France — honour and glory are all.

Books by Sir Arthur Conan Doyle
Published by The House of Ulverscroft:

A STUDY IN SCARLET

THE SIGN OF FOUR

THE ADVENTURES OF
SHERLOCK HOLMES

MEMOIRS OF SHERLOCK HOLMES

THE HOUND OF THE BASKERVILLES

THE RETURN OF SHERLOCK HOLMES

THE VALLEY OF FEAR

HIS LAST BOW

THE CASE BOOK OF
SHERLOCK HOLMES

SIR ARTHUR CONAN DOYLE

THE EXPLOITS
OF
BRIGADIER GERARD

Complete and Unabridged

ULVERSCROFT
Leicester

First published in Great Britain in 1896

This Large Print Edition
published 2013

A catalogue record for this book is available
from the British Library.

ISBN 978–1–4448–1603–7

Published by
F. A. Thorpe (Publishing)
Anstey, Leicestershire

Set by Words & Graphics Ltd.
Anstey, Leicestershire
Printed and bound in Great Britain by
T. J. International Ltd., Padstow, Cornwall

This book is printed on acid-free paper

Contents

1

How the Brigadier Came
to the Castle of Gloom

You do very well, my friends, to treat me with some little reverence, for in honouring me you are honouring both France and yourselves. It is not merely an old, grey-moustached officer whom you see eating his omelette or draining his glass, but it is a fragment of history. In me you see one of the last of those wonderful men, the men who were veterans when they were yet boys, who learned to use a sword earlier than a razor, and who during a hundred battles had never once let the enemy see the colour of their knapsacks. For twenty years we were teaching Europe how to fight, and even when they had learned their lesson it was only the thermometer, and never the bayonet, which could break the Grand Army down. Berlin, Naples, Vienna, Madrid, Lisbon, Moscow — we stabled our horses in them all. Yes, my friends, I say again that you do well to send your children to me with flowers, for these ears have heard the trumpet calls of France, and these eyes have seen her standards in lands where they may never be seen again.

Even now, when I doze in my arm-chair, I can see those great warriors stream before me — the green-jacketed chasseurs, the giant cuirassiers, Poniatowsky's lancers, the white-mantled dragoons, the nodding bearskins of the horse grenadiers. And then there comes the thick, low rattle of the drums, and through wreaths of dust and smoke I see the line of high bonnets, the row of brown faces, the swing and toss of the long, red plumes amid the sloping lines of steel. And there rides Ney with his red head, and Lefebvre with his bulldog jaw, and Lannes with his Gascon swagger; and then amidst the gleam of brass and the flaunting feathers I catch a glimpse of *him*, the man with the pale smile, the rounded shoulders, and the far-off eyes. There is an end of my sleep, my friends, for up I spring from my chair, with a cracked voice calling and a silly hand outstretched, so that Madame Titaux has one more laugh at the old fellow who lives among the shadows.

Although I was a full Chief of Brigade when the wars came to an end, and had every hope of soon being made a General of Division, it is still rather to my earlier days that I turn when I wish to talk of the glories and the trials of a soldier's life. For you will understand that when an officer has so many men and horses under him, he has his mind full of recruits and remounts, fodder and farriers, and quarters, so that even when he is not in the face of the enemy, life is a very serious matter for him. But when he is only a lieutenant or a captain he has nothing heavier than his epaulettes upon his shoulders, so that he can clink his spurs and swing his dolman, drain his glass and kiss his girl, thinking of nothing save of enjoying a gallant life. That is the time when he is likely to have adventures, and it is often to that time that I shall turn in the stories which I may have for you. So it will be tonight when I tell you of my visit to the Castle of Gloom; of the strange mission of Sub-Lieutenant Duroc, and of the horrible affair of the man who was once known as Jean Carabin, and afterwards as the Baron Straubenthal.

You must know, then, that in the February of 1807, immediately after the taking of Danzig, Major Legendre and I were commissioned to bring four hundred remounts from Prussia into Eastern Poland.

The hard weather, and especially the great battle at Eylau, had killed so many of the horses that there was some danger of our beautiful Tenth of Hussars becoming a battalion of light infantry. We knew, therefore, both the Major and I, that we should be very welcome at the front. We did not advance very rapidly, however, for the snow was deep, the roads detestable, and we had but twenty returning invalids to assist us. Besides, it is impossible, when you have a daily change of forage, and sometimes none at all, to move horses faster than a walk. I am aware that in the story-books the cavalry whirls past at the maddest of gallops; but for my own part, after twelve campaigns, I should be very satisfied to know that my brigade could always walk upon the march and trot in the presence of the enemy. This I say of the hussars and chasseurs, mark you, so that it is far more the case with cuirassiers or dragoons.

For myself I am fond of horses, and to have four hundred of them, of every age and shade and character, all under my own hands, was a very great pleasure to me. They were from Pomerania for the most part, though some were from Normandy and some from Alsace, and it amused us to notice that they differed in character as much as the people of those provinces. We observed also, what I have often proved since, that the nature of a horse can be told by his colour, from the coquettish light bay, full of fancies and nerves, to the hardy chestnut, and from the docile roan to the pig-headed rusty-black. All this has nothing in the world to do with my story, but how is an officer of cavalry to get on with his tale when he finds four hundred horses waiting for him at the outset? It is my habit, you see, to talk of that which interests myself and so I hope that I may interest you.

We crossed the Vistula opposite Marien-werder, and had got as far as Riesenberg, when Major Legendre came into my room in the post-house with an open paper in his hand.

'You are to leave me,' said he, with despair upon his face.

It was no very great grief to me to do that, for he was, if I may say so, hardly worthy to have such a subaltern. I saluted, however, in silence.

'It is an order from General Lasalle,' he continued; 'you are to proceed to Rossel instantly, and to report yourself at the headquarters of the regiment.'

No message could have pleased me better. I was already very well thought of by my superior officers. It was evident to me, therefore, that this sudden order meant that the regiment was about to see service once more, and that Lasalle understood how incomplete my squadron would be without me. It is true that it came at an inconvenient moment, for the keeper of the post-house had a daughter — one of those ivory-skinned, black-haired Polish girls — with whom I had hoped to have some further talk. Still, it is not for the pawn to argue when the fingers of the player move him from the square; so down I went, saddled my big black charger, Rataplan, and set off instantly upon my lonely journey.

My word, it was a treat for those poor Poles and Jews, who have so little to brighten their dull lives, to see such a picture as that before their doors! The frosty morning air made Rataplan's great black limbs and the beautiful curves of his back and sides gleam and shimmer with every gambade. As for me, the rattle of hoofs upon a road, and the jingle of bridle chains which comes with every toss of a saucy head, would even now set my blood dancing through my veins. You may think, then, how I carried myself in my five-and-twentieth year — I, Etienne Gerard, the picked horseman and surest blade in the ten regiments of hussars. Blue was our colour in the Tenth — a sky-blue dolman and pelisse with a scarlet front — and it was said of us in the army that we could set a whole population running, the women towards us, and the men away. There were bright eyes in the Riesenberg windows that morning which seemed to beg me to tarry; but what can a soldier do, save to kiss his hand and shake his bridle as he rides upon his way?

It was a bleak season to ride through the poorest and ugliest country in Europe, but there was a cloudless sky above, and a bright, cold sun, which shimmered on the huge snowfields. My breath reeked into the frosty air, and Rataplan sent up two feathers of steam from his nostrils, while the icicles drooped from the side-irons of his bit. I let him trot to warm his limbs, while for my own part I had too much to think of to give much heed to the cold. To north and south stretched the great plains, mottled over with dark clumps of fir and lighter patches of larch. A few cottages peeped out here and there, but it was only three months since the Grand Army had passed that way, and you know what that meant to a country. The Poles were our friends, it was true, but out of a hundred thousand men, only the Guard had waggons, and the rest had to live as best they might. It did not surprise me, therefore, to see no signs of cattle and no smoke from the silent houses. A weal had been left across the country where the great host had passed, and it was said that even the rats were starved wherever the Emperor had led his men.

By midday I had got as far as the village of Saalfeldt, but as I was on the direct road for Osterode, where the Emperor was wintering, and also for the main camp of the seven divisions of infantry, the highway was choked with carriages and carts. What with artillery caissons and waggons and couriers, and the ever-thickening stream of recruits and stragglers, it seemed to me that it would be a very long time before I should join my comrades. The plains, however, were five feet deep in snow, so there was nothing for it but to plod upon our way. It was with joy, therefore, that I found a second road which branched away from the other, trending through a fir-wood towards the north. There was a small auberge at the cross-roads, and a patrol of the Third Hussars of Conflans — the very regiment of which I was afterwards colonel — were mounting their horses at the door. On the steps stood their officer, a slight, pale young man, who looked more like a young priest from a seminary than a leader of the devil-may-care rascals before him.

'Good-day, sir,' said he, seeing that I pulled up my horse.

'Good-day,' I answered. 'I am Lieutenant Etienne Gerard, of the Tenth.'

I could see by his face that he had heard of me. Everybody had heard of me since my duel with the six fencing masters. My manner, however, served to put him at his ease with me.

'I am Sub-Lieutenant Duroc, of the Third,' said he.

'Newly joined?' I asked.

'Last week.'

I had thought as much, from his white face and from the way in which he let his men lounge upon their horses. It was not so long, however, since I had learned myself what it was like when a schoolboy has to give orders to veteran troopers. It made me blush, I remember, to shout abrupt commands to men who had seen more battles than I had years, and it would have come more natural for me to say, 'With your permission, we shall now wheel into line,' or, 'If you think it best, we shall trot.' I did not think the less of the lad, therefore, when I observed that his men were somewhat out of hand, but I gave them a glance which stiffened them in their saddles.

'May I ask, monsieur, whether you are going by this northern road?' I asked.

'My orders are to patrol it as far as Arensdorf,' said he.

'Then I will, with your permission, ride so far with you,' said I. 'It is very clear that the longer way will be the faster.'

So it proved, for this road led away from the army into a country which was given over to Cossacks and marauders, and it was as bare as the other was crowded. Duroc and I rode in front, with our six troopers clattering in the rear. He was a good boy, this Duroc, with his head full of the nonsense that they teach at St Cyr, knowing more about Alexander and Pompey than how to mix a horse's fodder or care for a horse's feet. Still, he was, as I have said, a good boy, unspoiled as yet by the camp. It pleased me to hear him prattle away about his sister Marie and about his mother in Amiens. Presently we found ourselves at the village of Hayenau. Duroc rode up to the post-house and asked to see the master.

'Can you tell me,' said he, 'whether the man who calls himself the Baron Straubenthal lives in these parts?'

The postmaster shook his head, and we rode upon our way. I took no notice of this, but when, at the next village, my comrade repeated the same question, with the same result, I could not help asking him who this Baron Straubenthal might be.

'He is a man,' said Duroc, with a sudden flush upon his boyish face, 'to whom I have a very important message to convey.'

Well, this was not satisfactory, but there was something in my companion's manner which told me that any further questioning would be distasteful to him. I said nothing more, therefore, but Duroc would still ask every peasant whom we met whether he could give him any news of the Baron Straubenthal.

For my own part I was endeavouring, as an officer of light cavalry should, to form an idea of the lay of the country, to note the course of the streams, and to mark the places where there should be fords. Every step was taking us farther from the camp round the flanks of which we were travelling. Far to the south a few plumes of grey smoke in the frosty air marked the position of some of our outposts. To the north, however, there was nothing between ourselves and the Russian winter quarters. Twice on the extreme horizon I caught a glimpse of the glitter of steel, and pointed it out to my companion. It was too distant for us to tell whence it came, but we had little doubt that it was from the lance-heads of marauding Cossacks.

The sun was just setting when we rode over a low hill and saw a small village upon our right, and on our left a high black castle, which jutted out from amongst the pine-woods. A farmer with his cart was approaching us — a matted-haired, downcast fellow, in a sheepskin jacket.

'What village is this?' asked Duroc.

'It is Arensdorf,' he answered, in his

barbarous German dialect.

'Then here I am to stay the night,' said my young companion. Then, turning to the farmer, he asked his eternal question, 'Can you tell me where the Baron Straubenthal lives?'

'Why, it is he who owns the Castle of Gloom,' said the farmer, pointing to the dark turrets over the distant fir forest.

Duroc gave a shout like the sportsman who sees his game rising in front of him. The lad seemed to have gone off his head — his eyes shining, his face deathly white, and such a grim set about his mouth as made the farmer shrink away from him. I can see him now, leaning forward on his brown horse, with his eager gaze fixed upon the great black tower.

'Why do you call it the Castle of Gloom?' I asked.

'Well, it's the name it bears upon the countryside,' said the farmer. 'By all accounts there have been some black doings up yonder. It's not for nothing that the wickedest man in Poland has been living there these fourteen years past.'

'A Polish nobleman?' I asked.

'Nay, we breed no such men in Poland,' he answered.

'A Frenchman, then?' cried Duroc.

'They say that he came from France.'

'And with red hair?'

'As red as a fox.'

'Yes, yes, it is my man,' cried my companion, quivering all over in his excitement. 'It is the hand of Providence which has led me here. Who can say that there is not justice in this world? Come, Monsieur Gerard, for I must see the men safely quartered before I can attend to this private matter.'

He spurred on his horse, and ten minutes later we were at the door of the inn of Arensdorf, where his men were to find their quarters for the night.

Well, all this was no affair of mine, and I could not imagine what the meaning of it might be. Rossel was still far off, but I determined to ride on for a few hours and take my chance of some wayside barn in which I could find shelter for Rataplan and myself. I had mounted my horse, therefore, after tossing off a cup of wine, when young Duroc came running out of the door and laid his hand upon my knee.

'Monsieur Gerard,' he panted, 'I beg of you not to abandon me like this!'

'My good sir,' said I, 'if you would tell me what is the matter and what you would wish me to do, I should be better able to tell you if I could be of any assistance to you.'

'You can be of the very greatest,' he cried. 'Indeed, from all that I have heard of you, Monsieur Gerard, you are the one man whom I should wish to have by my side tonight.'

'You forget that I am riding to join my regiment.'

'You cannot, in any case, reach it tonight. Tomorrow will bring you to Rossel. By staying with me you will confer the very greatest kindness upon me, and you will aid me in a matter which concerns my own honour and the honour of my family. I am compelled, however, to confess to you that some personal danger may possibly be involved.'

It was a crafty thing for him to say. Of course, I sprang from Rataplan's back and ordered the groom to lead him back into the stables.

'Come into the inn,' said I, 'and let me know exactly what it is that you wish me to do.'

He led the way into a sitting-room, and fastened the door lest we should be interrupted. He was a well-grown lad, and as he stood in the glare of the lamp, with the light beating upon his earnest face and upon his uniform of silver grey, which suited him to a marvel, I felt my heart warm towards him.

14

Without going so far as to say that he carried himself as I had done at his age, there was at least similarity enough to make me feel in sympathy with him.

'I can explain it all in a few words,' said he. 'If I have not already satisfied your very natural curiosity, it is because the subject is so painful a one to me that I can hardly bring myself to allude to it. I cannot, however, ask for your assistance without explaining to you exactly how the matter lies.

'You must know, then, that my father was the well-known banker, Christophe Duroc, who was murdered by the people during the September massacres. As you are aware, the mob took possession of the prisons, chose three so-called judges to pass sentence upon the unhappy aristocrats, and then tore them to pieces when they were passed out into the street. My father had been a benefactor of the poor all his life. There were many to plead for him. He had the fever, too, and was carried in, half-dead, upon a blanket. Two of the judges were in favour of acquitting him; the third, a young Jacobin, whose huge body and brutal mind had made him a leader among these wretches, dragged him, with his own hands, from the litter, kicked him again and again with his heavy boots, and hurled him out of the door, where in an instant he was torn limb from limb under circumstances which are too horrible for me to describe. This, as you perceive, was murder, even under their own unlawful laws, for two of their own judges had pronounced in my father's favour.

'Well, when the days of order came back again, my elder brother began to make inquiries about this man. I was only a child then, but it was a family matter, and it was discussed in my presence. The fellow's name was Carabin. He was one of Sansterre's Guard, and a noted duellist. A foreign lady named the Baroness Straubenthal having been dragged before the Jacobins, he had gained her liberty for her on the promise that she with her money and estates should be his. He had married her, taken her name and title, and escaped out of France at the time of the fall of Robespierre. What had become of him we had no means of learning.

'You will think, doubtless, that it would be easy for us to find him, since we had both his name and his title. You must remember, however, that the Revolution left us without money, and that without money such a search is very difficult. Then came the Empire, and it became more difficult still, for, as you are aware, the Emperor considered that the 18th

Brumaire brought all accounts to a settlement, and that on that day a veil had been drawn across the past. None the less, we kept our own family story and our own family plans.

'My brother joined the army, and passed with it through all Southern Europe, asking everywhere for the Baron Straubenthal. Last October he was killed at Jena, with his mission still unfulfilled. Then it became my turn, and I have the good fortune to hear of the very man of whom I am in search at one of the first Polish villages which I have to visit, and within a fortnight of joining my regiment. And then, to make the matter even better, I find myself in the company of one whose name is never mentioned throughout the army save in connection with some daring and generous deed.'

This was all very well, and I listened to it with the greatest interest, but I was none the clearer as to what young Duroc wished me to do.

'How can I be of service to you?' I asked.

'By coming up with me.'

'To the Castle?'

'Precisely.'

'When?'

'At once.'

'But what do you intend to do?'

17

'I shall know what to do. But I wish you to be with me, all the same.'

Well, it was never in my nature to refuse an adventure, and, besides, I had every sympathy with the lad's feelings. It is very well to forgive one's enemies, but one wishes to give them something to forgive also. I held out my hand to him, therefore.

'I must be on my way for Rossel tomorrow morning, but tonight I am yours,' said I.

We left our troopers in snug quarters, and, as it was but a mile to the Castle, we did not disturb our horses. To tell the truth, I hate to see a cavalry man walk, and I hold that just as he is the most gallant thing upon earth when he has his saddle-flaps between his knees, so he is the most clumsy when he has to loop up his sabre and his sabre-tasche in one hand and turn in his toes for fear of catching the rowels of his spurs. Still, Duroc and I were of the age when one can carry things off, and I dare swear that no woman at least would have quarrelled with the appearance of the two young hussars, one in blue and one in grey, who set out that night from the Arensdorf post-house. We both carried our swords, and for my own part I slipped a pistol from my holster into the inside of my pelisse, for it seemed to me that there might be some wild work before us.

The track which led to the Castle wound through a pitch-black fir-wood, where we could see nothing save the ragged patch of stars above our heads. Presently, however, it opened up, and there was the Castle right in front of us, about as far as a carbine would carry. It was a huge, uncouth place, and bore every mark of being exceedingly old, with turrets at every corner, and a square keep on the side which was nearest to us. In all its great shadow there was no sign of light save from a single window, and no sound came from it. To me there was something awful in its size and its silence, which corresponded so well with its sinister name. My companion pressed on eagerly, and I followed him along the ill-kept path which led to the gate.

There was no bell or knocker upon the great iron-studded door, and it was only by pounding with the hilts of our sabres that we could attract attention. A thin, hawk-faced man, with a beard up to his temples, opened it at last. He carried a lantern in one hand, and in the other a chain which held an enormous black hound. His manner at the first moment was threatening, but the sight of our uniforms and of our faces turned it into one of sulky reserve.

'The Baron Straubenthal does not receive visitors at so late an hour,' said he, speaking in very excellent French.

'You can inform Baron Straubenthal that I have come eight hundred leagues to see him, and that I will not leave until I have done so,' said my companion. I could not myself have said it with a better voice and manner.

The fellow took a sidelong look at us, and tugged at his black beard in his perplexity.

'To tell the truth, gentlemen,' said he, 'the Baron has a cup or two of wine in him at this hour, and you would certainly find him a more entertaining companion if you were to come again in the morning.'

He had opened the door a little wider as he spoke, and I saw by the light of the lamp in the hall behind him that three other rough fellows were standing there, one of whom held another of these monstrous hounds. Duroc must have seen it also, but it made no difference to his resolution.

'Enough talk,' said he, pushing the man to one side. 'It is with your master that I have to deal.'

The fellows in the hall made way for him as he strode in among them, so great is the power of one man who knows what he wants over several who are not sure of themselves. My companion tapped one of them upon the shoulder with as much assurance as though he owned him.

'Show me to the Baron,' said he.

The man shrugged his shoulders, and answered something in Polish. The fellow with the beard, who had shut and barred the front door, appeared to be the only one among them who could speak French.

'Well, you shall have your way,' said he, with a sinister smile. 'You shall see the Baron. And perhaps, before you have finished, you will wish that you had taken my advice.'

We followed him down the hall, which was stone-flagged and very spacious, with skins scattered upon the floor, and the heads of wild beasts upon the walls. At the farther end he threw open a door, and we entered.

It was a small room, scantily furnished, with the same marks of neglect and decay which met us at every turn. The walls were hung with discoloured tapestry, which had come loose at one corner, so as to expose the rough stonework behind. A second door, hung with a curtain, faced us upon the other side. Between lay a square table, strewn with dirty dishes and the sordid remains of a meal. Several bottles were scattered over it. At the head of it, and facing us, there sat a huge man with a lion-like head and a great shock of orange-coloured hair. His beard was of the same glaring hue; matted and tangled and coarse as a horse's mane. I have seen some strange faces in my time, but never one more brutal than that, with its small, vicious, blue eyes, its white, crumpled cheeks, and the thick, hanging lip which protruded over his monstrous beard. His head swayed about on his shoulders, and he looked at us with the vague, dim gaze of a drunken man. Yet he was not so drunk but that our uniforms carried their message to him.

'Well, my brave boys,' he hiccoughed. 'What is the latest news from Paris, eh? You're going to free Poland, I hear, and have meantime all become slaves yourselves — slaves to a little aristocrat with his grey coat and his three-cornered hat. No more citizens either, I am told, and nothing but monsieur and madame. My faith, some more heads will have to roll into the sawdust basket some of these mornings.'

Duroc advanced in silence, and stood by the ruffian's side.

'Jean Carabin,' said he.

The Baron started, and the film of drunkenness seemed to be clearing from his eyes.

'Jean Carabin,' said Duroc, once more.

He sat up and grasped the arms of his chair.

'What do you mean by repeating that name, young man?' he asked.

'Jean Carabin, you are a man whom I have long wished to meet.'

'Supposing that I once had such a name, how can it concern you, since you must have been a child when I bore it?'

'My name is Duroc.'

'Not the son of — ?'

'The son of the man you murdered.'

The Baron tried to laugh, but there was terror in his eyes.

'We must let bygones be bygones, young man,' he cried. 'It was our life or theirs in those days: the aristocrats or the people. Your father was of the Gironde. He fell. I was of the mountain. Most of my comrades fell. It was all the fortune of war. We must forget all this and learn to know each other better, you and I.' He held out a red, twitching hand as he spoke.

'Enough,' said young Duroc. 'If I were to pass my sabre through you as you sit in that chair, I should do what is just and right. I dishonour my blade by crossing it with yours. And yet you are a Frenchman, and have even held a commission under the same flag as myself. Rise, then, and defend yourself!'

'Tut, tut!' cried the Baron. 'It is all very well for you young bloods — '

Duroc's patience could stand no more. He swung his open hand into the centre of the great orange beard. I saw a lip fringed with blood, and two glaring blue eyes above it.

'You shall die for that blow.'

'That is better,' said Duroc.

'My sabre!' cried the other. 'I will not keep you waiting, I promise you!' and he hurried from the room.

I have said that there was a second door covered with a curtain. Hardly had the Baron vanished when there ran from behind it a woman, young and beautiful. So swiftly and noiselessly did she move that she was between us in an instant, and it was only the shaking curtains which told us whence she had come.

'I have seen it all,' she cried. 'Oh, sir, you have carried yourself splendidly.' She stooped to my companion's hand, and kissed it again and again ere he could disengage it from her grasp.

'Nay, madame, why should you kiss my hand?' he cried.

'Because it is the hand which struck him on his vile, lying mouth. Because it may be the hand which will avenge my mother. I am his step-daughter. The woman whose heart he broke was my mother. I loathe him, I fear him. Ah, there is his step!' In an instant she had vanished as suddenly as she had come. A moment later, the Baron entered with a drawn sword in his hand, and the fellow who had admitted us at his heels.

'This is my secretary,' said he. 'He will be my friend in this affair. But we shall need more elbow-room than we can find here. Perhaps you will kindly come with me to a more spacious apartment.'

It was evidently impossible to fight in a chamber which was blocked by a great table. We followed him out, therefore, into the dimly-lit hall. At the farther end a light was shining through an open door.

'We shall find what we want in here,' said the man with the dark beard. It was a large, empty room, with rows of barrels and cases round the walls. A strong lamp stood upon a shelf in the corner. The floor was level and true, so that no swordsman could ask for more. Duroc drew his sabre and sprang into it. The Baron stood back with a bow and motioned me to follow my companion. Hardly were my heels over the threshold when the heavy door crashed behind us and the key screamed in the lock. We were taken in a trap.

For a moment we could not realize it. Such incredible baseness was outside all our experiences. Then, as we understood how foolish we had been to trust for an instant a man with such a history, a flush of rage came over us, rage against his villainy and against our own stupidity. We rushed at the door together, beating it with our fists and kicking with our heavy boots. The sound of our blows and of our execrations must have resounded through the Castle. We called to this villain, hurling at him every name which might pierce even into his hardened soul. But the door was enormous — such a door as one finds in mediaeval castles — made of huge beams clamped together with iron. It was as easy to break as a square of the Old Guard. And our cries appeared to be of as little avail as our blows, for they only brought for answer the clattering echoes from the high roof above us. When you have done some soldiering, you soon learn to put up with what cannot be altered. It was I, then, who first recovered my calmness, and prevailed upon Duroc to join with me in examining the apartment which had become our dungeon.

There was only one window, which had no glass in it, and was so narrow that one could not so much as get one's head through. It was high up, and Duroc had to stand upon a barrel in order to see from it.

'What can you see?' I asked.

'Fir-woods and an avenue of snow between them,' said he. 'Ah!' he gave a cry of surprise.

I sprang upon the barrel beside him. There was, as he said, a long, clear strip of snow in front. A man was riding down it, flogging his horse and galloping like a madman. As we watched, he grew smaller and smaller, until he was swallowed up by the black shadows of the forest.

'What does that mean?' asked Duroc.

'No good for us,' said I. 'He may have gone for some brigands to cut our throats. Let us see if we cannot find a way out of this mouse-trap before the cat can arrive.'

The one piece of good fortune in our favour was that beautiful lamp. It was nearly full of oil, and would last us until morning. In the dark our situation would have been far more difficult. By its light we proceeded to examine the packages and cases which lined the walls. In some places there was only a single line of them, while in one corner they were piled nearly to the ceiling. It seemed that we were in the storehouse of the Castle, for there were a great number of cheeses, vegetables of various kinds, bins full of dried fruits, and a line of wine barrels. One of these had a spigot in it, and as I had eaten little during the day, I was glad of a cup of claret and some food. As to Duroc, he would take nothing, but paced up and down the room in a fever of anger and impatience. 'I'll have him yet!' he cried, every now and then. 'The rascal shall not escape me!'

This was all very well, but it seemed to me, as I sat on a great round cheese eating my supper, that this youngster was thinking rather too much of his own family affairs and too little of the fine scrape into which he had got me. After all, his father had been dead fourteen years, and nothing could set that right; but here was Etienne Gerard, the most dashing lieutenant in the whole Grand Army, in imminent danger of being cut off at the very outset of his brilliant career. Who was ever to know the heights to which I might have risen if I were knocked on the head in this hole-and-corner business, which had nothing whatever to do with France or the Emperor? I could not help thinking what a fool I had been, when I had a fine war before me and everything which a man could desire, to go off on a hare-brained expedition of this sort, as if it were not enough to have a quarter of a million Russians to fight against, without plunging into all sorts of private quarrels as well.

'That is all very well,' I said at last, as I heard Duroc muttering his threats. 'You may do what you like to him when you get the upper hand. At present the question rather is, what is *he* going to do to us?'

'Let him do his worst!' cried the boy. 'I owe a duty to my father.'

'That is mere foolishness,' said I. 'If you owe a duty to your father, I owe one to my mother, which is to get out of this business safe and sound.'

My remark brought him to his senses.

'I have thought too much of myself!' he cried. 'Forgive me, Monsieur Gerard. Give me your advice as to what I should do.'

'Well,' said I, 'it is not for our health that they have shut us up here among the cheeses. They mean to make an end of us if they can. That is certain. They hope that no one knows that we have come here, and that none will trace us if we remain. Do your hussars know where you have gone to?'

'I said nothing.'

'Hum! It is clear that we cannot be starved here. They must come to us if they are to kill us. Behind a barricade of barrels we could hold our own against the five rascals whom we have seen. That is, probably, why they have sent that messenger for assistance.'

'We must get out before he returns.'

'Precisely, if we are to get out at all.'

'Could we not burn down this door?' he cried.

'Nothing could be easier,' said I. 'There are several casks of oil in the corner. My only objection is that we should ourselves be nicely toasted, like two little oyster pâtés.'

'Can you not suggest something?' he cried, in despair. 'Ah, what is that?'

There had been a low sound at our little window, and a shadow came between the stars and ourselves. A small, white hand was stretched into the lamplight. Something glittered between the fingers.

'Quick! quick!' cried a woman's voice.

We were on the barrel in an instant.

'They have sent for the Cossacks. Your lives are at stake. Ah, I am lost! I am lost!'

There was the sound of rushing steps, a hoarse oath, a blow, and the stars were once more twinkling through the window. We stood helpless upon the barrel with our blood cold with horror. Half a minute afterwards we heard a smothered scream, ending in a choke. A great door slammed somewhere in the silent night.

'Those ruffians have seized her. They will kill her,' I cried.

Duroc sprang down with the inarticulate shouts of one whose reason has left him. He struck the door so frantically with his naked hands that he left a blotch of blood with every blow.

'Here is the key!' I shouted, picking one from the floor. 'She must have thrown it in at the instant that she was torn away.'

My companion snatched it from me with a

shriek of joy. A moment later he dashed it down upon the boards. It was so small that it was lost in the enormous lock. Duroc sank upon one of the boxes with his head between his hands. He sobbed in his despair. I could have sobbed, too, when I thought of the woman and how helpless we were to save her.

But I am not easily baffled. After all, this key must have been sent to us for a purpose. The lady could not bring us that of the door, because this murderous stepfather of hers would most certainly have it in his pocket. Yet this other must have a meaning, or why should she risk her life to place it in our hands? It would say little for our wits if we could not find out what that meaning might be.

I set to work moving all the cases out from the wall, and Duroc, gaining new hope from my courage, helped me with all his strength. It was no light task, for many of them were large and heavy. On we went, working like maniacs, slinging barrels, cheeses, and boxes pell-mell into the middle of the room. At last there only remained one huge barrel of vodka, which stood in the corner. With our united strength we rolled it out, and there was a little low wooden door in the wainscot behind it. The key fitted, and with a cry of delight we saw it swing open before us. With the lamp in my hand, I squeezed my way in, followed by my companion.

We were in the powder-magazine of the Castle — a rough, walled cellar, with barrels all round it, and one with the top staved in in the centre. The powder from it lay in a black heap upon the floor. Beyond there was another door, but it was locked.

'We are no better off than before,' cried Duroc. 'We have no key.'

'We have a dozen!' I cried.

'Where?'

I pointed to the line of powder barrels.

'You would blow this door open?'

'Precisely.'

'But you would explode the magazine.'

It was true, but I was not at the end of my resources.

'We will blow open the store-room door,' I cried.

I ran back and seized a tin box which had been filled with candles. It was about the size of my busby — large enough to hold several pounds of powder. Duroc filled it while I cut off the end of a candle. When we had finished, it would have puzzled a colonel of engineers to make a better petard. I put three cheeses on the top of each other and placed it above them, so as to lean against the lock. Then we lit our candle-end and ran for shelter, shutting the door of the magazine behind us.

It is no joke, my friends, to be among all those tons of powder, with the knowledge that if the flame of the explosion should penetrate through one thin door our blackened limbs would be shot higher than the Castle keep. Who could have believed that a half-inch of candle could take so long to burn? My ears were straining all the time for the thudding of the hoofs of the Cossacks who were coming to destroy us. I had almost made up my mind that the candle must have gone out when there was a smack like a bursting bomb, our door flew to bits, and pieces of cheese, with a shower of turnips, apples, and splinters of cases, were shot in among us. As we rushed out we had to stagger through an impenetrable smoke, with all sorts of débris beneath our feet, but there was a glimmering square where the dark door had been. The petard had done its work.

In fact, it had done more for us than we had even ventured to hope. It had shattered gaolers as well as gaol. The first thing that I saw as I came out into the hall was a man with a butcher's axe in his hand, lying flat upon his back, with a gaping wound across his forehead. The second was a huge dog, with two of its legs broken, twisting in agony upon the floor. As it raised itself up I saw the two broken ends flapping like flails. At the same instant I heard a cry, and there was Duroc, thrown against the wall, with the other hound's teeth in his throat. He pushed it off with his left hand, while again and again he passed his sabre through its body, but it was not until I blew out its brains with my pistol that the iron jaws relaxed, and the fierce, bloodshot eyes were glazed in death.

There was no time for us to pause. A woman's scream from in front — a scream of mortal terror — told us that even now we might be too late. There were two other men in the hall, but they cowered away from our drawn swords and furious faces. The blood was streaming from Duroc's neck and dyeing the grey fur of his pelisse. Such was the lad's fire, however, that he shot in front of me, and it was only over his shoulder that I caught a glimpse of the scene as we rushed into the chamber in which we had first seen the master of the Castle of Gloom.

The Baron was standing in the middle of the room, his tangled mane bristling like an angry lion. He was, as I have said, a huge man with enormous shoulders; and as he stood there, with his face flushed with rage and his sword advanced, I could not but think that, in spite of all his villainies, he had a proper figure for a grenadier. The lady lay cowering in a chair behind him. A weal across one of her white arms and a dog-whip upon the floor were enough to show that our escape had hardly been in time to save her from his brutality. He gave a howl like a wolf as we broke in, and was upon us in an instant, hacking and driving, with a curse at every blow.

I have already said that the room gave no space for swordsmanship. My young companion was in front of me in the narrow passage between the table and the wall, so that I could only look on without being able to aid him. The lad knew something of his weapon, and was as fierce and active as a wild cat, but in so narrow a space the weight and strength of the giant gave him the advantage. Besides, he was an admirable swordsman. His parade and riposte were as quick as lightning. Twice he touched Duroc upon the shoulder, and then, as the lad slipped on a lunge, he whirled up his sword to finish him before he could recover his feet. I was quicker than he, however, and took the cut upon the pommel of my sabre.

'Excuse me,' said I, 'but you have still to deal with Etienne Gerard.'

He drew back and leaned against the tapestry-covered wall, breathing in little, hoarse gasps, for his foul living was against him.

'Take your breath,' said I. 'I will await your convenience.'

'You have no cause of quarrel against me,' he panted.

'I owe you some little attention,' said I, 'for having shut me up in your store-room. Besides, if all other were wanting, I see cause enough upon that lady's arm.'

'Have your way, then!' he snarled, and leaped at me like a madman. For a minute I saw only the blazing blue eyes, and the red glazed point which stabbed and stabbed, rasping off to right or to left, and yet ever back at my throat and my breast. I had never thought that such good sword-play was to be found at Paris in the days of the Revolution. I do not suppose that in all my little affairs I have met six men who had a better knowledge of their weapon. But he knew that I was his master. He read death in my eyes, and I could see that he read it. The flush died from his face. His breath came in shorter and in thicker gasps. Yet he fought on, even after the final thrust had come, and died still hacking and cursing, with foul cries upon his lips, and his blood clotting upon his orange beard. I who speak to you have seen so many battles, that my old memory can scarce contain their names, and yet of all the terrible sights which these eyes have rested upon, there is none which I care to think of less than of that orange beard with the crimson stain in the centre, from which I had drawn my sword-point.

It was only afterwards that I had time to think of all this. His monstrous body had hardly crashed down upon the floor before the woman in the corner sprang to her feet, clapping her hands together and screaming out in her delight. For my part I was disgusted to see a woman take such delight in a deed of blood, and I gave no thought as to the terrible wrongs which must have befallen her before she could so far forget the gentleness of her sex. It was on my tongue to tell her sharply to be silent, when a strange, choking smell took the breath from my nostrils, and a sudden, yellow glare brought out the figures upon the faded hangings.

'Duroc, Duroc!' I shouted, tugging at his shoulder. 'The Castle is on fire!'

The boy lay senseless upon the ground, exhausted by his wounds. I rushed out into the hall to see whence the danger came. It was our explosion which had set alight to the dry frame-work of the door. Inside the store-room some of the boxes were already blazing. I glanced in, and as I did so my blood was turned to water by the sight of the powder barrels beyond, and of the loose heap upon the floor. It might be seconds, it could not be more than minutes, before the flames would be at the edge of it. These eyes will be closed in death, my friends, before they cease to see those crawling lines of fire and the black heap beyond.

How little I can remember what followed. Vaguely I can recall how I rushed into the chamber of death, how I seized Duroc by one limp hand and dragged him down the hall, the woman keeping pace with me and pulling at the other arm. Out of the gateway we rushed, and on down the snow-covered path until we were on the fringe of the fir forest. It was at that moment that I heard a crash behind me, and, glancing round, saw a great spout of fire shoot up into the wintry sky. An instant later there seemed to come a second crash, far louder than the first. I saw the fir trees and the stars whirling round me, and I fell unconscious across the body of my comrade.

★　★　★

It was some weeks before I came to myself in the post-house of Arensdorf, and longer still before I could be told all that had befallen me. It was Duroc, already able to go soldiering, who came to my bedside and gave me an account of it. He it was who told me how a piece of timber had struck me on the head and laid me almost dead upon the ground. From him, too, I learned how the Polish girl had run to Arensdorf, how she had roused our hussars, and how she had only just brought them back in time to save us from the spears of the Cossacks who had been summoned from their bivouac by that same black-bearded secretary whom we had seen galloping so swiftly over the snow. As to the brave lady who had twice saved our lives, I could not learn very much about her at that moment from Duroc, but when I chanced to meet him in Paris two years later, after the campaign of Wagram, I was not very much surprised to find that I needed no introduction to his bride, and that by the queer turns of fortune he had himself, had he chosen to use it, that very name and title of the Baron Straubenthal, which showed him to be the owner of the blackened ruins of the Castle of Gloom.

2

How the Brigadier Slew
the Brothers of Ajaccio

When the Emperor needed an agent he was
always very ready to do me the honour of
recalling the name of Etienne Gerard, though
it occasionally escaped him when rewards
were to be distributed. Still, I was a colonel at
twenty-eight, and the chief of a brigade at
thirty-one, so that I have no reason to be
dissatisfied with my career. Had the wars
lasted another two or three years I might have
grasped my bâton, and the man who had his
hand upon that was only one stride from a
throne. Murat had changed his hussar's cap
for a crown, and another light cavalry man
might have done as much. However, all those
dreams were driven away by Waterloo, and,
although I was not able to write my name
upon history, it is sufficiently well known by
all who served with me in the great wars of
the Empire.

What I want to tell you tonight is about the
very singular affair which first started me
upon my rapid upward course, and which

had the effect of establishing a secret bond between the Emperor and myself.

There is just one little word of warning which I must give you before I begin. When you hear me speak, you must always bear in mind that you are listening to one who has seen history from the inside. I am talking about what my ears have heard and my eyes have seen, so you must not try to confute me by quoting the opinions of some student or man of the pen, who has written a book of history or memoirs. There is much which is unknown by such people, and much which never will be known by the world. For my own part, I could tell you some very surprising things were it discreet to do so. The facts which I am about to relate to you tonight were kept secret by me during the Emperor's lifetime, because I gave him my promise that it should be so, but I do not think that there can be any harm now in my telling the remarkable part which I played.

You must know, then, that at the time of the Treaty of Tilsit I was a simple lieutenant in the 10th Hussars, without money or interest. It is true that my appearance and my gallantry were in my favour, and that I had already won a reputation as being one of the best swordsmen in the army; but amongst the host of brave men who surrounded the

41

Emperor it needed more than this to insure a rapid career. I was confident, however, that my chance would come, though I never dreamed that it would take so remarkable a form.

When the Emperor returned to Paris, after the declaration of peace in the year 1807, he spent much of his time with the Empress and the Court at Fontainebleau. It was the time when he was at the pinnacle of his career. He had in three successive campaigns humbled Austria, crushed Prussia, and made the Russians very glad to get upon the right side of the Niemen. The old Bulldog over the Channel was still growling, but he could not get very far from his kennel. If we could have made a perpetual peace at that moment, France would have taken a higher place than any nation since the days of the Romans. So I have heard the wise folk say, though for my part I had other things to think of. All the girls were glad to see the army back after its long absence, and you may be sure that I had my share of any favours that were going. You may judge how far I was a favourite in those days when I say that even now, in my sixtieth year — but why should I dwell upon that which is already sufficiently well known?

Our regiment of hussars was quartered with the horse chasseurs of the guard at

Fontainebleau. It is, as you know, but a little place, buried in the heart of the forest, and it was wonderful at this time to see it crowded with Grand Dukes and Electors and Princes, who thronged round Napoleon like puppies round their master, each hoping that some bone might be thrown to him. There was more German than French to be heard in the street, for those who had helped us in the late war had come to beg for a reward, and those who had opposed us had come to try and escape their punishment.

And all the time our little man, with his pale face and his cold, grey eyes, was riding to the hunt every morning, silent and brooding, all of them following in his train, in the hope that some word would escape him. And then, when the humour seized him, he would throw a hundred square miles to that man, or tear as much off the other, round off one kingdom by a river, or cut off another by a chain of mountains. That was how he used to do business, this little artilleryman, whom we had raised so high with our sabres and our bayonets. He was very civil to us always, for he knew where his power came from. We knew also, and showed it by the way in which we carried ourselves. We were agreed, you understand, that he was the finest leader in the world, but we did not forget that he had the finest men to lead.

Well, one day I was seated in my quarters playing cards with young Morat, of the horse chasseurs, when the door opened and in walked Lasalle, who was our Colonel. You know what a fine, swaggering fellow he was, and the sky-blue uniform of the Tenth suited him to a marvel. My faith, we youngsters were so taken by him that we all swore and diced and drank and played the deuce whether we liked it or no, just that we might resemble our Colonel! We forgot that it was not because he drank or gambled that the Emperor was going to make him the head of the light cavalry, but because he had the surest eye for the nature of a position or for the strength of a column, and the best judgment as to when infantry could be broken, or whether guns were exposed, of any man in the army. We were too young to understand all that, however, so we waxed our moustaches and clicked our spurs and let the ferrules of our scabbards wear out by trailing them along the pavement in the hope that we should all become Lasalles. When he came clanking into my quarters, both Morat and I sprang to our feet.

'My boy,' said he, clapping me on the shoulder, 'the Emperor wants to see you at four o'clock.'

The room whirled round me at the words, and I had to lean my hands upon the edge of the card-table.

'What?' I cried. 'The Emperor!'

'Precisely,' said he, smiling at my astonishment.

'But the Emperor does not know of my existence, Colonel,' I protested. 'Why should he send for me?'

'Well, that's just what puzzles me,' cried Lasalle, twirling his moustache. 'If he wanted the help of a good sabre, why should he descend to one of my lieutenants when he might have found all that he needed at the head of the regiment? However,' he added, clapping me on the shoulder again in his hearty fashion, 'every man has his chance. I have had mine, otherwise I should not be Colonel of the Tenth. I must not grudge you yours. Forwards, my boy, and may it be the first step towards changing your busby for a cocked hat.'

It was but two o'clock, so he left me, promising to come back and to accompany me to the palace. My faith, what a time I passed, and how many conjectures did I make as to what it was that the Emperor could want of me! I paced up and down my little room in a fever of anticipation. Sometimes I thought that perhaps he had heard of the guns which we had taken at Austerlitz; but, then, there were so many who had taken guns at Austerlitz, and two years had passed since the battle. Or it might be that he wished to reward me for my affair with the *aide-de-camp* of the Russian Emperor. But then again a cold fit would seize me, and I would fancy that he had sent for me to reprimand me. There were a few duels which he might have taken in ill part, and there were one or two little jokes in Paris since the peace.

But, no! I considered the words of Lasalle. 'If he had need of a brave man,' said Lasalle.

It was obvious that my Colonel had some idea of what was in the wind. If he had not known that it was to my advantage, he would not have been so cruel as to congratulate me. My heart glowed with joy as this conviction grew upon me, and I sat down to write to my mother and to tell her that the Emperor was waiting, at that very moment, to have my opinion upon a matter of importance. It made me smile as I wrote it to think that, wonderful as it appeared to me, it would probably only confirm my mother in her opinion of the Emperor's good sense.

At half-past three I heard a sabre come clanking against every step of my wooden stair. It was Lasalle, and with him was a lame gentleman, very neatly dressed in black with dapper ruffles and cuffs. We did not know many civilians, we of the army, but, my word, this was one whom we could not afford to ignore! I had only to glance at those twinkling eyes, the comical, upturned nose, and the straight, precise mouth, to know that I was in the presence of the one man in France whom even the Emperor had to consider.

'This is Monsieur Etienne Gerard, Monsieur de Talleyrand,' said Lasalle.

I saluted, and the statesman took me in from the top of my panache to the rowel of my spur, with a glance that played over me like a rapier point.

'Have you explained to the lieutenant the circumstances under which he is summoned to the Emperor's presence?' he asked, in his dry, creaking voice.

They were such a contrast, these two men, that I could not help glancing from one to the other of them: the black, sly politician, and the big, sky-blue hussar with one fist on his hip and the other on the hilt of his sabre. They both took their seats as I looked, Talleyrand without a sound, and Lasalle with a clash and a jingle like a prancing charger.

'It's this way, youngster,' said he, in his brusque fashion; 'I was with the Emperor in his private cabinet this morning when a note was brought in to him. He opened it, and as he did so he gave such a start that it fluttered down on to the floor. I handed it up to him again, but he was staring at the wall in front of him as if he had seen a ghost. 'Fratelli dell' Ajaccio,' he muttered; and then again, 'Fratelli dell' Ajaccio.' I don't pretend to know more Italian than a man can pick up in two campaigns, and I could make nothing of this. It seemed to me that he had gone out of his mind; and you would have said so also, Monsieur de Talleyrand, if you had seen the look in his eyes. He read the note, and then he sat for half an hour or more without moving.'

'And you?' asked Talleyrand.

'Why, I stood there not knowing what I ought to do. Presently he seemed to come back to his senses.

' 'I suppose, Lasalle,' said he, 'that you have some gallant young officers in the Tenth?'

' 'They are all that, sire,' I answered.

' 'If you had to pick one who was to be depended upon for action, but who would not think too much — you understand me, Lasalle — which would you select?' he asked.

'I saw that he needed an agent who would not penetrate too deeply into his plans.

' 'I have one,' said I, 'who is all spurs and moustaches, with never a thought beyond women and horses.'

'"That is the man I want,' said Napoleon. 'Bring him to my private cabinet at four o'clock.'

'So, youngster, I came straight away to you at once, and mind that you do credit to the 10th Hussars.'

I was by no means flattered by the reasons which had led to my Colonel's choice, and I must have shown as much in my face, for he roared with laughter and Talleyrand gave a dry chuckle also.

'Just one word of advice before you go, Monsieur Gerard,' said he: 'you are now coming into troubled waters, and you might find a worse pilot than myself. We have none of us any idea as to what this little affair means, and, between ourselves, it is very important for us, who have the destinies of France upon our shoulders, to keep ourselves in touch with all that goes on. You understand me, Monsieur Gerard?'

I had not the least idea what he was driving at, but I bowed and tried to look as if it was clear to me.

'Act very guardedly, then, and say nothing to anybody,' said Talleyrand. 'Colonel de Lasalle and I will not show ourselves in public with you, but we will await you here, and we will give you our advice when you have told us what has passed between the

Emperor and yourself. It is time that you started now, for the Emperor never forgives unpunctuality.'

Off I went on foot to the palace, which was only a hundred paces off. I made my way to the antechamber, where Duroc, with his grand new scarlet and gold coat, was fussing about among the crowd of people who were waiting. I heard him whisper to Monsieur de Caulaincourt that half of them were German Dukes who expected to be made Kings, and the other half German Dukes who expected to be made paupers. Duroc, when he heard my name, showed me straight in, and I found myself in the Emperor's presence.

I had, of course, seen him in camp a hundred times, but I had never been face to face with him before. I have no doubt that if you had met him without knowing in the least who he was, you would simply have said that he was a sallow little fellow with a good forehead and fairly well-turned calves. His tight white cashmere breeches and white stockings showed off his legs to advantage. But even a stranger must have been struck by the singular look of his eyes, which could harden into an expression which would frighten a grenadier. It is said that even Auguereau, who was a man who had never known what fear was, quailed before

Napoleon's gaze, at a time, too, when the Emperor was but an unknown soldier. He looked mildly enough at me, however, and motioned me to remain by the door. De Meneval was writing to his dictation, looking up at him between each sentence with his spaniel eyes.

'That will do. You can go,' said the Emperor, abruptly. Then, when the secretary had left the room, he strode across with his hands behind his back, and he looked me up and down without a word. Though he was a small man himself, he was very fond of having fine-looking fellows about him, and so I think that my appearance gave him pleasure. For my own part, I raised one hand to the salute and held the other upon the hilt of my sabre, looking straight ahead of me, as a soldier should.

'Well, Monsieur Gerard,' said he, at last, tapping his forefinger upon one of the brandebourgs of gold braid upon the front of my pelisse, 'I am informed that you are a very deserving young officer. Your Colonel gives me an excellent account of you.'

I wished to make a brilliant reply, but I could think of nothing save Lasalle's phrase that I was all spurs and moustaches, so it ended in my saying nothing at all. The Emperor watched the struggle which must have shown itself upon my features, and when, finally, no answer came he did not appear to be displeased.

'I believe that you are the very man that I want,' said he. 'Brave and clever men surround me upon every side. But a brave man who — ' He did not finish his sentence, and for my own part I could not understand what he was driving at. I contented myself with assuring him that he could count upon me to the death.

'You are, as I understand, a good swordsman?' said he.

'Tolerable, sire,' I answered.

'You were chosen by your regiment to fight the champion of the Hussars of Chambarant?' said he.

I was not sorry to find that he knew so much of my exploits.

'My comrades, sire, did me that honour,' said I.

'And for the sake of practice you insulted six fencing masters in the week before your duel?'

'I had the privilege of being out seven times in as many days, sire,' said I.

'And escaped without a scratch?'

'The fencing master of the 23rd Light Infantry touched me on the left elbow, sire.'

'Let us have no more child's play of the

sort, monsieur,' he cried, turning suddenly to that cold rage of his which was so appalling. 'Do you imagine that I place veteran soldiers in these positions that you may practise quarte and tierce upon them? How am I to face Europe if my soldiers turn their points upon each other? Another word of your duelling, and I break you between these fingers.'

I saw his plump white hands flash before my eyes as he spoke, and his voice had turned to the most discordant hissing and growling. My word, my skin pringled all over as I listened to him, and I would gladly have changed my position for that of the first man in the steepest and narrowest breach that ever swallowed up a storming party. He turned to the table, drank off a cup of coffee, and then when he faced me again every trace of this storm had vanished, and he wore that singular smile which came from his lips but never from his eyes.

'I have need of your services, Monsieur Gerard,' said he. 'I may be safer with a good sword at my side, and there are reasons why yours should be the one which I select. But first of all I must bind you to secrecy. Whilst I live what passes between us today must be known to none but ourselves.'

I thought of Talleyrand and of Lasalle, but I promised.

'In the next place, I do not want your opinions or conjectures, and I wish you to do exactly what you are told.'

I bowed.

'It is your sword that I need, and not your brains. I will do the thinking. Is that clear to you?'

'Yes, sire.'

'You know the Chancellor's Grove, in the forest?'

I bowed.

'You know also the large double fir-tree where the hounds assembled on Tuesday?'

Had he known that I met a girl under it three times a week, he would not have asked me. I bowed once more without remark.

'Very good. You will meet me there at ten o'clock tonight.'

I had got past being surprised at anything which might happen. If he had asked me to take his place upon the imperial throne I could only have nodded my busby.

'We shall then proceed into the wood together,' said the Emperor. 'You will be armed with a sword, but not with pistols. You must address no remark to me, and I shall say nothing to you. We will advance in silence. You understand?'

'I understand, sire.'

'After a time we shall see a man, or more probably two men, under a certain tree. We shall approach them together. If I signal to you to defend me, you will have your sword ready. If, on the other hand, I speak to these men, you will wait and see what happens. If you are called upon to draw, you must see that neither of them, in the event of there being two, escapes from us. I shall myself assist you.'

'Sire,' I cried, 'I have no doubt that two would not be too many for my sword; but would it not be better that I should bring a comrade than that you should be forced to join in such a struggle?'

'Ta, ta, ta,' said he. 'I was a soldier before I was an Emperor. Do you think, then, that artillerymen have not swords as well as the hussars? But I ordered you not to argue with me. You will do exactly what I tell you. If swords are once out, neither of these men is to get away alive.'

'They shall not, sire,' said I.

'Very good. I have no more instructions for you. You can go.'

I turned to the door, and then an idea occurring to me I turned.

'I have been thinking, sire — ' said I.

He sprang at me with the ferocity of a wild

beast. I really thought he would have struck me.

'Thinking!' he cried. 'You, *you*! Do you imagine I chose you out because you could think? Let me hear of your doing such a thing again! You, the one man — but, there! You meet me at the fir-tree at ten o'clock.'

My faith, I was right glad to get out of the room. If I have a good horse under me, and a sword clanking against my stirrup-iron, I know where I am. And in all that relates to green fodder or dry, barley and oats and rye, and the handling of squadrons upon the march, there is no one who can teach me very much. But when I meet a Chamberlain and a Marshal of the Palace, and have to pick my words with an Emperor, and find that everybody hints instead of talking straight out, I feel like a troop-horse who has been put in a lady's calèche. It is not my trade, all this mincing and pretending. I have learned the manners of a gentleman, but never those of a courtier. I was right glad then to get into the fresh air again, and I ran away up to my quarters like a schoolboy who has just escaped from the seminary master.

But as I opened the door, the very first thing that my eye rested upon was a long pair of sky-blue legs with hussar boots, and a short pair of black ones with knee breeches and buckles. They both sprang up together to greet me.

'Well, what news?' they cried, the two of them.

'None,' I answered.

'The Emperor refused to see you?'

'No, I have seen him.'

'And what did he say?'

'Monsieur de Talleyrand,' I answered, 'I regret to say that it is quite impossible for me to tell you anything about it. I have promised the Emperor.'

'Pooh, pooh, my dear young man,' said he, sidling up to me, as a cat does when it is about to rub itself against you. 'This is all among friends, you understand, and goes no farther than these four walls. Besides, the Emperor never meant to include me in this promise.'

'It is but a minute's walk to the palace, Monsieur de Talleyrand,' I answered; 'if it would not be troubling you too much to ask you to step up to it and bring back the Emperor's written statement that he did not mean to include you in this promise, I shall be happy to tell you every word that passed.'

He showed his teeth at me then like the old fox that he was.

'Monsieur Gerard appears to be a little puffed up,' said he. 'He is too young to see things in their just proportion. As he grows older he may understand that it is not always very discreet for a subaltern of cavalry to give such very abrupt refusals.'

I did not know what to say to this, but Lasalle came to my aid in his downright fashion.

'The lad is quite right,' said he. 'If I had known that there was a promise I should not have questioned him. You know very well, Monsieur de Talleyrand, that if he had answered you, you would have laughed in your sleeve and thought as much about him as I think of the bottle when the burgundy is gone. As for me, I promise you that the Tenth would have had no room for him, and that we should have lost our best swordsman if I had heard him give up the Emperor's secret.'

But the statesman became only the more bitter when he saw that I had the support of my Colonel.

'I have heard, Colonel de Lasalle,' said he, with an icy dignity, 'that your opinion is of great weight upon the subject of light cavalry. Should I have occasion to seek information about that branch of the army, I shall be very happy to apply to you. At present, however, the matter concerns diplomacy, and you will permit me to form my own views upon that question. As long as the welfare of France and the safety of the Emperor's person are largely committed to my care, I will use every means in my power to secure them, even if it should be against the Emperor's own temporary wishes. I have the honour, Colonel de Lasalle, to wish you a very good-day!'

He shot a most unamiable glance in my direction, and, turning upon his heel, he walked with little, quick, noiseless steps out of the room.

I could see from Lasalle's face that he did not at all relish finding himself at enmity with the powerful Minister. He rapped out an oath or two, and then, catching up his sabre and his cap, he clattered away down the stairs. As I looked out of the window I saw the two of them, the big blue man and the limping black one, going up the street together. Talleyrand was walking very rigidly, and Lasalle was waving his hands and talking, so I suppose he was trying to make his peace.

The Emperor had told me not to think, and I endeavoured to obey him. I took up the cards from the table where Morat had left them, and I tried to work out a few combinations at écarté. But I could not remember which were trumps, and I threw them under the table in despair. Then I drew my sabre and practised giving point until I was weary, but it was all of no use at all. My mind *would* work, in spite of myself. At ten o'clock I was to meet the Emperor in the forest. Of all extraordinary combinations of events in the whole world, surely this was the last which would have occurred to me when I rose from my couch that morning. But the responsibility — the dreadful responsibility! It was all upon my shoulders. There was no one to halve it with me. It made me cold all over. Often as I have faced death upon the battlefield, I have never known what real fear was until that moment. But then I considered that after all I could but do my best like a brave and honourable gentleman, and above all obey the orders which I had received, to the very letter. And, if all went well, this would surely be the foundation of my fortunes. Thus, swaying between my fears and my hopes, I spent the long, long evening until it was time to keep my appointment.

I put on my military overcoat, as I did not know how much of the night I might have to spend in the woods, and I fastened my sword outside it. I pulled off my hussar boots also, and wore a pair of shoes and gaiters, that I might be lighter upon my feet. Then I stole out of my quarters and made for the forest, feeling very much easier in my mind, for I am always at my best when the time of thought has passed and the moment for action arrived.

I passed the barracks of the Chasseurs of the Guards, and the line of cafes all filled with uniforms. I caught a glimpse as I went by of the blue and gold of some of my comrades, amid the swarm of dark infantry coats and the light green of the Guides. There they sat, sipping their wine and smoking their cigars, little dreaming what their comrade had on hand. One of them, the chief of my squadron, caught sight of me in the lamplight, and came shouting after me into the street. I hurried on, however, pretending not to hear him, so he, with a curse at my deafness, went back at last to his wine bottle.

It is not very hard to get into the forest at Fontainebleau. The scattered trees steal their way into the very streets, like the tirailleurs in front of a column. I turned into a path, which led to the edge of the woods, and then I pushed rapidly forward towards the old fir-tree. It was a place which, as I have hinted, I had my own reasons for knowing well, and I could only thank the Fates that it was not one of the nights upon which Léonie would be waiting for me. The poor child would have died of terror at sight of the Emperor. He might have been too harsh with her — and worse still, he might have been too kind.

There was a half moon shining, and, as I came up to our trysting-place, I saw that I was not the first to arrive. The Emperor was pacing up and down, his hands behind him and his face sunk somewhat forward upon his breast. He wore a grey great-coat with a capote over his head. I had seen him in such a dress in our winter campaign in Poland, and it was said that he used it because the hood was such an excellent disguise. He was always fond, whether in the camp or in Paris, of walking round at night, and overhearing the talk in the cabarets or round the fires. His figure, however, and his way of carrying his head and his hands were so well known that he was always recognized, and then the talkers would say whatever they thought would please him best.

My first thought was that he would be angry with me for having kept him waiting, but as I approached him, we heard the big church clock of Fontainebleau clang out the hour of ten. It was evident, therefore, that it was he who was too soon, and not I too late. I remembered his order that I should make no remark, so contented myself with halting within four paces of him, clicking my spurs together, grounding my sabre, and saluting. He glanced at me, and then without a word he turned and walked slowly through the forest, I keeping always about the same distance behind him. Once or twice he seemed to me to look apprehensively to right and to left, as if he feared that someone was observing us. I looked also, but although I have the keenest sight, it was quite impossible to see anything except the ragged patches of moonshine between the great black shadows of the trees. My ears are as quick as my eyes, and once or twice I thought that I heard a twig crack; but you know how many sounds there are in a forest at night, and how difficult it is even to say what direction they come from.

We walked for rather more than a mile, and I knew exactly what our destination was, long before we got there. In the centre of one of the glades, there is the shattered stump of what must at some time have been a most gigantic tree. It is called the Abbot's Beech, and there are so many ghostly stories about it, that I know many a brave soldier who would not care about mounting sentinel over it. However, I cared as little for such folly as the Emperor did, so we crossed the glade and made straight for the old broken trunk. As we approached, I saw that two men were waiting for us beneath it.

When I first caught sight of them they were standing rather behind it, as if they were not anxious to be seen, but as we came nearer they emerged from its shadow and walked forward to meet us. The Emperor glanced back at me, and slackened his pace a little so that I came within arm's length of him. You may think that I had my hilt well to the front, and that I had a very good look at these two people who were approaching us.

The one was tall, remarkably so, and of very spare frame, while the other was rather below the usual height, and had a brisk, determined way of walking. They each wore black cloaks, which were slung right across their figures, and hung down upon one side, like the mantles of Murat's dragoons. They had flat black caps, like those I have since seen in Spain, which threw their faces into darkness, though I could see the gleam of their eyes from beneath them. With the moon behind them and their long black shadows walking in front, they were such figures as one might expect to meet at night near the Abbot's Beech. I can remember that they had a stealthy way of moving, and that as they approached, the moonshine formed two white diamonds between their legs and the legs of their shadows.

The Emperor had paused, and these two strangers came to a stand also within a few paces of us. I had drawn up close to my

64

companion's elbow, so that the four of us were facing each other without a word spoken. My eyes were particularly fixed upon the taller one, because he was slightly the nearer to me, and I became certain as I watched him that he was in the last state of nervousness. His lean figure was quivering all over, and I heard a quick, thin panting like that of a tired dog. Suddenly one of them gave a short, hissing signal. The tall man bent his back and his knees like a diver about to spring, but before he could move, I had jumped with drawn sabre in front of him. At the same instant the smaller man bounded past me, and buried a long poniard in the Emperor's heart.

My God! the horror of that moment! It is a marvel that I did not drop dead myself. As in a dream, I saw the grey coat whirl convulsively round, and caught a glimpse in the moonlight of three inches of red point which jutted out from between the shoulders. Then down he fell with a dead man's gasp upon the grass, and the assassin, leaving his weapon buried in his victim, threw up both his hands and shrieked with joy. But I — I drove my sword through his midriff with such frantic force, that the mere blow of the hilt against the end of his breast-bone sent him six paces before he fell, and left my reeking blade ready for the other. I sprang round upon him with such a lust for blood upon me as I had never felt, and never have felt, in all my days. As I turned, a dagger flashed before my eyes, and I felt the cold wind of it pass my neck and the villain's wrist jar upon my shoulder. I shortened my sword, but he winced away from me, and an instant afterwards was in full flight, bounding like a deer across the glade in the moonlight.

But he was not to escape me thus. I knew that the murderer's poniard had done its work. Young as I was, I had seen enough of war to know a mortal blow. I paused but for an instant to touch the cold hand.

'Sire! Sire!' I cried, in an agony; and then as no sound came back and nothing moved, save an ever-widening dark circle in the moonlight, I knew that all was indeed over. I sprang madly to my feet, threw off my great-coat, and ran at the top of my speed after the remaining assassin.

Ah, how I blessed the wisdom which had caused me to come in shoes and gaiters! And the happy thought which had thrown off my coat. He could not get rid of his mantle, this wretch, or else he was too frightened to think of it. So it was that I gained upon him from the beginning. He must have been out of his wits, for he never tried to bury himself in the darker parts of the woods, but he flew on from glade to glade, until he came to the heath-land which leads up to the great Fontainebleau quarry. There I had him in full sight, and knew that he could not escape me. He ran well, it is true — ran as a coward runs when his life is the stake. But I ran as Destiny runs when it gets behind a man's heels. Yard by yard I drew in upon him. He was rolling and staggering. I could hear the rasping and crackling of his breath. The great gulf of the quarry suddenly yawned in front of his path, and glancing at me over his shoulder, he gave a shriek of despair. The next instant he had vanished from my sight.

Vanished utterly, you understand. I rushed to the spot, and gazed down into the black abyss. Had he hurled himself over? I had almost made up my mind that he had done so, when a gentle sound rising and falling came out of the darkness beneath me. It was his breathing once more, and it showed me where he must be. He was hiding in the tool-house.

At the edge of the quarry and beneath the summit there is a small platform upon which stands a wooden hut for the use of the labourers. It was into this, then, that he had darted. Perhaps he had thought, the fool, that, in the darkness, I would not venture to follow him. He little knew Etienne Gerard. With a spring I was on the platform, with another I was through the doorway, and then, hearing him in the corner, I hurled myself down upon the top of him.

He fought like a wild cat, but he never had a chance with his shorter weapon. I think that I must have transfixed him with that first mad lunge, for, though he struck and struck, his blows had no power in them, and presently his dagger tinkled down upon the floor. When I was sure that he was dead, I rose up and passed out into the moonlight. I climbed on to the heath again, and wandered across it as nearly out of my mind as a man could be.

With the blood singing in my ears, and my naked sword still clutched in my hand, I walked aimlessly on until, looking round me, I found that I had come as far as the glade of the Abbot's Beech, and saw in the distance that gnarled stump which must ever be associated with the most terrible moment of my life. I sat down upon a fallen trunk with my sword across my knees and my head between my hands, and I tried to think about what had happened and what would happen in the future.

The Emperor had committed himself to my care. The Emperor was dead. Those were the two thoughts which clanged in my head, until I had no room for any other ones. He had come with me and he was dead. I had done what he had ordered when living. I had revenged him when dead. But what of all that? The world would look upon me as responsible. They might even look upon me as the assassin. What could I prove? What witnesses had I? Might I not have been the accomplice of these wretches? Yes, yes, I was eternally dishonoured — the lowest, most despicable creature in all France. This, then, was the end of my fine military ambitions — of the hopes of my mother. I laughed bitterly at the thought. And what was I to do now? Was I to go into Fontainebleau, to wake up the palace, and to inform them that the great Emperor had been murdered within a pace of me? I could not do it — no, I could not do it! There was but one course for an honourable gentleman whom Fate had placed in so cruel a position. I would fall upon my dishonoured sword, and so share, since I could not avert, the Emperor's fate. I rose with my nerves strung to this last piteous deed, and as I did so, my eyes fell upon something which struck the breath from my lips. The Emperor was standing before me!

He was not more than ten yards off, with the moon shining straight upon his cold, pale face. He wore his grey overcoat, but the hood was turned back, and the front open, so that I could see the green coat of the Guides, and the white breeches. His hands were clasped behind his back, and his chin sunk forward upon his breast, in the way that was usual with him.

'Well,' said he, in his hardest and most abrupt voice, 'what account do you give of yourself?'

I believe that, if he had stood in silence for another minute, my brain would have given way. But those sharp military accents were exactly what I needed to bring me to myself. Living or dead, here was the Emperor standing before me and asking me questions. I sprang to the salute.

'You have killed one, I see,' said he, jerking his head towards the beech.

'Yes, sire.'

'And the other escaped?'

'No, sire, I killed him also.'

'What!' he cried. 'Do I understand that you have killed them both?' He approached me as he spoke with a smile which set his teeth gleaming in the moonlight.

'One body lies there, sire,' I answered. 'The other is in the tool-house at the quarry.'

'Then the Brothers of Ajaccio are no more,' he cried, and after a pause, as if speaking to himself: 'The shadow has passed me for ever.'

Then he bent forward and laid his hand upon my shoulder.

'You have done very well, my young friend,' said he. 'You have lived up to your reputation.'

He was flesh and blood, then, this Emperor. I could feel the little, plump palm that rested upon me. And yet I could not get over what I had seen with my own eyes, and so I stared at him in such bewilderment that he broke once more into one of his smiles.

'No, no, Monsieur Gerard,' said he, 'I am not a ghost, and you have not seen me killed. You will come here, and all will be clear to you.'

He turned as he spoke, and led the way towards the great beech stump.

The bodies were still lying upon the ground, and two men were standing beside them. As we approached I saw from the turbans that they were Roustem and Mustafa, the two Mameluke servants. The Emperor paused when he came to the grey figure upon the ground, and turning back the hood which shrouded the features, he showed a face which was very different from his own.

'Here lies a faithful servant who has given up his life for his master,' said he. 'Monsieur de Goudin resembles me in figure and in manner, as you must admit.'

What a delirium of joy came upon me when these few words made everything clear to me. He smiled again as he saw the delight which urged me to throw my arms round him and to embrace him, but he moved a step away, as if he had divined my impulse.

'You are unhurt?' he asked.

'I am unhurt, sire. But in another minute I should in my despair — '

'Tut, tut!' he interrupted. 'You did very well. He should himself have been more on his guard. I saw everything which passed.'

'You saw it, sire!'

'You did not hear me follow you through the wood, then? I hardly lost sight of you from the moment that you left your quarters until poor De Goudin fell. The counterfeit Emperor was in front of you and the real one behind. You will now escort me back to the palace.'

He whispered an order to his Mamelukes, who saluted in silence and remained where they were standing. For my part, I followed the Emperor with my pelisse bursting with pride. My word, I have always carried myself as a hussar should, but Lasalle himself never strutted and swung his dolman as I did that night. Who should clink his spurs and clatter his sabre if it were not I — I, Etienne Gerard — the confidant of the Emperor, the chosen swordsman of the light cavalry, the man who slew the would-be assassins of Napoleon? But he noticed my bearing and turned upon me like a blight.

'Is that the way you carry yourself on a secret mission?' he hissed, with that cold glare in his eyes. 'Is it thus that you will make your comrades believe that nothing remarkable has occurred? Have done with this nonsense, monsieur, or you will find yourself transferred to the sappers, where you would have harder work and duller plumage.'

That was the way with the Emperor. If ever he thought that anyone might have a claim upon him, he took the first opportunity to show him the gulf that lay between. I saluted and was silent, but I must confess to you that it hurt me after all that had passed between us. He led on to the palace, where we passed through the side door and up into his own cabinet. There were a couple of grenadiers at the staircase, and their eyes started out from under their fur caps, I promise you, when they saw a young lieutenant of hussars going up to the Emperor's room at midnight. I stood by the door, as I had done in the afternoon, while he flung himself down in an arm-chair, and remained silent so long that it seemed to me that he had forgotten all about me. I ventured at last upon a slight cough to remind him.

'Ah, Monsieur Gerard,' said he, 'you are very curious, no doubt, as to the meaning of all this?'

'I am quite content, sire, if it is your pleasure not to tell me,' I answered.

'Ta, ta, ta,' said he impatiently. 'These are only words. The moment that you were outside that door you would begin making inquiries about what it means. In two days your brother officers would know about it, in three days it would be all over Fontainebleau, and it would be in Paris on the fourth. Now, if I tell you enough to appease your curiosity, there is some reasonable hope that you may be able to keep the matter to yourself.'

He did not understand me, this Emperor, and yet I could only bow and be silent.

'A few words will make it clear to you,' said he, speaking very swiftly and pacing up and down the room. 'They were Corsicans, these two men. I had known them in my youth. We had belonged to the same society — Brothers of Ajaccio, as we called ourselves. It was founded in the old Paoli days, you understand, and we had some strict rules of our own which were not infringed with impunity.'

A very grim look came over his face as he

spoke, and it seemed to me that all that was French had gone out of him, and that it was the pure Corsican, the man of strong passions and of strange revenges, who stood before me. His memory had gone back to those early days of his, and for five minutes, wrapped in thought, he paced up and down the room with his quick little tiger steps. Then with an impatient wave of his hands he came back to his palace and to me.

'The rules of such a society,' he continued, 'are all very well for a private citizen. In the old days there was no more loyal brother than I. But circumstances change, and it would be neither for my welfare nor for that of France that I should now submit myself to them. They wanted to hold me to it, and so brought their fate upon their own heads. These were the two chiefs of the order, and they had come from Corsica to summon me to meet them at the spot which they named. I knew what such a summons meant. No man had ever returned from obeying one. On the other hand, if I did not go, I was sure that disaster would follow. I am a brother myself, you remember, and I know their ways.'

Again there came that hardening of his mouth and cold glitter of his eyes.

'You perceive my dilemma, Monsieur Gerard,' said he. 'How would you have acted yourself, under such circumstances?'

'Given the word to the 10th Hussars, sire,' I cried. 'Patrols could have swept the woods from end to end, and brought these two rascals to your feet.'

He smiled, but he shook his head.

'I had very excellent reasons why I did not wish them taken alive,' said he. 'You can understand that an assassin's tongue might be as dangerous a weapon as an assassin's dagger. I will not disguise from you that I wished to avoid scandal at all cost. That was why I ordered you to take no pistols with you. That also is why my Mamelukes will remove all traces of the affair, and nothing more will be heard about it. I thought of all possible plans, and I am convinced that I selected the best one. Had I sent more than one guard with De Goudin into the woods, then the brothers would not have appeared. They would not change their plans nor miss their chance for the sake of a single man. It was Colonel Lasalle's accidental presence at the moment when I received the summons which led to my choosing one of his hussars for the mission. I selected you, Monsieur Gerard, because I wanted a man who could handle a sword, and who would not pry more deeply into the affair than I desired. I trust that, in this respect, you will justify my choice as well as you have done in your bravery and skill.'

'Sire,' I answered, 'you may rely upon it.'

'As long as I live,' said he, 'you never open your lips upon this subject.'

'I dismiss it entirely from my mind, sire. I will efface it from my recollection as if it had never been. I will promise you to go out of your cabinet at this moment exactly as I was when I entered it at four o'clock.'

'You cannot do that,' said the Emperor, smiling. 'You were a lieutenant at that time. You will permit me, Captain, to wish you a very good-night.'

3

How the Brigadier Held the King

Here, upon the lapel of my coat, you may see the ribbon of my decoration, but the medal itself I keep in a leathern pouch at home, and I never venture to take it out unless one of the modern peace generals, or some foreigner of distinction who finds himself in our little town, takes advantage of the opportunity to pay his respects to the well-known Brigadier Gerard. Then I place it upon my breast, and I give my moustache the old Marengo twist which brings a grey point into either eye. Yet with it all I fear that neither they, nor you either, my friends, will ever realize the man that I was. You know me only as a civilian — with an air and a manner, it is true — but still merely as a civilian. Had you seen me as I stood in the doorway of the inn at Alamo, on the 1st of July, in the year 1810, you would then have known what the hussar may attain to.

For a month I had lingered in that accursed village, and all on account of a lance-thrust in my ankle, which made it impossible for me to put my foot to the ground. There were three besides myself at first: old Bouvet, of the Hussars of Bercheny, Jacques Regnier, of the Cuirassiers, and a funny little voltigeur captain whose name I forget; but they all got well and hurried on to the front, while I sat gnawing my fingers and tearing my hair, and even, I must confess, weeping from time to time as I thought of my Hussars of Conflans, and the deplorable condition in which they must find themselves when deprived of their colonel. I was not a chief of brigade yet, you understand, although I already carried myself like one, but I was the youngest colonel in the whole service, and my regiment was wife and children to me. It went to my heart that they should be so bereaved. It is true that Villaret, the senior major, was an excellent soldier; but still, even among the best there are degrees of merit.

Ah, that happy July day of which I speak, when first I limped to the door and stood in the golden Spanish sunshine! It was but the evening before that I had heard from the regiment. They were at Pastores, on the other side of the mountains, face to face with the English — not forty miles from me by road. But how was I to get to them? The same thrust which had pierced my ankle had slain my charger. I took advice both from Gomez, the landlord, and from an old priest who had slept that night in the inn, but neither of them could do more than assure me that there was not so much as a colt left upon the whole countryside.

The landlord would not hear of my crossing the mountains without an escort, for he assured me that El Cuchillo, the Spanish guerilla chief, was out that way with his band, and that it meant a death by torture to fall into his hands. The old priest observed, however, that he did not think a French hussar would be deterred by that, and if I had had any doubts, they would of course have been decided by his remark.

But a horse! How was I to get one? I was standing in the doorway, plotting and planning, when I heard the clink of shoes, and, looking up, I saw a great bearded man, with a blue cloak frogged across in military fashion, coming towards me. He was riding a big black horse with one white stocking on his near fore-leg.

'Halloa, comrade!' said I, as he came up to me.

'Halloa!' said he.

'I am Colonel Gerard, of the Hussars,' said I. 'I have lain here wounded for a month, and I am now ready to rejoin my regiment at Pastores.'

'I am Monsieur Vidal, of the commissariat,' he answered, 'and I am myself upon my way to Pastores. I should be glad to have your company, Colonel, for I hear that the mountains are far from safe.'

'Alas,' said I, 'I have no horse. But if you will sell me yours, I will promise that an escort of hussars shall be sent back for you.'

He would not hear of it, and it was in vain that the landlord told him dreadful stories of the doings of El Cuchillo, and that I pointed out the duty which he owed to the army and to the country. He would not even argue, but called loudly for a cup of wine. I craftily asked him to dismount and to drink with me, but he must have seen something in my face, for he shook his head; and then, as I approached him with some thought of seizing him by the leg, he jerked his heels into his horse's flanks, and was off in a cloud of dust.

My faith! it was enough to make a man mad to see this fellow riding away so gaily to join his beef-barrels, and his brandy-casks, and then to think of my five hundred beautiful hussars without their leader. I was gazing after him with bitter thoughts in my mind, when who should touch me on the elbow but the little priest whom I have mentioned.

'It is I who can help you,' he said. 'I am

myself travelling south.'

I put my arms about him and, as my ankle gave way at the same moment, we nearly rolled upon the ground together.

'Get me to Pastores,' I cried, 'and you shall have a rosary of golden beads.' I had taken one from the Convent of Spiritu Santo. It shows how necessary it is to take what you can when you are upon a campaign, and how the most unlikely things may become useful.

'I will take you,' he said, in very excellent French, 'not because I hope for any reward, but because it is my way always to do what I can to serve my fellow-man, and that is why I am so beloved wherever I go.'

With that he led me down the village to an old cow-house, in which we found a tumble-down sort of diligence, such as they used to run early in this century, between some of our remote villages. There were three old mules, too, none of which were strong enough to carry a man, but together they might draw the coach. The sight of their gaunt ribs and spavined legs gave me more delight than the whole two hundred and twenty hunters of the Emperor which I have seen in their stalls at Fontainebleau. In ten minutes the owner was harnessing them into the coach, with no very good will, however, for he was in mortal dread of this terrible

Cuchillo. It was only by promising him riches in this world, while the priest threatened him with perdition in the next, that we at last got him safely upon the box with the reins between his fingers. Then he was in such a hurry to get off, out of fear lest we should find ourselves in the dark in the passes, that he hardly gave me time to renew my vows to the innkeeper's daughter. I cannot at this moment recall her name, but we wept together as we parted, and I can remember that she was a very beautiful woman. You will understand, my friends, that when a man like me, who has fought the men and kissed the women in fourteen separate kingdoms, gives a word of praise to the one or the other, it has a little meaning of its own.

The little priest had seemed a trifle grave when we kissed good-bye, but he soon proved himself the best of companions in the diligence. All the way he amused me with tales of his little parish up in the mountains, and I in my turn told him stories about the camp; but, my faith, I had to pick my steps, for when I said a word too much he would fidget in his seat and his face would show the pain that I had given him. And of course it is not the act of a gentleman to talk in anything but a proper manner to a religious man, though, with all the care in the world, one's words may get out of hand sometimes.

He had come from the north of Spain, as he told me, and was going to see his mother in a village of Estremadura, and as he spoke about her little peasant home, and her joy in seeing him, it brought my own mother so vividly to my thoughts that the tears started to my eyes. In his simplicity he showed me the little gifts which he was taking to her, and so kindly was his manner that I could readily believe him when he said he was loved wherever he went. He examined my own uniform with as much curiosity as a child, admiring the plume of my busby, and passing his fingers through the sable with which my dolman was trimmed. He drew my sword, too, and then when I told him how many men I had cut down with it, and set my finger on the notch made by the shoulder-bone of the Russian Emperor's aide-de-camp, he shuddered and placed the weapon under the leathern cushion, declaring that it made him sick to look at it.

Well, we had been rolling and creaking on our way whilst this talk had been going forward, and as we reached the base of the mountains we could hear the rumbling of cannon far away upon the right. This came from Massena, who was, as I knew, besieging Ciudad Rodrigo. There was nothing I should have wished better than to have gone straight to him, for if, as some said, he had Jewish blood in his veins, he was the best Jew that I have heard of since Joshua's time. If you were in sight of his beaky nose and bold, black eyes, you were not likely to miss much of what was going on. Still, a siege is always a poor sort of a pick-and-shovel business, and there were better prospects with my hussars in front of the English. Every mile that passed, my heart grew lighter and lighter, until I found myself shouting and singing like a young ensign fresh from St Cyr, just to think of seeing all my fine horses and my gallant fellows once more.

As we penetrated the mountains the road grew rougher and the pass more savage. At first we had met a few muleteers, but now the whole country seemed deserted, which is not to be wondered at when you think that the French, the English, and the guerillas had each in turn had command over it. So bleak and wild was it, one great brown wrinkled cliff succeeding another, and the pass growing narrower and narrower, that I ceased to look out, but sat in silence, thinking of this and that, of women whom I had loved and of horses which I had handled. I was suddenly brought back from my dreams, however, by observing the difficulties of my companion, who was trying with a sort of brad-awl, which he had drawn out, to bore a hole through the leathern strap which held up his water-flask. As he worked with twitching fingers the strap escaped his grasp, and the wooden bottle fell at my feet. I stooped to pick it up, and as I did so the priest silently leaped upon my shoulders and drove his brad-awl into my eye!

My friends, I am, as you know, a man steeled to face every danger. When one has served from the affair of Zurich to that last fatal day of Waterloo, and has had the special medal, which I keep at home in a leathern pouch, one can afford to confess when one is frightened. It may console some of you, when your own nerves play you tricks, to remember that you have heard even me, Brigadier Gerard, say that I have been scared. And besides my terror at this horrible attack, and the maddening pain of my wound, there was a sudden feeling of loathing such as you might feel were some filthy tarantula to strike its fangs into you.

I clutched the creature in both hands, and, hurling him on to the floor of the coach, I stamped on him with my heavy boots. He had drawn a pistol from the front of his soutane, but I kicked it out of his hand, and again I fell with my knees upon his chest. Then, for the first time, he screamed horribly, while I, half blinded, felt about for the sword which he had so cunningly concealed. My hand had just lighted upon it, and I was dashing the blood from my face to see where he lay that I might transfix him, when the whole coach turned partly over upon its side, and my weapon was jerked out of my grasp by the shock.

Before I could recover myself the door was burst open, and I was dragged by the heels on to the road. But even as I was torn out on to the flint stones, and realized that thirty ruffians were standing around me, I was filled with joy, for my pelisse had been pulled over my head in the struggle and was covering one of my eyes, and it was with my wounded eye that I was seeing this gang of brigands. You see for yourself by this pucker and scar how the thin blade passed between socket and ball, but it was only at that moment, when I was dragged from the coach, that I understood that my sight was not gone for ever. The creature's intention, doubtless, was to drive it through into my brain, and indeed he loosened some portion of the inner bone of my head, so that I afterwards had more trouble from that wound than from any one of the seventeen which I have received.

They dragged me out, these sons of dogs, with curses and execrations, beating me with their fists and kicking me as I lay upon the ground. I had frequently observed that the mountaineers wore cloth swathed round their feet, but never did I imagine that I should have so much cause to be thankful for it. Presently, seeing the blood upon my head, and that I lay quiet, they thought that I was unconscious, whereas I was storing every ugly face among them into my memory, so that I might see them all safely hanged if ever my chance came round. Brawny rascals they were, with yellow handkerchiefs round their heads, and great red sashes stuffed with weapons. They had rolled two rocks across the path, where it took a sharp turn, and it was these which had torn off one of the wheels of the coach and upset us. As to this reptile, who had acted the priest so cleverly and had told me so much of his parish and his mother, he, of course, had known where the ambuscade was laid, and had attempted to put me beyond all resistance at the moment when we reached it.

I cannot tell you how frantic their rage was when they drew him out of the coach and saw the state to which I had reduced him. If he had not got all his deserts, he had, at least, something as a souvenir of his meeting with Etienne Gerard, for his legs dangled aimlessly about, and though the upper part of his body was convulsed with rage and pain, he sat straight down upon his feet when they tried to set him upright. But all the time his two little black eyes, which had seemed so kindly and so innocent in the coach, were glaring at me like a wounded cat, and he spat, and spat, and spat in my direction. My faith! when the wretches jerked me on to my feet again, and when I was dragged off up one of the mountain paths, I understood that a time was coming when I was to need all my courage and resource. My enemy was carried upon the shoulders of two men behind me, and I could hear his hissing and his reviling, first in one ear and then in the other, as I was hurried up the winding track.

I suppose that it must have been for an hour that we ascended, and what with my wounded ankle and the pain from my eye, and the fear lest this wound should have spoiled my appearance, I have made no journey to which I look back with less pleasure. I have never been a good climber at any time, but it is astonishing what you can do, even with a stiff ankle, when you have a copper-coloured brigand at each elbow and a nine-inch blade within touch of your whiskers.

We came at last to a place where the path wound over a ridge, and descended upon the other side through thick pine-trees into a valley which opened to the south. In time of peace I had little doubt that the villains were all smugglers, and that these were the secret paths by which they crossed the Portuguese frontier. There were many mule-tracks, and once I was surprised to see the marks of a large horse where a stream had softened the track. These were explained when, on reaching a place where there was a clearing in the fir wood, I saw the animal itself haltered to a fallen tree. My eyes had hardly rested upon it, when I recognized the great black limbs and the white near fore-leg. It was the very horse which I had begged for in the morning.

What, then, had become of Commissariat Vidal? Was it possible that there was another Frenchman in as perilous a plight as myself? The thought had hardly entered my head when our party stopped and one of them uttered a peculiar cry. It was answered from among the brambles which lined the base of a cliff at one side of a clearing, and an instant later ten or a dozen more brigands came out from amongst them, and the two parties greeted each other. The newcomers surrounded my friend of the brad-awl with cries of grief and sympathy, and then, turning upon me, they brandished their knives and howled at me like the gang of assassins that they were. So frantic were their gestures that I was convinced that my end had come, and was just bracing myself to meet it in a manner which should be worthy of my past reputation, when one of them gave an order and I was dragged roughly across the little glade to the brambles from which this new band had emerged.

A narrow pathway led through them to a deep grotto in the side of the cliff. The sun was already setting outside, and in the cave itself it would have been quite dark but for a pair of torches which blazed from a socket on either side. Between them there was sitting at a rude table a very singular-looking person, whom I saw instantly, from the respect with which the others addressed him, could be none other than the brigand chief who had received, on account of his dreadful character, the sinister name of El Cuchillo.

The man whom I had injured had been carried in and placed upon the top of a barrel, his helpless legs dangling about in front of him, and his cat's eyes still darting glances of hatred at me. I understood, from the snatches of talk which I could follow between the chief and him, that he was the lieutenant of the band, and that part of his duties was to lie in wait with his smooth tongue and his peaceful garb for travellers like myself. When I thought of how many gallant officers may have been lured to their death by this monster of hypocrisy, it gave me a glow of pleasure to think that I had brought his villainies to an end — though I feared it would be at the price of a life which neither the Emperor nor the army could well spare.

As the injured man still supported upon the barrel by two comrades, was explaining in Spanish all that had befallen him, I was held by several of the villains in front of the table at which the chief was seated, and had an excellent opportunity of observing him. I have seldom seen any man who was less like my idea of a brigand, and especially of a brigand with such a reputation that in a land of cruelty he had earned so dark a nickname. His face was bluff and broad and bland, with ruddy cheeks and comfortable little tufts of side-whiskers, which gave him the appearance of a well-to-do grocer of the Rue St Antoine. He had not any of those flaring sashes or gleaming weapons which distinguished his followers, but on the contrary he wore a good broadcloth coat like a respectable father of a family, and save for his brown leggings there was nothing to indicate a life among the mountains. His surroundings, too, corresponded with himself, and beside his snuff-box upon the table there stood a great brown book, which looked like a commercial ledger. Many other books were ranged along a plank between two powder-casks, and there was a great litter of papers, some of which had verses scribbled upon them. All this I took in while he, leaning indolently back in his chair, was listening to the report of his lieutenant. Having heard everything, he ordered the cripple to be carried out again, and I was left with my three guards, waiting to hear my fate. He took up his pen, and tapping his forehead with the handle of it, he pursed up his lips and looked out of the corner of his eyes at the roof of the grotto.

'I suppose,' said he at last, speaking very excellent French, 'that you are not able to suggest a rhyme for the word Covilha.'

I answered him that my acquaintance with the Spanish language was so limited that I was unable to oblige him.

'It is a rich language,' said he, 'but less prolific in rhymes than either the German or the English. That is why our best work has been done in blank verse, a form of composition which is capable of reaching great heights. But I fear that such subjects are somewhat outside the range of a hussar.'

I was about to answer that if they were good enough for a guerilla, they could not be too much for the light cavalry, but he was already stooping over his half-finished verse. Presently he threw down the pen with an exclamation of satisfaction, and declaimed a few lines which drew a cry of approval from the three ruffians who held me. His broad face blushed like a young girl who receives her first compliment.

'The critics are in my favour, it appears,' said he; 'we amuse ourselves in our long evenings by singing our own ballads, you understand. I have some little facility in that direction, and I do not at all despair of seeing some of my poor efforts in print before long, and with 'Madrid' upon the title-page, too. But we must get back to business. May I ask what your name is?'

'Etienne Gerard.'

'Rank?'

'Colonel.'

'Corps?'

'The Third Hussars of Conflans.'

'You are young for a colonel.'

'My career has been an eventful one.'

'Tut, that makes it the sadder,' said he, with his bland smile.

I made no answer to that, but I tried to show him by my bearing that I was ready for the worst which could befall me.

'By the way, I rather fancy that we have had

some of your corps here,' said he, turning over the pages of his big brown register. 'We endeavour to keep a record of our operations. Here is a heading under June 24th. Have you not a young officer named Soubiron, a tall, slight youth with light hair?'

'Certainly.'

'I see that we buried him upon that date.'

'Poor lad!' I cried. 'And how did he die?'

'We buried him.'

'But before you buried him?'

'You misunderstand me, Colonel. He was not dead before we buried him.'

'You buried him alive!'

For a moment I was too stunned to act. Then I hurled myself upon the man, as he sat with that placid smile of his upon his lips, and I would have torn his throat out had the three wretches not dragged me away from him. Again and again I made for him, panting and cursing, shaking off this man and that, straining and wrenching, but never quite free. At last, with my jacket torn nearly off my back and blood dripping from my wrists, I was hauled backwards in the bight of a rope and cords passed round my ankles and my arms.

'You sleek hound!' I cried. 'If ever I have you at my sword's point, I will teach you to maltreat one of my lads. You will find, you bloodthirsty beast, that my Emperor has long arms, and though you lie here like a rat in its hole, the time will come when he will tear you out of it, and you and your vermin will perish together.'

My faith, I have a rough side to my tongue, and there was not a hard word that I had learned in fourteen campaigns which I did not let fly at him; but he sat with the handle of his pen tapping against his forehead and his eyes squinting up at the roof as if he had conceived the idea of some new stanza. It was this occupation of his which showed me how I might get my point into him.

'You spawn!' said I; 'you think that you are safe here, but your life may be as short as that of your absurd verses, and God knows that it could not be shorter than that.'

Ah, you should have seen him bound from his chair when I said the words. This vile monster, who dispensed death and torture as a grocer serves out his figs, had one raw nerve then which I could prod at pleasure. His face grew livid, and those little bourgeois side-whiskers quivered and thrilled with passion.

'Very good, Colonel. You have said enough,' he cried, in a choking voice. 'You say that you have had a very distinguished career. I promise you also a very distinguished ending. Colonel Etienne Gerard of the Third Hussars shall have a death of his own.'

'And I only beg,' said I, 'that you will not commemorate it in verse.' I had one or two little ironies to utter, but he cut me short by a furious gesture which caused my three guards to drag me from the cave.

Our interview, which I have told you as nearly as I can remember it, must have lasted some time, for it was quite dark when we came out, and the moon was shining very clearly in the heavens. The brigands had lighted a great fire of the dried branches of the firtrees; not, of course, for warmth, since the night was already very sultry, but to cook their evening meal. A huge copper pot hung over the blaze, and the rascals were lying all round in the yellow glare, so that the scene looked like one of those pictures which Junot stole out of Madrid. There are some soldiers who profess to care nothing for art and the like, but I have always been drawn towards it myself, in which respect I show my good taste and my breeding. I remember, for example, that when Lefebvre was selling the plunder after the fall of Danzig, I bought a very fine picture, called 'Nymphs Surprised in a Wood,' and I carried it with me through two campaigns, until my charger had the misfortune to put his hoof through it.

I only tell you this, however, to show you

that I was never a mere rough soldier like Rapp or Ney. As I lay in that brigands' camp, I had little time or inclination to think about such matters. They had thrown me down under a tree, the three villains squatting round and smoking their cigarettes within hands' touch of me. What to do I could not imagine. In my whole career I do not suppose that I have ten times been in as hopeless a situation. 'But courage,' thought I. 'Courage, my brave boy! You were not made a Colonel of Hussars at twenty-eight because you could dance a cotillon. You are a picked man, Etienne; a man who has come through more than two hundred affairs, and this little one is surely not going to be the last.' I began eagerly to glance about for some chance of escape, and as I did so I saw something which filled me with great astonishment.

I have already told you that a large fire was burning in the centre of the glade. What with its glare, and what with the moonlight, everything was as clear as possible. On the other side of the glade there was a single tall fir-tree which attracted my attention because its trunk and lower branches were discoloured, as if a large fire had recently been lit underneath it. A clump of bushes grew in front of it which concealed the base. Well, as I looked towards it, I was surprised to see projecting above the bush, and fastened apparently to the tree, a pair of fine riding boots with the toes upwards. At first I thought that they were tied there, but as I looked harder I saw that they were secured by a great nail which was hammered through the foot of each. And then, suddenly, with a thrill of horror, I understood that these were not empty boots; and moving my head a little to the right, I was able to see who it was that had been fastened there, and why a fire had been lit beneath the tree. It is not pleasant to speak or to think of horrors, my friends, and I do not wish to give any of you bad dreams tonight — but I cannot take you among the Spanish guerillas without showing you what kind of men they were, and the sort of warfare that they waged. I will only say that I understood why Monsieur Vidal's horse was waiting masterless in the grove, and that I hoped he had met this terrible fate with sprightliness and courage, as a good French-man ought.

It was not a very cheering sight for me, as you can imagine. When I had been with their chief in the grotto I had been so carried away by my rage at the cruel death of young Soubiron, who was one of the brightest lads who ever threw his thigh over a charger, that I had never given a thought to my own position. Perhaps it would have been more politic had I spoken the ruffian fair, but it was too late now. The cork was drawn and I must drain the wine. Besides, if the harmless commissariat man were put to such a death, what hope was there for me, who had snapped the spine of their lieutenant? No, I was doomed in any case, and it was as well perhaps that I should have put the best face on the matter. This beast could bear witness that Etienne Gerard had died as he had lived, and that one prisoner at least had not quailed before him. I lay there thinking of the various girls who would mourn for me, and of my dear old mother, and of the deplorable loss which I should be, both to my regiment and to the Emperor, and I am not ashamed to confess to you that I shed tears as I thought of the general consternation which my premature end would give rise to.

But all the time I was taking the very keenest notice of everything which might possibly help me. I am not a man who would lie like a sick horse waiting for the farrier sergeant and the pole-axe. First I would give a little tug at my ankle cords, and then another at those which were round my wrists, and all the time that I was trying to loosen them I was peering round to see if I could find something which was in my favour.

There was one thing which was very evident. A hussar is but half formed without a horse, and there was my other half quietly grazing within thirty yards of me. Then I observed yet another thing. The path by which we had come over the mountains was so steep that a horse could only be led across it slowly and with difficulty, but in the other direction the ground appeared to be more open, and to lead straight down into a gently-sloping valley. Had I but my feet in yonder stirrups and my sabre in my hand, a single bold dash might take me out of the power of these vermin of the rocks.

I was still thinking it over and straining with my wrists and my ankles, when their chief came out from his grotto, and after some talk with his lieutenant, who lay groaning near the fire, they both nodded their heads and looked across at me. He then said some few words to the band, who clapped their hands and laughed uproariously. Things looked ominous, and I was delighted to feel that my hands were so far free that I could easily slip them through the cords if I wished. But with my ankles I feared that I could do nothing, for when I strained it brought such pain into my lance-wound that I had to gnaw my moustache to keep from crying out. I could only lie still, half-free and half-bound, and see what turn things were likely to take.

For a little I could not make out what they were after. One of the rascals climbed up a well-grown firtree upon one side of the glade, and tied a rope round the top of the trunk. He then fastened another rope in the same fashion to a similar tree upon the other side. The two loose ends were now dangling down, and I waited with some curiosity, and just a little trepidation also, to see what they would do next. The whole band pulled upon one of the ropes until they had bent the strong young tree down into a semi-circle, and they then fastened it to a stump, so as to hold it so. When they had bent the other tree down in a similar fashion, the two summits were within a few feet of each other, though, as you understand, they would each spring back into their original position the instant that they were released. I already saw the diabolical plan which these miscreants had formed.

'I presume that you are a strong man, Colonel,' said the chief, coming towards me with his hateful smile.

'If you will have the kindness to loosen these cords,' I answered, 'I will show you how strong I am.'

'We were all interested to see whether you were as strong as these two young saplings,' said he. 'It is our intention, you see, to tie one end of each rope round your ankles and then let the trees go. If you are stronger than the trees, then, of course, no harm would be done; if, on the other hand, the trees are stronger than you, why, in that case, Colonel, we may have a souvenir of you upon each side of our little glade.'

He laughed as he spoke, and at the sight of it the whole forty of them laughed also. Even now if I am in my darker humour, or if I have a touch of my old Lithuanian ague, I see in my sleep that ring of dark, savage faces, with their cruel eyes, and the firelight flashing upon their strong white teeth.

It is astonishing — and I have heard many make the same remark — how acute one's senses become at such a crisis as this. I am convinced that at no moment is one living so vividly, so acutely, as at the instant when a violent and foreseen death overtakes one. I could smell the resinous fagots, I could see every twig upon the ground, I could hear every rustle of the branches, as I have never smelled or seen or heard save at such times of danger. And so it was that long before anyone else, before even the time when the chief had addressed me, I had heard a low, monotonous sound, far away indeed, and yet coming nearer at every instant. At first it was but a murmur, a rumble, but by the time he had finished speaking, while the assassins were untying my ankles in order to lead me to the scene of my murder, I heard, as plainly as ever I heard anything in my life, the clinking of horseshoes and the jingling of bridle-chains, with the clank of sabres against stirrup-irons. Is it likely that I, who had lived with the light cavalry since the first hair shaded my lip, would mistake the sound of troopers on the march?

'Help, comrades, help!' I shrieked, and though they struck me across the mouth and tried to drag me up to the trees, I kept on yelling, 'Help me, my brave boys! Help me, my children! They are murdering your colonel!'

For the moment my wounds and my troubles had brought on a delirium, and I looked for nothing less than my five hundred hussars, kettle-drums and all, to appear at the opening of the glade.

But that which really appeared was very different to anything which I had conceived. Into the clear space there came galloping a fine young man upon a most beautiful roan horse. He was fresh-faced and pleasant-looking, with the most debonair bearing in the world and the most gallant way of carrying himself — a way which reminded me somewhat of my own. He wore a singular coat which had once been red all over, but which was now stained to the colour of a withered oak-leaf wherever the weather could reach it. His shoulder-straps, however, were of golden lace, and he had a bright metal helmet upon his head, with a coquettish white plume upon one side of its crest. He trotted his horse up the glade, while behind him rode four cavaliers in the same dress — all clean-shaven, with round, comely faces, looking to me more like monks than dragoons. At a short, gruff order they halted with a rattle of arms, while their leader cantered forward, the fire beating upon his eager face and the beautiful head of his charger. I knew, of course, by the strange coats that they were English. It was the first sight that I had ever had of them, but from their stout bearing and their masterful way I could see at a glance that what I had always been told was true, and that they were excellent people to fight against.

'Well, well, well!' cried the young officer, in sufficiently bad French, 'what game are you up to here? Who was that who was yelling for help, and what are you trying to do to him?'

It was at that moment that I learned to bless those months which Obriant, the descendant of the Irish kings, had spent in teaching me the tongue of the English. My ankles had just been freed, so that I had only to slip my hands out of the cords, and with a single rush I had flown across, picked up my sabre where it lay by the fire, and hurled myself on to the saddle of poor Vidal's horse. Yes, for all my wounded ankle, I never put foot to stirrup, but was in the seat in a single bound. I tore the halter from the tree, and before these villains could so much as snap a pistol at me I was beside the English officer.

'I surrender to you, sir,' I cried; though I daresay my English was not very much better than his French. 'If you will look at that tree to the left you will see what these villains do to the honourable gentlemen who fall into their hands.'

The fire had flared up at that moment, and there was poor Vidal exposed before them, as horrible an object as one could see in a nightmare. 'Godam!' cried the officer, and 'Godam!' cried each of the four troopers, which is the same as with us when we cry 'Mon Dieu!' Out rasped the five swords, and the four men closed up. One, who wore a sergeant's chevrons, laughed and clapped me on the shoulder.

'Fight for your skin, froggy,' said he.

Ah, it was so fine to have a horse between my thighs and a weapon in my grip. I waved it above my head and shouted in my exultation.

The chief had come forward with that odious smiling face of his.

'Your excellency will observe that this Frenchman is our prisoner,' said he.

'You are a rascally robber,' said the Englishman, shaking his sword at him. 'It is a disgrace to us to have such allies. By my faith, if Lord Wellington were of my mind we would swing you up on the nearest tree.'

'But my prisoner?' said the brigand, in his suave voice.

'He shall come with us to the British camp.'

'Just a word in your ear before you take him.'

He approached the young officer, and then turning as quick as a flash, he fired his pistol in my face. The bullet scored its way through my hair and burst a hole on each side of my busby. Seeing that he had missed me, he raised the pistol and was about to hurl it at me when the English sergeant, with a single back-handed cut, nearly severed his head from his body. His blood had not reached the ground, nor the last curse died on his lips, before the whole horde was upon us, but with a dozen bounds and as many slashes we were all safely out of the glade, and galloping down the winding track which led to the valley.

It was not until we had left the ravine far

behind us and were right out in the open fields that we ventured to halt, and to see what injuries we had sustained. For me, wounded and weary as I was, my heart was beating proudly, and my chest was nearly bursting my tunic to think that I, Etienne Gerard, had left this gang of murderers so much by which to remember me. My faith, they would think twice before they ventured again to lay hands upon one of the Third Hussars. So carried away was I that I made a small oration to these brave Englishmen, and told them who it was that they had helped to rescue. I would have spoken of glory also, and of the sympathies of brave men, but the officer cut me short.

'That's all right,' said he. 'Any injuries, Sergeant?'

'Trooper Jones's horse hit with a pistol bullet on the fetlock.'

'Trooper Jones to go with us. Sergeant Halliday, with troopers Harvey and Smith, to keep to the right until they touch the vedettes of the German Hussars.'

So these three jingled away together, while the officer and I, followed at some distance by the trooper whose horse had been wounded, rode straight down in the direction of the English camp. Very soon we had opened our hearts, for we each liked the other from the beginning. He was of the nobility, this brave lad, and he had been sent out scouting by Lord Wellington to see if there were any signs of our advancing through the mountains. It is one advantage of a wandering life like mine, that you learn to pick up those bits of knowledge which distinguish the man of the world. I have, for example, hardly ever met a Frenchman who could repeat an English title correctly. If I had not travelled I should not be able to say with confidence that this young man's real name was Milor the Hon. Sir Russell, Bart., this last being an honourable distinction, so that it was as the Bart that I usually addressed him, just as in Spanish one might say 'the Don.'

As we rode beneath the moonlight in the lovely Spanish night, we spoke our minds to each other, as if we were brothers. We were both of an age, you see, both of the light cavalry also (the Sixteenth Light Dragoons was his regiment), and both with the same hopes and ambitions. Never have I learned to know a man so quickly as I did the Bart. He gave me the name of a girl whom he had loved at a garden called Vauxhall, and, for my own part, I spoke to him of little Coralie, of the Opera. He took a lock of hair from his bosom, and I a garter. Then we nearly quarrelled over hussar and dragoon, for he was absurdly proud of his regiment, and you should have seen him curl his lip and clap his hand to his hilt when I said that I hoped it might never be its misfortune to come in the way of the Third. Finally, he began to speak about what the English call sport, and he told such stories of the money which he had lost over which of two cocks could kill the other, or which of two men could strike the other the most in a fight for a prize, that I was filled with astonishment. He was ready to bet upon anything in the most wonderful manner, and when I chanced to see a shooting star he was anxious to bet that he would see more than me, twenty-five francs a star, and it was only when I explained that my purse was in the hands of the brigands that he would give over the idea.

Well, we chatted away in this very amiable fashion until the day began to break, when suddenly we heard a great volley of musketry from somewhere in front of us. It was very rocky and broken ground, and I thought, although I could see nothing, that a general engagement had broken out. The Bart laughed at my idea, however, and explained that the sound came from the English camp, where every man emptied his piece each morning so as to make sure of having a dry priming.

'In another mile we shall be up with the outposts,' said he.

I glanced round at this, and I perceived that we had trotted along at so good a pace during the time that we were keeping up our pleasant chat, that the dragoon with the lame horse was altogether out of sight. I looked on every side, but in the whole of that vast rocky valley there was no one save only the Bart and I — both of us armed, you understand, and both of us well mounted. I began to ask myself whether after all it was quite necessary that I should ride that mile which would bring me to the British outposts.

Now, I wish to be very clear with you on this point, my friends, for I would not have you think that I was acting dishonourably or ungratefully to the man who had helped me away from the brigands. You must remember that of all duties the strongest is that which a commanding officer owes to his men. You must also bear in mind that war is a game which is played under fixed rules, and when these rules are broken one must at once claim the forfeit. If, for example, I had given a parole, then I should have been an infamous wretch had I dreamed of escaping. But no parole had been asked of me. Out of over-confidence, and the chance of the lame horse dropping behind, the Bart had permitted me to get upon equal terms with him. Had it been I who had taken him, I should have used him as courteously as he had me, but, at the same time, I should have respected his enterprise so far as to have deprived him of his sword, and seen that I had at least one guard beside myself. I reined up my horse and explained this to him, asking him at the same time whether he saw any breach of honour in my leaving him.

He thought about it, and several times repeated that which the English say when they mean 'Mon Dieu.'

'You would give me the slip, would you?' said he.

'If you can give no reason against it.'

'The only reason that I can think of,' said the Bart, 'is that I should instantly cut your head off if you were to attempt it.'

'Two can play at that game, my dear Bart,' said I.

'Then we'll see who can play at it best,' he cried, pulling out his sword.

I had drawn mine also, but I was quite determined not to hurt this admirable young man who had been my benefactor.

'Consider,' said I, 'you say that I am your prisoner. I might with equal reason say that you are mine. We are alone here, and though I have no doubt that you are an excellent swordsman, you can hardly hope to hold your own against the best blade in the six light cavalry brigades.'

His answer was a cut at my head. I parried and shore off half of his white plume. He thrust at my breast. I turned his point and cut away the other half of his cockade.

'Curse your monkey-tricks!' he cried, as I wheeled my horse away from him.

'Why should you strike at me?' said I. 'You see that I will not strike back.'

'That's all very well,' said he; 'but you've got to come along with me to the camp.'

'I shall never see the camp,' said I.

'I'll lay you nine to four you do,' he cried, as he made at me, sword in hand.

But those words of his put something new into my head. Could we not decide the matter in some better way than fighting? The Bart was placing me in such a position that I should have to hurt him, or he would certainly hurt me. I avoided his rush, though his sword-point was within an inch of my neck.

'I have a proposal,' I cried. 'We shall throw dice as to which is the prisoner of the other.'

He smiled at this. It appealed to his love of sport.

'Where are your dice?' he cried.

'I have none.'

'Nor I. But I have cards.'

'Cards let it be,' said I.

'And the game?'

'I leave it to you.'

'Écarté, then — the best of three.'

I could not help smiling as I agreed, for I do not suppose that there were three men in France who were my masters at the game. I told the Bart as much as we dismounted. He smiled also as he listened.

'I was counted the best player at Watier's,' said he. 'With even luck you deserve to get off if you beat me.'

So we tethered our two horses and sat down one on either side of a great flat rock. The Bart took a pack of cards out of his tunic, and I had only to see him shuffle to convince me that I had no novice to deal with. We cut, and the deal fell to him.

My faith, it was a stake worth playing for. He wished to add a hundred gold pieces a game, but what was money when the fate of Colonel Etienne Gerard hung upon the cards? I felt as though all those who had reason to be interested in the game — my mother, my hussars, the Sixth Corps d'Armée, Ney, Massena, even the Emperor himself — were forming a ring round us in that desolate valley. Heavens, what a blow to one and all of them should the cards go against me! But I was confident, for my écarté play was as famous as my swordsmanship, and save old Bouvet of the Hussars of Bercheny, who won seventy-six out of one hundred and fifty games off me, I have always had the best of a series.

The first game I won right off, though I must confess that the cards were with me, and that my adversary could have done no more. In the second, I never played better and saved a trick by a finesse, but the Bart voled me once, marked the king, and ran out in the second hand. My faith, we were so excited that he laid his helmet down beside him and I my busby.

'I'll lay my roan mare against your black horse,' said he.

'Done!' said I.

'Sword against sword.'

'Done!' said I.

'Saddle, bridle, and stirrups!' he cried.

'Done!' I shouted.

I had caught this spirit of sport from him. I would have laid my hussars against his dragoons had they been ours to pledge.

And then began the game of games. Oh, he played, this Englishman — he played in a way that was worthy of such a stake. But I, my friends, I was superb! Of the five which I had to make to win, I gained three on the first hand. The Bart bit his moustache and drummed his hands, while I already felt myself at the head of my dear little rascals. On the second, I turned the king, but lost two tricks — and my score was four to his two. When I saw my next hand I could not but give a cry of delight. 'If I cannot gain my freedom on this,' thought I, 'I deserve to remain for ever in chains.'

Give me the cards, landlord, and I will lay them out on the table for you.

Here was my hand: knave and ace of clubs, queen and knave of diamonds, and king of hearts. Clubs were trumps, mark you, and I had but one point between me and freedom. He knew it was the crisis, and he undid his tunic. I threw my dolman on the ground. He led the ten of spades. I took it with my ace of trumps. One point in my favour. The correct play was to clear the trumps, and I led the knave. Down came the queen upon it, and the game was equal. He led the eight of spades, and I could only discard my queen of diamonds. Then came the seven of spades, and the hair stood straight up on my head. We each threw down a king at the final. He had won two points, and my beautiful hand had been mastered by his inferior one. I could have rolled on the ground as I thought of it. They used to play very good écarté at Watier's in the year '10. I say it — I, Brigadier Gerard.

The last game was now four all. This next hand must settle it one way or the other. He undid his sash, and I put away my sword-belt. He was cool, this Englishman, and I tried to be so also, but the perspiration would trickle into my eyes. The deal lay with him, and I may confess to you, my friends, that my hands shook so that I could hardly pick my cards from the rock. But when I raised them, what was the first thing that my eyes rested upon? It was the king, the king, the glorious king of trumps! My mouth was open to declare it when the words were frozen upon my lips by the appearance of my comrade.

He held his cards in his hand, but his jaw had fallen, and his eyes were staring over my shoulder with the most dreadful expression of consternation and surprise. I whisked round, and I was myself amazed at what I saw.

Three men were standing quite close to us — fifteen mètres at the farthest. The middle one was of a good height, and yet not too tall — about the same height, in fact, that I am myself. He was clad in a dark uniform with a small cocked hat, and some sort of white plume upon the side. But I had little thought of his dress. It was his face, his gaunt cheeks, his beak-like nose, his masterful blue eyes, his thin, firm slit of a mouth which made one feel

117

that this was a wonderful man, a man of a million. His brows were tied into a knot, and he cast such a glance at my poor Bart from under them that one by one the cards came fluttering down from his nerveless fingers. Of the two other men, one, who had a face as brown and hard as though it had been carved out of old oak, wore a bright red coat, while the other, a fine portly man with bushy side-whiskers, was in a blue jacket with gold facings. Some little distance behind, three orderlies were holding as many horses, and an escort of dragoons was waiting in the rear.

'Heh, Crauford, what the deuce is this?' asked the thin man.

'D'you hear, sir?' cried the man with the red coat. 'Lord Wellington wants to know what this means.'

My poor Bart broke into an account of all that had occurred, but that rock-face never softened for an instant.

'Pretty fine, 'pon my word, General Crauford,' he broke in. 'The discipline of this force must be maintained, sir. Report yourself at headquarters as a prisoner.'

It was dreadful to me to see the Bart mount his horse and ride off with hanging head. I could not endure it. I threw myself before this English General. I pleaded with him for my friend. I told him how I, Colonel

Gerard, would witness what a dashing young officer he was. Ah, my eloquence might have melted the hardest heart; I brought tears to my own eyes, but none to his. My voice broke, and I could say no more.

'What weight do you put on your mules, sir, in the French service?' he asked. Yes, that was all this phlegmatic Englishman had to answer to these burning words of mine. That was his reply to what would have made a Frenchman weep upon my shoulder.

'What weight on a mule?' asked the man with the red coat.

'Two hundred and ten pounds,' said I.

'Then you load them deucedly badly,' said Lord Wellington. 'Remove the prisoner to the rear.'

His dragoons closed in upon me, and I — I was driven mad, as I thought that the game had been in my hands, and that I ought at that moment to be a free man. I held the cards up in front of the General.

'See, my lord!' I cried; 'I played for my freedom and I won, for, as you perceive, I hold the king.'

For the first time a slight smile softened his gaunt face.

'On the contrary,' said he, as he mounted his horse, 'it is I who won, for, as you perceive, my King holds you.'

4

How the King Held the Brigadier

Murat was undoubtedly an excellent cavalry officer, but he had too much swagger, which spoils many a good soldier. Lasalle, too, was a very dashing leader, but he ruined himself with wine and folly. Now I, Etienne Gerard, was always totally devoid of swagger, and at the same time I was very abstemious, except, maybe, at the end of a campaign, or when I met an old comrade-in-arms. For these reasons I might, perhaps, had it not been for a certain diffidence, have claimed to be the most valuable officer in my own branch of the Service. It is true that I never rose to be more than a chief of brigade, but then, as everyone knows, no one had a chance of rising to the top unless he had the good fortune to be with the Emperor in his early campaigns. Except Lasalle, and Labau, and Drouet, I can hardly remember any one of the generals who had not already made his name before the Egyptian business. Even I, with all my brilliant qualities, could only attain the head of my brigade, and also the special medal of honour, which I received from the Emperor himself, and which I keep at home in a leathern pouch.

But though I never rose higher than this, my qualities were very well known to those who had served with me, and also to the English. After they had captured me in the way which I described to you the other night, they kept a very good guard over me at Oporto, and I promise you that they did not give such a formidable opponent a chance of slipping through their fingers. It was on the 10th of August that I was escorted on board the transport which was to take us to England, and behold me before the end of the month in the great prison which had been built for us at Dartmoor!

'L'hôtel Français, et Pension,' we used to call it, for you understand that we were all brave men there, and that we did not lose our spirits because we were in adversity.

It was only those officers who refused to give their parole who were confined at Dartmoor, and most of the prisoners were seamen, or from the ranks. You ask me, perhaps, why it was that I did not give this parole, and so enjoy the same good treatment as most of my brother officers. Well, I had two reasons, and both of them were sufficiently strong.

In the first place, I had so much confidence in myself, that I was quite convinced that I could escape. In the second, my family, though of good repute, has never been wealthy, and I could not bring myself to take anything from the small income of my mother. On the other hand, it would never do for a man like me to be outshone by the bourgeois society of an English country town, or to be without the means of showing courtesies and attentions to those ladies whom I should attract. It was for these reasons that I preferred to be buried in the dreadful prison of Dartmoor. I wish now to tell you of my adventures in England, and how far Milor Wellington's words were true when he said that his King would hold me.

And first of all I may say that if it were not that I have set off to tell you about what befell myself, I could keep you here until morning with my stories about Dartmoor itself, and about the singular things which occurred there. It was one of the very strangest places in the whole world, for there, in the middle of that great desolate waste, were herded together seven or eight thousand men — warriors, you understand, men of experience and courage. Around there were a double wall and a ditch, and warders and soldiers; but, my faith! you could not coop men like that up like rabbits in a hutch! They would escape by twos and tens and twenties, and then the cannon would boom, and the search parties run, and we, who were left behind, would laugh and dance and shout 'Vive l'Empereur' until the warders would turn their muskets upon us in their passion. And then we would have our little mutinies, too, and up would come the infantry and the guns from Plymouth, and that would set us yelling 'Vive l'Empereur' once more, as though we wished them to hear us in Paris. We had lively moments at Dartmoor, and we contrived that those who were about us should be lively also.

You must know that the prisoners there had their own Courts of Justice, in which they tried their own cases, and inflicted their own punishments. Stealing and quarrelling were punished — but most of all treachery. When I came there first there was a man, Meunier, from Rheims, who had given information of some plot to escape. Well, that night, owing to some form or other which had to be gone through, they did not take him out from among the other prisoners, and though he wept and screamed, and grovelled upon the ground, they left him there amongst the comrades whom he had betrayed. That night there was a trial with a whispered accusation and a whispered defence, a gagged prisoner, and a judge whom none could see. In the morning, when they came for their man with papers for his release, there was not as much of him left as you could put upon your thumb-nail. They were ingenious people, these prisoners, and they had their own way of managing.

We officers, however, lived in a separate wing, and a very singular group of people we were. They had left us our uniforms, so that there was hardly a corps which had served under Victor, or Massena, or Ney, which was not represented there, and some had been there from the time when Junot was beaten at Vimiera. We had chasseurs in their green tunics, and hussars, like myself, and blue-coated dragoons, and white-fronted lancers, and voltigeurs, and grenadiers, and the men of the artillery and engineers. But the greater part were naval officers, for the English had had the better of us upon the seas. I could never understand this until I journeyed myself from Oporto to Plymouth, when I lay for seven days upon my back, and could not have stirred had I seen the eagle of the regiment carried off before my eyes. It was in perfidious weather like this that Nelson took advantage of us.

I had no sooner got into Dartmoor than I

began to plan to get out again, and you can readily believe that, with wits sharpened by twelve years of warfare, it was not very long before I saw my way.

You must know, in the first place, that I had a very great advantage in having some knowledge of the English language. I learned it during the months that I spent before Danzig, from Adjutant Obriant, of the Regiment Irlandais, who was sprung from the ancient kings of the country. I was quickly able to speak it with some facility, for I do not take long to master anything to which I set my mind. In three months I could not only express my meaning, but I could use the idioms of the people. It was Obriant who taught me to say 'Be jabers,' just as we might say 'Ma foi'; and also 'The curse of Crummle!' which means 'Ventre bleu!' Many a time I have seen the English smile with pleasure when they have heard me speak so much like one of themselves.

We officers were put two in a cell, which was very little to my taste, for my room-mate was a tall, silent man named Beaumont, of the Flying Artillery, who had been taken by the English cavalry at Astorga.

It is seldom I meet a man of whom I cannot make a friend, for my disposition and manners are — as you know them. But this fellow had never a smile for my jests, nor an ear for my sorrows, but would sit looking at me with his sullen eyes, until sometimes I thought that his two years of captivity had driven him crazy. Ah, how I longed that old Bouvet, or any of my comrades of the hussars, was there, instead of this mummy of a man. But such as he was I had to make the best of him, and it was very evident that no escape could be made unless he were my partner in it, for what could I possibly do without him observing me? I hinted at it, therefore, and then by degrees I spoke more plainly, until it seemed to me that I had prevailed upon him to share my lot.

I tried the walls, and I tried the floor, and I tried the ceiling, but though I tapped and probed, they all appeared to be very thick and solid. The door was of iron, shutting with a spring lock, and provided with a small grating, through which a warder looked twice in every night. Within there were two beds, two stools, two washstands — nothing more. It was enough for my wants, for when had I had as much during those twelve years spent in camps? But how was I to get out? Night after night I thought of my five hundred hussars, and had dreadful nightmares, in which I fancied that the whole regiment needed shoeing, or that my horses were all bloated with green fodder, or that they were foundered from bogland, or that six squadrons were clubbed in the presence of the Emperor. Then I would awake in a cold sweat, and set to work picking and tapping at the walls once more; for I knew very well that there is no difficulty which cannot be overcome by a ready brain and a pair of cunning hands.

There was a single window in our cell, which was too small to admit a child. It was further defended by a thick iron bar in the centre. It was not a very promising point of escape, as you will allow, but I became more and more convinced that our efforts must be directed towards it. To make matters worse, it only led out into the exercise yard, which was surrounded by two high walls. Still, as I said to my sullen comrade, it is time to talk of the Vistula when you are over the Rhine. I got a small piece of iron, therefore, from the fittings of my bed, and I set to work to loosen the plaster at the top and the bottom of the bar. Three hours I would work, and then leap into my bed upon the sound of the warder's step. Then another three hours, and then very often another yet, for I found that Beaumont was so slow and clumsy at it that it was on myself only that I could rely.

I pictured to myself my Third of Hussars

waiting just outside that window, with kettle-drums and standards and leopard-skin schabraques all complete. Then I would work like a madman, until my iron was crusted with blood, as if with rust. And so, night by night, I loosened that stony plaster, and hid it away in the stuffing of my pillow, until the hour came when the iron shook; and then with one good wrench it came off in my hand, and my first step had been made towards freedom.

You will ask me what better off I was, since, as I have said, a child could not have fitted through the opening. I will tell you. I had gained two things — a tool and a weapon. With the one I might loosen the stone which flanked the window. With the other I might defend myself when I had scrambled through. So now I turned my attention to that stone, and I picked and picked with the sharpened end of my bar until I had worked out the mortar all round. You understand, of course, that during the day I replaced everything in its position, and that the warder was never permitted to see a speck upon the floor. At the end of three weeks I had separated the stone, and had the rapture of drawing it through, and seeing a hole left with ten stars shining through it, where there had been but four before. All was ready for us now, and I had replaced the stone, smearing the edges of it round with a little fat and soot, so as to hide the cracks where the mortar should have been. In three nights the moon would be gone, and that seemed the best time for our attempt.

I had now no doubt at all about getting into the yards, but I had very considerable misgivings as to how I was to get out again. It would be too humiliating, after trying here, and trying there, to have to go back to my hole again in despair, or to be arrested by the guards outside, and thrown into those damp underground cells which are reserved for prisoners who are caught in escaping. I set to work, therefore, to plan what I should do. I have never, as you know, had the chance of showing what I could do as a general. Sometimes, after a glass or two of wine, I have found myself capable of thinking out surprising combinations, and have felt that if Napoleon had intrusted me with an army corps, things might have gone differently with him. But however that may be, there is no doubt that in the small stratagems of war, and in that quickness of invention which is so necessary for an officer of light cavalry, I could hold my own against anyone. It was now that I had need of it, and I felt sure that it would not fail me.

The inner wall which I had to scale was built of bricks, 12ft. high, with a row of iron spikes, 3in. apart upon the top. The outer I had only caught a glimpse of once or twice, when the gate of the exercise yard was open. It appeared to be about the same height, and was also spiked at the top. The space between the walls was over twenty feet, and I had reason to believe that there were no sentries there, except at the gates. On the other hand, I knew that there was a line of soldiers outside. Behold the little nut, my friends, which I had to open with no crackers, save these two hands.

One thing upon which I relied was the height of my comrade Beaumont. I have already said that he was a very tall man, six feet at least, and it seemed to me that if I could mount upon his shoulders, and get my hands upon the spikes, I could easily scale the wall. Could I pull my big companion up after me? That was the question, for when I set forth with a comrade, even though it be one for whom I bear no affection, nothing on earth would make me abandon him. If I climbed the wall and he could not follow me, I should be compelled to return to him. He did not seem to concern himself much about it, however, so I hoped that he had confidence in his own activity.

Then another very important matter was the choice of the sentry who should be on duty in front of my window at the time of our attempt. They were changed every two hours to insure their vigilance, but I, who watched them closely each night out of my window, knew that there was a great difference between them. There were some who were so keen that a rat could not cross the yard unseen, while others thought only of their own ease, and could sleep as soundly leaning upon a musket as if they were at home upon a feather bed. There was one especially, a fat, heavy man, who would retire into the shadow of the wall and doze so comfortably during his two hours, that I have dropped pieces of plaster from my window at his very feet, without his observing it. By good luck, this fellow's watch was due from twelve to two upon the night which we had fixed upon for our enterprise.

As the last day passed, I was so filled with nervous agitation that I could not control myself, but ran ceaselessly about my cell, like a mouse in a cage. Every moment I thought that the warder would detect the looseness of the bar, or that the sentry would observe the unmortared stone, which I could not conceal outside, as I did within. As for my companion, he sat brooding upon the end of

131

his bed, looking at me in a sidelong fashion from time to time, and biting his nails like one who is deep in thought.

'Courage, my friend!' I cried, slapping him upon the shoulder. 'You will see your guns before another month be past.'

'That is very well,' said he. 'But whither will you fly when you get free?'

'To the coast,' I answered. 'All comes right for a brave man, and I shall make straight for my regiment.'

'You are more likely to make straight for the underground cells, or for the Portsmouth hulks,' said he.

'A soldier takes his chances,' I remarked. 'It is only the poltroon who reckons always upon the worst.'

I raised a flush in each of his sallow cheeks at that, and I was glad of it, for it was the first sign of spirit which I had ever observed in him. For a moment he put his hand out towards his water-jug, as though he would have hurled it at me, but then he shrugged his shoulders and sat in silence once more, biting his nails, and scowling down at the floor. I could not but think, as I looked at him, that perhaps I was doing the Flying Artillery a very bad service by bringing him back to them.

I never in my life have known an evening

pass as slowly as that one. Towards nightfall a wind sprang up, and as the darkness deepened it blew harder and harder, until a terrible gale was whistling over the moor. As I looked out of my window I could not catch a glimpse of a star, and the black clouds were flying low across the heavens. The rain was pouring down, and what with its hissing and splashing, and the howling and screaming of the wind, it was impossible for me to hear the steps of the sentinels. 'If I cannot hear them,' thought I, 'then it is unlikely that they can hear me'; and I waited with the utmost impatience until the time when the inspector should have come round for his nightly peep through our grating. Then having peered through the darkness, and seen nothing of the sentry, who was doubtless crouching in some corner out of the rain, I felt that the moment was come. I removed the bar, pulled out the stone, and motioned to my companion to pass through.

'After you, Colonel,' said he.

'Will you not go first?' I asked.

'I had rather you showed me the way.'

'Come after me, then, but come silently, as you value your life.'

In the darkness I could hear the fellow's teeth chattering, and I wondered whether a man ever had such a partner in a desperate enterprise. I seized the bar, however, and mounting upon my stool, I thrust my head and shoulders into the hole. I had wriggled through as far as my waist, when my companion seized me suddenly by the knees, and yelled at the top of his voice: 'Help! Help! A prisoner is escaping!'

Ah, my friends, what did I not feel at that moment! Of course, I saw in an instant the game of this vile creature. Why should he risk his skin in climbing walls when he might be sure of a free pardon from the English for having prevented the escape of one so much more distinguished than himself? I had recognized him as a poltroon and a sneak, but I had not understood the depth of baseness to which he could descend. One who has spent his life among gentlemen and men of honour does not think of such things until they happen.

The blockhead did not seem to understand that he was lost more certainly than I. I writhed back in the darkness, and seizing him by the throat, I struck him twice with my iron bar. At the first blow he yelped as a little cur does when you tread upon its paw. At the second, down he fell with a groan upon the floor. Then I seated myself upon my bed, and waited resignedly for whatever punishment my gaolers might inflict upon me.

But a minute passed and yet another, with no sound save the heavy, snoring breathing of the senseless wretch upon the floor. Was it possible, then, that amid the fury of the storm his warning cries had passed unheeded? At first it was but a tiny hope, another minute and it was probable, another and it was certain. There was no sound in the corridor, none in the courtyard. I wiped the cold sweat from my brow, and asked myself what I should do next.

One thing seemed certain. The man on the floor must die. If I left him I could not tell how short a time it might be before he gave the alarm. I dare not strike a light, so I felt about in the darkness until my hand came upon something wet, which I knew to be his head. I raised my iron bar, but there was something, my friends, which prevented me from bringing it down. In the heat of fight I have slain many men — men of honour, too, who had done me no injury. Yet here was this wretch, a creature too foul to live, who had tried to work me so great a mischief, and yet I could not bring myself to crush his skull in. Such deeds are very well for a Spanish partida — or for that matter a sansculotte of the Faubourg St Antoine — but not for a soldier and a gentleman like me.

However, the heavy breathing of the fellow

made me hope that it might be a very long time before he recovered his senses. I gagged him, therefore, and bound him with strips of blanket to the bed, so that in his weakened condition there was good reason to think that, in any case, he might not get free before the next visit of the warder. But now again I was faced with new difficulties, for you will remember that I had relied upon his height to help me over the walls. I could have sat down and shed tears of despair had not the thought of my mother and of the Emperor come to sustain me. 'Courage!' said I. 'If it were anyone but Etienne Gerard he would be in a bad fix now; that is a young man who is not so easily caught.'

I set to work therefore upon Beaumont's sheet as well as my own, and by tearing them into strips and then plaiting them together, I made a very excellent rope. This I tied securely to the centre of my iron bar, which was a little over a foot in length. Then I slipped out into the yard, where the rain was pouring and the wind screaming louder than ever. I kept in the shadow of the prison wall, but it was as black as the ace of spades, and I could not see my own hand in front of me. Unless I walked into the sentinel I felt that I had nothing to fear from him. When I had come under the wall I threw up my bar, and to my joy it stuck the very first time between the spikes at the top. I climbed up my rope, pulled it after me, and dropped down on the other side. Then I scaled the second wall, and was sitting astride among the spikes upon the top, when I saw something twinkle in the darkness beneath me. It was the bayonet of the sentinel below, and so close was it (the second wall being rather lower than the first) that I could easily, by leaning over, have unscrewed it from its socket. There he was, humming a tune to himself, and cuddling up against the wall to keep himself warm, little thinking that a desperate man within a few feet of him was within an ace of stabbing him to the heart with his own weapon. I was already bracing myself for the spring when the fellow, with an oath, shouldered his musket, and I heard his steps squelching through the mud as he resumed his beat. I slipped down my rope, and, leaving it hanging, I ran at the top of my speed across the moor.

Heavens, how I ran! The wind buffeted my face and buzzed in my nostrils. The rain pringled upon my skin and hissed past my ears. I stumbled into holes. I tripped over bushes. I fell among brambles. I was torn and breathless and bleeding. My tongue was like leather, my feet like lead, and my heart beating like a kettle-drum. Still I ran, and I ran, and I ran.

But I had not lost my head, my friends. Everything was done with a purpose. Our fugitives always made for the coast. I was determined to go inland, and the more so as I had told Beaumont the opposite. I would fly to the north, and they would seek me in the south. Perhaps you will ask me how I could tell which was which on such a night. I answer that it was by the wind. I had observed in the prison that it came from the north, and so, as long as I kept my face to it, I was going in the right direction.

Well, I was rushing along in this fashion when, suddenly, I saw two yellow lights shining out of the darkness in front of me. I paused for a moment, uncertain what I should do. I was still in my hussar uniform, you understand, and it seemed to me that the very first thing that I should aim at was to get some dress which should not betray me. If these lights came from a cottage, it was probable enough that I might find what I wanted there. I approached, therefore, feeling very sorry that I had left my iron bar behind; for I was determined to fight to the death before I should be retaken.

But very soon I found that there was no cottage there. The lights were two lamps hung upon each side of a carriage, and by their glare I saw that a broad road lay in front of me. Crouching among the bushes, I observed that there were two horses to the equipage, that a small post-boy was standing at their heads, and that one of the wheels was lying in the road beside him. I can see them now, my friends: the steaming creatures, the stunted lad with his hands to their bits, and the big, black coach, all shining with the rain, and balanced upon its three wheels. As I looked, the window was lowered, and a pretty little face under a bonnet peeped out from it.

'What shall I do?' the lady cried to the post-boy, in a voice of despair. 'Sir Charles is certainly lost, and I shall have to spend the night upon the moor.'

'Perhaps I can be of some assistance to madame,' said I, scrambling out from among the bushes into the glare of the lamps. A woman in distress is a sacred thing to me, and this one was beautiful. You must not forget that, although I was a colonel, I was only eight-and-twenty years of age.

My word, how she screamed, and how the post-boy stared! You will understand that after that long race in the darkness, with my shako broken in, my face smeared with dirt, and my uniform all stained and torn with brambles, I was not entirely the sort of gentleman whom one would choose to meet in the middle of a lonely moor. Still, after the first surprise, she soon understood that I was her very humble servant, and I could even read in her pretty eyes that my manner and bearing had not failed to produce an impression upon her.

'I am sorry to have startled you, madame,' said I. 'I chanced to overhear your remark, and I could not refrain from offering you my assistance.' I bowed as I spoke. You know my bow, and can realize what its effect was upon the lady.

'I am much indebted to you, sir,' said she. 'We have had a terrible journey since we left Tavistock. Finally, one of our wheels came off, and here we are helpless in the middle of the moor. My husband, Sir Charles, has gone on to get help, and I much fear that he must have lost his way.'

I was about to attempt some consolation, when I saw beside the lady a black travelling coat, faced with astrakhan, which her companion must have left behind him. It was exactly what I needed to conceal my uniform. It is true that I felt very much like a highway robber, but then, what would you have? Necessity has no law, and I was in an enemy's country.

'I presume, madame, that this is your

husband's coat,' I remarked. 'You will, I am sure, forgive me, if I am compelled to — ' I pulled it through the window as I spoke.

I could not bear to see the look of surprise and fear and disgust which came over her face.

'Oh, I have been mistaken in you!' she cried. 'You came to rob me, then, and not to help me. You have the bearing of a gentleman, and yet you steal my husband's coat.'

'Madame,' said I, 'I beg that you will not condemn me until you know everything. It is quite necessary that I should take this coat, but if you will have the goodness to tell me who it is who is fortunate enough to be your husband, I shall see that the coat is sent back to him.'

Her face softened a little, though she still tried to look severe. 'My husband,' she answered, 'is Sir Charles Meredith, and he is travelling to Dartmoor Prison, upon important Government business. I only ask you, sir, to go upon your way, and to take nothing which belongs to him.'

'There is only one thing which belongs to him that I covet,' said I.

'And you have taken it from the carriage,' she cried.

'No,' I answered. 'It still remains there.'

She laughed in her frank English way.

'If, instead of paying me compliments, you were to return my husband's coat — ' she began.

'Madame,' I answered, 'what you ask is quite impossible. If you will allow me to come into the carriage, I will explain to you how necessary this coat is to me.'

Heaven knows into what foolishness I might have plunged myself had we not, at this instant, heard a faint halloa in the distance, which was answered by a shout from the little post-boy. In the rain and the darkness, I saw a lantern some distance from us, but approaching rapidly.

'I am sorry, madame, that I am forced to leave you,' said I. 'You can assure your husband that I shall take every care of his coat.' Hurried as I was, I ventured to pause a moment to salute the lady's hand, which she snatched through the window with an admirable pretence of being offended at my presumption. Then, as the lantern was quite close to me, and the post-boy seemed inclined to interfere with my flight, I tucked my precious overcoat under my arm, and dashed off into the darkness.

And now I set myself to the task of putting as broad a stretch of moor between the prison and myself as the remaining hours of darkness would allow. Setting my face to the wind once more, I ran until I fell from exhaustion. Then, after five minutes of panting among the heather, I made another start, until again my knees gave way beneath me. I was young and hard, with muscles of steel, and a frame which had been toughened by twelve years of camp and field. Thus I was able to keep up this wild flight for another three hours, during which I still guided myself, you understand, by keeping the wind in my face. At the end of that time I calculated that I had put nearly twenty miles between the prison and myself. Day was about to break, so I crouched down among the heather upon the top of one of those small hills which abound in that country, with the intention of hiding myself until nightfall. It was no new thing for me to sleep in the wind and the rain, so, wrapping myself up in my thick warm cloak, I soon sank into a doze.

But it was not a refreshing slumber. I tossed and tumbled amid a series of vile dreams, in which everything seemed to go wrong with me. At last, I remember, I was charging an unshaken square of Hungarian Grenadiers, with a single squadron upon spent horses, just as I did at Elchingen. I stood in my stirrups to shout 'Vive l'Empereur!' and as I did so, there came the answering roar from my hussars, 'Vive l'Empereur!' I sprang from my rough bed, with the words still ringing in my ears, and then, as I rubbed my eyes, and wondered if I were mad, the same cry came again, five thousand voices in one long-drawn yell. I looked out from my screen of brambles, and saw in the clear light of morning the very last thing that I should either have expected or chosen.

It was Dartmoor Prison! There it stretched, grim and hideous, within a furlong of me. Had I run on for a few more minutes in the dark, I should have butted my shako against the wall. I was so taken aback at the sight, that I could scarcely realize what had happened. Then it all became clear to me, and I struck my head with my hands in my despair. The wind had veered from north to south during the night, and I, keeping my face always towards it, had run ten miles out and ten miles in, winding up where I had started. When I thought of my hurry, my falls, my mad rushing and jumping, all ending in this, it seemed so absurd, that my grief changed suddenly to amusement, and I fell among the brambles, and laughed, and laughed, until my sides were sore. Then I rolled myself up in my cloak and considered seriously what I should do.

One lesson which I have learned in my

roaming life, my friends, is never to call anything a misfortune until you have seen the end of it. Is not every hour a fresh point of view? In this case I soon perceived that accident had done for me as much as the most profound cunning. My guards naturally commenced their search from the place where I had taken Sir Charles Meredith's coat, and from my hiding-place I could see them hurrying along the road to that point. Not one of them ever dreamed that I could have doubled back from there, and I lay quite undisturbed in the little bush-covered cup at the summit of my knoll. The prisoners had, of course, learned of my escape, and all day exultant yells, like that which had aroused me in the morning, resounded over the moor, bearing a welcome message of sympathy and companionship to my ears. How little did they dream that on the top of that very mound, which they could see from their windows, was lying the comrade whose escape they were celebrating? As for me — I could look down upon this poor herd of idle warriors, as they paced about the great exercise yard, or gathered in little groups, gesticulating joyfully over my success. Once I heard a howl of execration, and I saw Beaumont, his head all covered with bandages, being led across the yard by two of the warders. I cannot tell you the pleasure which this sight gave me, for it proved that I had not killed him, and also that the others knew the true story of what had passed. They had all known me too well to think that I could have abandoned him.

All that long day I lay behind my screen of bushes, listening to the bells which struck the hours below.

My pockets were filled with bread which I had saved out of my allowance, and on searching my borrowed overcoat I came upon a silver flask, full of excellent brandy and water, so that I was able to get through the day without hardship. The only other things in the pockets were a red silk handkerchief, a tortoise-shell snuff-box, and a blue envelope, with a red seal, addressed to the Governor of Dartmoor Prison. As to the first two, I determined to send them back when I should return the coat itself.

The letter caused me more perplexity, for the Governor had always shown me every courtesy, and it offended my sense of honour that I should interfere with his correspondence. I had almost made up my mind to leave it under a stone upon the roadway within musket-shot of the gate. This would guide them in their search for me, however, and so, on the whole, I saw no better way than just to carry the letter with me in the hope that I might find some means of sending it back to him. Meanwhile I packed it safely away in my inner-most pocket.

There was a warm sun to dry my clothes, and when night fell I was ready for my journey. I promise you that there were no mistakes this time. I took the stars for my guides, as every hussar should be taught to do, and I put eight good leagues between myself and the prison. My plan now was to obtain a complete suit of clothes from the first person whom I could waylay, and I should then find my way to the north coast, where there were many smugglers and fishermen who would be ready to earn the reward which was paid by the Emperor to those who brought escaping prisoners across the Channel. I had taken the panache from my shako so that it might escape notice, but even with my fine overcoat I feared that sooner or later my uniform would betray me. My first care must be to provide myself with a complete disguise.

When day broke, I saw a river upon my right and a small town upon my left — the blue smoke reeking up above the moor. I should have liked well to have entered it, because it would have interested me to see something of the customs of the English, which differ very much from those of other nations. Much as I should have wished, however, to have seen them eat their raw meat and sell their wives, it would have been dangerous until I had got rid of my uniform. My cap, my moustache, and my speech would all help to betray me. I continued to travel towards the north therefore, looking about me continually, but never catching a glimpse of my pursuers.

About midday I came to where, in a secluded valley, there stood a single small cottage without any other building in sight. It was a neat little house, with a rustic porch and a small garden in front of it, with a swarm of cocks and hens. I lay down among the ferns and watched it, for it seemed to be exactly the kind of place where I might obtain what I wanted. My bread was finished, and I was exceedingly hungry after my long journey; I determined, therefore, to make a short reconnaissance, and then to march up to this cottage, summon it to surrender, and help myself to all that I needed. It could at least provide me with a chicken and with an omelette. My mouth watered at the thought.

As I lay there, wondering who could live in this lonely place, a brisk little fellow came out through the porch, accompanied by another older man, who carried two large clubs in his hands. These he handed to his young companion, who swung them up and down, and round and round, with extraordinary swiftness. The other, standing beside him, appeared to watch him with great attention, and occasionally to advise him. Finally he took a rope, and began skipping like a girl, the other still gravely observing him. As you may think, I was utterly puzzled as to what these people could be, and could only surmise that the one was a doctor, and the other a patient who had submitted himself to some singular method of treatment.

Well, as I lay watching and wondering, the older man brought out a great-coat, and held it while the other put it on and buttoned it to his chin. The day was a warmish one, so that this proceeding amazed me even more than the other. 'At least,' thought I, 'it is evident that his exercise is over'; but, far from this being so, the man began to run, in spite of his heavy coat, and as it chanced, he came right over the moor in my direction. His companion had re-entered the house, so that this arrangement suited me admirably. I would take the small man's clothing, and hurry on to some village where I could buy provisions. The chickens were certainly tempting, but still there were at least two men in the house, so perhaps it would be wiser for me, since I had no arms, to keep away from it.

I lay quietly then among the ferns. Presently I heard the steps of the runner, and there he was quite close to me, with his huge coat, and the perspiration running down his face. He seemed to be a very solid man — but small — so small that I feared that his clothes might be of little use to me. When I jumped out upon him he stopped running, and looked at me in the greatest astonishment.

'Blow my dickey,' said he, 'give it a name, guv'nor! Is it a circus, or what?'

That was how he talked, though I cannot pretend to tell you what he meant by it.

'You will excuse me, sir,' said I, 'but I am under the necessity of asking you to give me your clothes.'

'Give you what?' he cried.

'Your clothes.'

'Well, if this don't lick cock-fighting!' said he. 'What am I to give you my clothes for?'

'Because I need them.'

'And suppose I won't?'

'Be jabers,' said I, 'I shall have no choice but to take them.'

He stood with his hands in the pockets of his greatcoat, and a most amused smile upon his square-jawed, clean-shaven face.

'You'll take them, will you?' said he. 'You're a very leery cove, by the look of you, but I can tell you that you've got the wrong sow by the ear this time. I know who you are. You're a runaway Frenchy, from the prison yonder, as anyone could tell with half an eye. But you don't know who I am, else you wouldn't try such a plant as that. Why, man, I'm the Bristol Bustler, nine stone champion, and them's my training quarters down yonder.'

He stared at me as if this announcement of his would have crushed me to the earth, but I smiled at him in my turn, and looked him up and down, with a twirl of my moustache.

'You may be a very brave man, sir,' said I, 'but when I tell you that you are opposed to Colonel Etienne Gerard, of the Hussars of Conflans, you will see the necessity of giving up your clothes without further parley.'

'Look here, mounseer, drop it!' he cried; 'this'll end by your getting pepper.'

'Your clothes, sir, this instant!' I shouted, advancing fiercely upon him.

For answer he threw off his heavy great-coat, and stood in a singular attitude, with one arm out, and the other across his chest, looking at me with a curious smile. For myself, I knew nothing of the methods of fighting which these people have, but on horse or on foot, with arms or without them,

I am always ready to take my own part. You understand that a soldier cannot always choose his own methods, and that it is time to howl when you are living among wolves. I rushed at him, therefore, with a warlike shout, and kicked him with both my feet. At the same moment my heels flew into the air, I saw as many flashes as at Austerlitz, and the back of my head came down with a crash upon a stone. After that I can remember nothing more.

When I came to myself I was lying upon a truckle-bed, in a bare, half-furnished room. My head was ringing like a bell, and when I put up my hand, there was a lump like a walnut over one of my eyes. My nose was full of a pungent smell, and I soon found that a strip of paper soaked in vinegar was fastened across my brow. At the other end of the room this terrible little man was sitting with his knee bare, and his elderly companion was rubbing it with some liniment. The latter seemed to be in the worst of tempers, and he kept up a continual scolding, which the other listened to with a gloomy face.

'Never heard tell of such a thing in my life,' he was saying. 'In training for a month with all the weight of it on my shoulders, and then when I get you as fit as a trout, and within two days of fighting the likeliest man on the list, you let yourself into a by-battle with a foreigner.'

'There, there! Stow your gab!' said the other, sulkily. 'You're a very good trainer, Jim, but you'd be better with less jaw.'

'I should think it was time to jaw,' the elderly man answered. 'If this knee don't get well before next Wednesday, they'll have it that you fought a cross, and a pretty job you'll have next time you look for a backer.'

'Fought a cross!' growled the other. 'I've won nineteen battles, and no man ever so much as dared to say the word 'cross' in my hearin'. How the deuce was I to get out of it when the cove wanted the very clothes off my back?'

'Tut, man; you knew that the beak and the guards were within a mile of you. You could have set them on to him as well then as now. You'd have got your clothes back again all right.'

'Well, strike me!' said the Bustler. 'I don't often break my trainin', but when it comes to givin' up my clothes to a Frenchy who couldn't hit a dint in a pat o' butter, why, it's more than I can swaller.'

'Pooh, man, what are the clothes worth? D'you know that Lord Rufton alone has five thousand pounds on you? When you jump the ropes on Wednesday, you'll carry every penny of fifty thousand into the ring. A pretty thing to turn up with a swollen knee and a story about a Frenchman!'

'I never thought he'd ha' kicked,' said the Bustler.

'I suppose you expected he'd fight Broughton's rules, and strict P.R.? Why, you silly, they don't know what fighting is in France.'

'My friends,' said I, sitting up on my bed, 'I do not understand very much of what you say, but when you speak like that it is foolishness. We know so much about fighting in France, that we have paid our little visit to nearly every capital in Europe, and very soon we are coming to London. But we fight like soldiers, you understand, and not like gamins in the gutter. You strike me on the head. I kick you on the knee. It is child's play. But if you will give me a sword, and take another one, I will show you how we fight over the water.'

They both stared at me in their solid, English way.

'Well, I'm glad you're not dead, mounseer,' said the elder one at last. 'There wasn't much sign of life in you when the Bustler and me carried you down. That head of yours ain't thick enough to stop the crook of the hardest hitter in Bristol.'

'He's a game cove, too, and he came for me like a bantam,' said the other, still rubbing his knee. 'I got my old left-right in, and he went over as if he had been pole-axed. It wasn't my fault, mounseer. I told you you'd get pepper if you went on.'

'Well, it's something to say all your life, that you've been handled by the finest light-weight in England,' said the older man, looking at me with an expression of congratulation upon his face. 'You've had him at his best, too — in the pink of condition, and trained by Jim Hunter.'

'I am used to hard knocks,' said I, unbuttoning my tunic, and showing my two musket wounds. Then I bared my ankle also, and showed the place in my eye where the guerilla had stabbed me.

'He can take his gruel,' said the Bustler.

'What a glutton he'd have made for the middle-weights,' remarked the trainer; 'with six months' coaching he'd astonish the fancy. It's a pity he's got to go back to prison.'

I did not like that last remark at all. I buttoned up my coat and rose from the bed.

'I must ask you to let me continue my journey,' said I.

'There's no help for it, mounseer,' the trainer answered. 'It's a hard thing to send such a man as you back to such a place, but business is business, and there's a twenty pound reward. They were here this morning, looking for you, and I expect they'll be round again.'

His words turned my heart to lead.

'Surely, you would not betray me!' I cried. 'I will send you twice twenty pounds on the day that I set foot upon France. I swear it upon the honour of a French gentleman.'

But I only got head-shakes for a reply. I pleaded, I argued, I spoke of the English hospitality and the fellowship of brave men, but I might as well have been addressing the two great wooden clubs which stood balanced upon the floor in front of me. There was no sign of sympathy upon their bull-faces.

'Business is business, mounseer,' the old trainer repeated. 'Besides, how am I to put the Bustler into the ring on Wednesday if he's jugged by the beak for aidin' and abettin' a prisoner of war? I've got to look after the Bustler, and I take no risks.'

This, then, was the end of all my struggles and strivings. I was to be led back again like a poor silly sheep who has broken through the hurdles. They little knew me who could fancy that I should submit to such a fate. I had heard enough to tell me where the weak point of these two men was, and I showed, as I have often showed before, that Etienne Gerard is never so terrible as when all hope seems to have deserted him. With a single spring I seized one of the clubs and swung it over the head of the Bustler.

'Come what may,' I cried, '*you* shall be spoiled for Wednesday.'

The fellow growled out an oath, and would have sprung at me, but the other flung his arms round him and pinned him to the chair.

'Not if I know it, Bustler,' he screamed. 'None of your games while I am by. Get away out of this, Frenchy. We only want to see your back. Run away, run away, or he'll get loose!'

It was good advice, I thought, and I ran to the door, but as I came out into the open air my head swam round and I had to lean against the porch to save myself from falling. Consider all that I had been through, the anxiety of my escape, the long, useless flight in the storm, the day spent amid wet ferns, with only bread for food, the second journey by night, and now the injuries which I had received in attempting to deprive the little man of his clothes. Was it wonderful that even I should reach the limits of my endurance?

I stood there in my heavy coat and my poor battered shako, my chin upon my chest, and my eyelids over my eyes. I had done my best, and I could do no more. It was the sound of horses' hoofs which made me at last raise my head, and there was the grey-moustached Governor of Dartmoor Prison not ten paces in front of me, with six mounted warders behind him!

'So, Colonel,' said he, with a bitter smile, 'we have found you once more.'

When a brave man has done his utmost, and has failed, he shows his breeding by the manner in which he accepts his defeat. For me, I took the letter which I had in my pocket, and stepping forward, I handed it with such grace of manner as I could summon to the Governor.

'It has been my misfortune, sir, to detain one of your letters,' said I.

He looked at me in amazement, and beckoned to the warders to arrest me. Then he broke the seal of the letter. I saw a curious expression come over his face as he read it.

'This must be the letter which Sir Charles Meredith lost,' said he.

'It was in the pocket of his coat.'

'You have carried it for two days?'

'Since the night before last.'

'And never looked at the contents?'

I showed him by my manner that he had committed an indiscretion in asking a question which one gentleman should not have put to another.

To my surprise he burst out into a roar of laughter.

'Colonel,' said he, wiping the tears from his eyes, 'you have really given both yourself and us a great deal of unnecessary trouble. Allow me to read the letter which you carried with you in your flight.'

And this was what I heard: —

'On receipt of this you are directed to release Colonel Etienne Gerard, of the 3rd Hussars, who has been exchanged against Colonel Mason, of the Horse Artillery, now in Verdun.'

And as he read it, he laughed again, and the warders laughed, and the two men from the cottage laughed, and then, as I heard this universal merriment, and thought of all my hopes and fears, and my struggles and dangers, what could a debonair soldier do but lean against the porch once more, and laugh as heartily as any of them? And of them all was it not I who had the best reason to laugh, since in front of me I could see my dear France, and my mother, and the Emperor, and my horsemen; while behind lay the gloomy prison, and the heavy hand of the English King?

5

How the Brigadier Took the Field
Against the Marshal Millefleurs

Massena was a thin, sour little fellow, and after his hunting accident he had only one eye, but when it looked out from under his cocked hat there was not much upon a field of battle which escaped it. He could stand in front of a battalion, and with a single sweep tell you if a buckle or a gaiter button were out of place. Neither the officers nor the men were very fond of him, for he was, as you know, a miser, and soldiers love that their leaders should be free-handed. At the same time, when it came to work they had a very high respect for him, and they would rather fight under him than under anyone except the Emperor himself, and Lannes, when he was alive. After all, if he had a tight grasp upon his money-bags, there was a day also, you must remember, when that same grip was upon Zurich and Genoa. He clutched on to his positions as he did to his strong box, and it took a very clever man to loosen him from either.

When I received his summons I went gladly to his headquarters, for I was always a great favourite of his, and there was no officer of whom he thought more highly. That was the best of serving with those good old generals, that they knew enough to be able to pick out a fine soldier when they saw one. He was seated alone in his tent, with his chin upon his hand, and his brow as wrinkled as if he had been asked for a subscription. He smiled, however, when he saw me before him.

'Good day, Colonel Gerard.'

'Good day, Marshal.'

'How is the Third of Hussars?'

'Seven hundred incomparable men upon seven hundred excellent horses.'

'And your wounds — are they healed?'

'My wounds never heal, Marshal,' I answered.

'And why?'

'Because I have always new ones.'

'General Rapp must look to his laurels,' said he, his face all breaking into wrinkles as he laughed. 'He has had twenty-one from the enemy's bullets, and as many from Larrey's knives and probes. Knowing that you were hurt, Colonel, I have spared you of late.'

'Which hurt me most of all.'

'Tut, tut! Since the English got behind these accursed lines of Torres Vedras, there

161

has been little for us to do. You did not miss much during your imprisonment at Dartmoor. But now we are on the eve of action.'

'We advance?'

'No, retire.'

My face must have shown my dismay. What, retire before this sacred dog of a Wellington — he who had listened unmoved to my words, and had sent me to his land of fogs? I could have sobbed as I thought of it.

'What would you have?' cried Massena impatiently. 'When one is in check, it is necessary to move the king.'

'Forwards,' I suggested.

He shook his grizzled head.

'The lines are not to be forced,' said he. 'I have already lost General St. Croix and more men than I can replace. On the other hand, we have been here at Santarem for nearly six months. There is not a pound of flour nor a jug of wine on the countryside. We must retire.'

'There are flour and wine in Lisbon,' I persisted.

'Tut, you speak as if an army could charge in and charge out again like your regiment of hussars. If Soult were here with thirty thousand men — but he will not come. I sent for you, however, Colonel Gerard, to say that I have a very singular and important expedition which I intend to place under your direction.'

I pricked up my ears, as you can imagine. The Marshal unrolled a great map of the country and spread it upon the table. He flattened it out with his little, hairy hands.

'This is Santarem,' he said pointing.

I nodded.

'And here, twenty-five miles to the east, is Almeixal, celebrated for its vintages and for its enormous Abbey.'

Again I nodded; I could not think what was coming.

'Have you heard of the Marshal Mille-fleurs?' asked Massena.

'I have served with all the Marshals,' said I, 'but there is none of that name.'

'It is but the nickname which the soldiers have given him,' said Massena. 'If you had not been away from us for some months, it would not be necessary for me to tell you about him. He is an Englishman, and a man of good breeding. It is on account of his manners that they have given him his title. I wish you to go to this polite Englishman at Almeixal.'

'Yes, Marshal.'

'And to hang him to the nearest tree.'

'Certainly, Marshal.'

I turned briskly upon my heels, but

Massena recalled me before I could reach the opening of his tent.

'One moment, Colonel,' said he; 'you had best learn how matters stand before you start. You must know, then, that this Marshal Millefleurs, whose real name is Alexis Morgan, is a man of very great ingenuity and bravery. He was an officer in the English Guards, but having been broken for cheating at cards, he left the army. In some manner he gathered a number of English deserters round him and took to the mountains. French stragglers and Portuguese brigands joined him, and he found himself at the head of five hundred men. With these he took possession of the Abbey of Almeixal, sent the monks about their business, fortified the place, and gathered in the plunder of all the country round.'

'For which it is high time he was hanged,' said I, making once more for the door.

'One instant!' cried the Marshal, smiling at my impatience. 'The worst remains behind. Only last week the Dowager Countess of La Ronda, the richest woman in Spain, was taken by these ruffians in the passes as she was journeying from King Joseph's Court to visit her grandson. She is now a prisoner in the Abbey, and is only protected by her — '

'Grandmotherhood,' I suggested.

'Her power of paying a ransom,' said Massena. 'You have three missions, then: To rescue this unfortunate lady; to punish this villain; and, if possible, to break up this nest of brigands. It will be a proof of the confidence which I have in you when I say that I can only spare you half a squadron with which to accomplish all this.'

My word, I could hardly believe my ears! I thought that I should have had my regiment at the least.

'I would give you more,' said he, 'but I commence my retreat today, and Wellington is so strong in horse that every trooper becomes of importance. I cannot spare you another man. You will see what you can do, and you will report yourself to me at Abrantes not later than tomorrow night.'

It was very complimentary that he should rate my powers so high, but it was also a little embarrassing. I was to rescue an old lady, to hang an Englishman, and to break up a band of five hundred assassins — all with fifty men. But after all, the fifty men were Hussars of Conflans, and they had an Etienne Gerard to lead them. As I came out into the warm Portuguese sunshine my confidence had returned to me, and I had already begun to wonder whether the medal which I had so often deserved might not be waiting for me at Almeixal.

You may be sure that I did not take my fifty men at haphazard. They were all old soldiers of the German wars, some of them with three stripes, and most of them with two. Oudet and Papilette, two of the best sub-officers in the regiment, were at their head. When I had them formed up in fours, all in silver grey and upon chestnut horses, with their leopard skin shabracks and their little red panaches, my heart beat high at the sight. I could not look at their weather-stained faces, with the great moustaches which bristled over their chin-straps, without feeling a glow of confidence, and, between ourselves, I have no doubt that that was exactly how they felt when they saw their young Colonel on his great black war-horse riding at their head.

Well, when we got free of the camp and over the Tagus, I threw out my advance and my flankers, keeping my own place at the head of the main body. Looking back from the hills above Santarem, we could see the dark lines of Massena's army, with the flash and twinkle of the sabres and bayonets as he moved his regiments into position for their retreat. To the south lay the scattered red patches of the English outposts, and behind the grey smoke-cloud which rose from

Wellington's camp — thick, oily smoke, which seemed to our poor starving fellows to bear with it the rich smell of seething camp-kettles. Away to the west lay a curve of blue sea flecked with the white sails of the English ships.

You will understand that as we were riding to the east, our road lay away from both armies. Our own marauders, however, and the scouting parties of the English, covered the country, and it was necessary with my small troop that I should take every precaution. During the whole day we rode over desolate hill-sides, the lower portions covered by the budding vines, but the upper turning from green to grey, and jagged along the skyline like the back of a starved horse. Mountain streams crossed our path, running west to the Tagus, and once we came to a deep, strong river, which might have checked us had I not found the ford by observing where houses had been built opposite each other upon either bank. Between them, as every scout should know, you will find your ford. There was none to give us information, for neither man nor beast, nor any living thing except great clouds of crows, was to be seen during our journey.

The sun was beginning to sink when we came to a valley clear in the centre, but shrouded by huge oak trees upon either side. We could not be more than a few miles from Almeixal, so it seemed to me to be best to keep among the groves, for the spring had been an early one and the leaves were already thick enough to conceal us. We were riding then in open order among the great trunks, when one of my flankers came galloping up.

'There are English across the valley, Colonel,' he cried, as he saluted.

'Cavalry or infantry?'

'Dragoons, Colonel,' said he; 'I saw the gleam of their helmets, and heard the neigh of a horse.'

Halting my men I hastened to the edge of the wood. There could be no doubt about it. A party of English cavalry was travelling in a line with us, and in the same direction. I caught a glimpse of their red coats and of their flashing arms glowing and twinkling among the tree-trunks. Once, as they passed through a small clearing, I could see their whole force, and I judged that they were of about the same strength as my own — a half squadron at the most.

You who have heard some of my little adventures will give me credit for being quick in my decisions, and prompt in carrying them out. But here I must confess that I was in two minds. On the one hand there was the chance of a fine cavalry skirmish with the English. On the other hand, there was my mission at the Abbey of Almeixal, which seemed already to be so much above my power. If I were to lose any of my men, it was certain that I should be unable to carry out my orders. I was sitting my horse, with my chin in my gauntlet, looking across at the rippling gleams of light from the further wood, when suddenly one of these red-coated Englishmen rode out from the cover, pointing at me and breaking into a shrill whoop and halloa as if I had been a fox. Three others joined him, and one who was a bugler sounded a call, which brought the whole of them into the open. They were, as I had thought, a half squadron, and they formed a double line with a front of twenty-five, their officer — the one who had whooped at me — at their head.

For my own part, I had instantly brought my own troopers into the same formation, so that there we were, hussars and dragoons, with only two hundred yards of grassy sward between us. They carried themselves well, those red-coated troopers, with their silver helmets, their high white plumes, and their long, gleaming swords; while, on the other hand, I am sure that they would acknowledge that they had never looked upon finer light horsemen than the fifty hussars of Conflans who were facing them. They were heavier, it is true, and they may have seemed the smarter, for Wellington used to make them burnish their metal work, which was not usual among us. On the other hand, it is well known that the English tunics were too tight for the sword-arm, which gave our men an advantage. As to bravery, foolish, inexperienced people of every nation always think that their own soldiers are braver than any others. There is no nation in the world which does not entertain this idea. But when one has seen as much as I have done, one understands that there is no very marked difference, and that although nations differ very much in discipline, they are all equally brave — except that the French have rather more courage than the rest.

Well, the cork was drawn and the glasses ready, when suddenly the English officer raised his sword to me as if in a challenge, and cantered his horse across the grassland. My word, there is no finer sight upon earth than that of a gallant man upon a gallant steed! I could have halted there just to watch him as he came with such careless grace, his sabre down by his horse's shoulder, his head thrown back, his white plume tossing — youth and strength and courage, with the violet evening sky above and the oak trees behind. But it was not for me to stand and stare. Etienne Gerard may have his faults, but, my faith, he was never accused of being backward in taking his own part. The old horse, Rataplan, knew me so well that he had started off before ever I gave the first shake to the bridle.

There are two things in this world that I am very slow to forget: the face of a pretty woman, and the legs of a fine horse. Well, as we drew together, I kept on saying, 'Where have I seen those great roan shoulders? Where have I seen that dainty fetlock?' Then suddenly I remembered, and as I looked up at the reckless eyes and the challenging smile, whom should I recognize but the man who had saved me from the brigands and played me for my freedom — he whose correct title was Milor the Hon. Sir Russell Bart!

'Bart!' I shouted.

He had his arm raised for a cut, and three parts of his body open to my point, for he did not know very much about the use of the sword. As I brought my hilt to the salute he dropped his hand and stared at me.

'Halloa!' said he. 'It's Gerard!' You would have thought by his manner that I had met him by appointment. For my own part, I would have embraced him had he but come an inch of the way to meet me.

171

'I thought we were in for some sport,' said he. 'I never dreamed that it was you.'

I found this tone of disappointment somewhat irritating. Instead of being glad at having met a friend, he was sorry at having missed an enemy.

'I should have been happy to join in your sport, my dear Bart,' said I. 'But I really cannot turn my sword upon a man who saved my life.'

'Tut, never mind about that.'

'No, it is impossible. I should never forgive myself.'

'You make too much of a trifle.'

'My mother's one desire is to embrace you. If ever you should be in Gascony — '

'Lord Wellington is coming there with 60,000 men.'

'Then one of them will have a chance of surviving,' said I, laughing. 'In the meantime, put your sword in your sheath!'

Our horses were standing head to tail, and the Bart put out his hand and patted me on the thigh.

'You're a good chap, Gerard,' said he. 'I only wish you had been born on the right side of the Channel.'

'I was,' said I.

'Poor devil!' he cried, with such an earnestness of pity that he set me laughing

172

again. 'But look here, Gerard,' he continued; 'this is all very well, but it is not business, you know. I don't know what Massena would say to it, but our Chief would jump out of his riding-boots if he saw us. We weren't sent out here for a picnic — either of us.'

'What would you have?'

'Well, we had a little argument about our hussars and dragoons, if you remember. I've got fifty of the Sixteenth all chewing their carbine bullets behind me. You've got as many fine-looking boys over yonder, who seem to be fidgeting in their saddles. If you and I took the right flanks we should not spoil each other's beauty — though a little blood-letting is a friendly thing in this climate.'

There seemed to me to be a good deal of sense in what he said. For the moment Mr Alexis Morgan and the Countess of La Ronda and the Abbey of Almeixal went right out of my head, and I could only think of the fine level turf and of the beautiful skirmish which we might have.

'Very good, Bart,' said I. 'We have seen the front of your dragoons. We shall now have a look at their backs.'

'Any betting?' he asked.

'The stake,' said I, 'is nothing less than the honour of the Hussars of Conflans.'

'Well, come on!' he answered. 'If we break you, well and good — if you break us, it will be all the better for Marshal Millefleurs.'

When he said that I could only stare at him in astonishment.

'Why for Marshal Millefleurs?' I asked.

'It is the name of a rascal who lives out this way. My dragoons have been sent by Lord Wellington to see him safely hanged.'

'Name of a name!' I cried. 'Why, my hussars have been sent by Massena for that very object.'

We burst out laughing at that, and sheathed our swords. There was a whirr of steel from behind us as our troopers followed our example.

'We are allies!' he cried.

'For a day.'

'We must join forces.'

'There is no doubt of it.'

And so, instead of fighting, we wheeled our half squadrons round and moved in two little columns down the valley, the shakos and the helmets turned inwards, and the men looking their neighbours up and down, like old fighting dogs with tattered ears who have learned to respect each other's teeth. The most were on the broad grin, but there were some on either side who looked black and challenging, especially the English sergeant and my own sub-officer Papilette. They were men of habit, you see, who could not change all their ways of thinking in a moment. Besides, Papilette had lost his only brother at Busaco. As for the Bart and me, we rode together at the head and chatted about all that had occurred to us since that famous game of écarté of which I have told you.

For my own part, I spoke to him of my adventures in England. They are a very singular people, these English. Although he knew that I had been engaged in twelve campaigns, yet I am sure that the Bart thought more highly of me because I had had an affair with the Bristol Bustler. He told me, too, that the Colonel who presided over his court-martial for playing cards with a prisoner acquitted him of neglect of duty, but nearly broke him because he thought that he had not cleared his trumps before leading his suit. Yes, indeed, they are a singular people.

At the end of the valley the road curved over some rising ground before winding down into another wider valley beyond. We called a halt when we came to the top; for there, right in front of us, at the distance of about three miles, was a scattered, grey town, with a single enormous building upon the flank of the mountain which overlooked it. We could not doubt that we were at last in sight of the

Abbey that held the gang of rascals whom we had come to disperse. It was only now, I think, that we fully understood what a task lay in front of us, for the place was a veritable fortress, and it was evident that cavalry should never have been sent out upon such an errand.

'That's got nothing to do with us,' said the Bart; 'Wellington and Massena can settle that between them.'

'Courage!' I answered. 'Piré took Leipzig with fifty hussars.'

'Had they been dragoons,' said the Bart, laughing, 'he would have had Berlin. But you are senior officer; give us a lead, and we'll see who will be the first to flinch.'

'Well,' said I, 'whatever we do must be done at once, for my orders are to be on my way to Abrantes by tomorrow night. But we must have some information first, and here is someone who should be able to give it to us.'

There was a square, whitewashed house standing by the roadside, which appeared, from the bush hanging over the door, to be one of those wayside tabernas which are provided for the muleteers. A lantern was hung in the porch, and by its light we saw two men, the one in the brown habit of a Capuchin monk, and the other girt with an apron, which showed him to be the landlord.

They were conversing together so earnestly that we were upon them before they were aware of us. The innkeeper turned to fly, but one of the Englishmen seized him by the hair, and held him tight.

'For mercy's sake, spare me,' he yelled. 'My house has been gutted by the French and harried by the English, and my feet have been burned by the brigands. I swear by the Virgin that I have neither money nor food in my inn, and the good Father Abbot, who is starving upon my doorstep, will be witness to it.'

'Indeed, sir,' said the Capuchin, in excellent French, 'what this worthy man says is very true. He is one of the many victims to these cruel wars, although his loss is but a feather-weight compared to mine. Let him go,' he added, in English, to the trooper, 'he is too weak to fly, even if he desired to.'

In the light of the lantern I saw that this monk was a magnificent man, dark and bearded, with the eyes of a hawk, and so tall that his cowl came up to Rataplan's ears. He wore the look of one who had been through much suffering, but he carried himself like a king, and we could form some opinion of his learning when we each heard him talk our own language as fluently as if he were born to it.

'You have nothing to fear,' said I, to the

trembling innkeeper. 'As to you, father, you are, if I am not mistaken, the very man who can give us the information which we require.'

'All that I have is at your service, my son. But,' he added, with a wan smile, 'my Lenten fare is always somewhat meagre, and this year it has been such that I must ask you for a crust of bread if I am to have the strength to answer your questions.'

We bore two days' rations in our haversacks, so that he soon had the little he asked for. It was dreadful to see the wolfish way in which he seized the piece of dried goat's flesh which I was able to offer him.

'Time presses, and we must come to the point,' said I. 'We want your advice as to the weak points of yonder Abbey, and concerning the habits of the rascals who infest it.'

He cried out something which I took to be Latin, with his hands clasped and his eyes upturned. 'The prayer of the just availeth much,' said he, 'and yet I had not dared to hope that mine would have been so speedily answered. In me you see the unfortunate Abbot of Almeixal, who has been cast out by this rabble of three armies with their heretical leader. Oh! to think of what I have lost!' his voice broke, and the tears hung upon his lashes.

'Cheer up, sir,' said the Bart. 'I'll lay nine to four that we have you back again by tomorrow night.'

'It is not of my own welfare that I think,' said he, 'nor even of that of my poor, scattered flock. But it is of the holy relics which are left in the sacrilegious hands of these robbers.'

'It's even betting whether they would ever bother their heads about them,' said the Bart. 'But show us the way inside the gates, and we'll soon clear the place out for you.'

In a few short words the good Abbot gave us the very points that we wished to know. But all that he said only made our task more formidable. The walls of the Abbey were forty feet high. The lower windows were barricaded, and the whole building loopholed for musketry fire. The gang preserved military discipline, and their sentries were too numerous for us to hope to take them by surprise. It was more than ever evident that a battalion of grenadiers and a couple of breaching pieces were what was needed. I raised my eyebrows, and the Bart began to whistle.

'We must have a shot at it, come what may,' said he.

The men had already dismounted, and, having watered their horses, were eating their suppers. For my own part I went into the sitting-room of the inn with the Abbot and the Bart, that we might talk about our plans.

I had a little cognac in my *sauve vie*, and I divided it among us — just enough to wet our moustaches.

'It is unlikely,' said I, 'that those rascals know anything about our coming. I have seen no signs of scouts along the road. My own plan is that we should conceal ourselves in some neighbouring wood, and then, when they open their gates, charge down upon them and take them by surprise.'

The Bart was of opinion that this was the best that we could do, but, when we came to talk it over, the Abbot made us see that there were difficulties in the way.

'Save on the side of the town, there is no place within a mile of the Abbey where you could shelter man or horse,' said he. 'As to the townsfolk, they are not to be trusted. I fear, my son, that your excellent plan would have little chance of success in the face of the vigilant guard which these men keep.'

'I see no other way,' answered I. 'Hussars of Conflans are not so plentiful that I can afford to run half a squadron of them against a forty-foot wall with five hundred infantry behind it.'

'I am a man of peace,' said the Abbot, 'and

yet I may, perhaps, give a word of counsel. I know these villains and their ways. Who should do so better, seeing that I have stayed for a month in this lonely spot, looking down in weariness of heart at the Abbey which was my own? I will tell you now what I should myself do if I were in your place.'

'Pray tell us, father,' we cried, both together.

'You must know that bodies of deserters, both French and English, are continually coming in to them, carrying their weapons with them. Now, what is there to prevent you and your men from pretending to be such a body, and so making your way into the Abbey?'

I was amazed at the simplicity of the thing, and I embraced the good Abbot. The Bart, however, had some objections to offer.

'That is all very well,' said he, 'but if these fellows are as sharp as you say, it is not very likely that they are going to let a hundred armed strangers into their crib. From all I have heard of Mr Morgan, or Marshal Millefleurs, or whatever the rascal's name is, I give him credit for more sense than that.'

'Well, then,' I cried, 'let us send fifty in, and let them at daybreak throw open the gates to the other fifty, who will be waiting outside.'

We discussed the question at great length

and with much foresight and discretion. If it had been Massena and Wellington instead of two young officers of light cavalry, we could not have weighed it all with more judgment. At last we agreed, the Bart and I, that one of us should indeed go with fifty men, under pretence of being deserters, and that in the early morning he should gain command of the gate and admit the others. The Abbot, it is true, was still of opinion that it was dangerous to divide our force, but finding that we were both of the same mind, he shrugged his shoulders and gave in.

'There is only one thing that I would ask,' said he. 'If you lay hands upon this Marshal Millefleurs — this dog of a brigand — what will you do with him?'

'Hang him,' I answered.

'It is too easy a death,' cried the Capuchin, with a vindictive glow in his dark eyes. 'Had I my way with him — but, oh, what thoughts are these for a servant of God to harbour!' He clapped his hands to his forehead like one who is half demented by his troubles, and rushed out of the room.

There was an important point which we had still to settle, and that was whether the French or the English party should have the honour of entering the Abbey first. My faith, it was asking a great deal of Etienne Gerard that he should give place to any man at such a time! But the poor Bart pleaded so hard, urging the few skirmishes which he had seen against my four-and-seventy engagements, that at last I consented that he should go. We had just clasped hands over the matter when there broke out such a shouting and cursing and yelling from the front of the inn, that out we rushed with our drawn sabres in our hands, convinced that the brigands were upon us.

You may imagine our feelings when, by the light of the lantern which hung from the porch, we saw a score of our hussars and dragoons all mixed in one wild heap, red coats and blue, helmets and busbies, pommelling each other to their hearts' content. We flung ourselves upon them, imploring, threatening, tugging at a lace collar, or at a spurred heel, until, at last, we had dragged them all apart. There they stood, flushed and bleeding, glaring at each other, and all panting together like a line of troop horses after a ten-mile chase. It was only with our drawn swords that we could keep them from each other's throats. The poor Capuchin stood in the porch in his long brown habit, wringing his hands and calling upon all the saints for mercy.

He was, indeed, as I found upon inquiry,

the innocent cause of all the turmoil, for, not understanding how soldiers look upon such things, he had made some remark to the English sergeant that it was a pity that his squadron was not as good as the French. The words were not out of his mouth before a dragoon knocked down the nearest hussar, and then, in a moment, they all flew at each other like tigers. We would trust them no more after that, but the Bart moved his men to the front of the inn, and I mine to the back, the English all scowling and silent, and our fellows shaking their fists and chattering, each after the fashion of their own people.

Well, as our plans were made, we thought it best to carry them out at once, lest some fresh cause of quarrel should break out between our followers. The Bart and his men rode off, therefore, he having first torn the lace from his sleeves, and the gorget and sash from his uniform, so that he might pass as a simple trooper. He explained to his men what it was that was expected of them, and though they did not raise a cry or wave their weapons as mine might have done, there was an expression upon their stolid and clean-shaven faces which filled me with confidence. Their tunics were left unbuttoned, their scabbards and helmets stained with dirt, and their harness badly fastened, so that they might look the part of deserters, without order or discipline. At six o'clock next morning they were to gain command of the main gate of the Abbey, while at that same hour my hussars were to gallop up to it from outside. The Bart and I pledged our words to it before he trotted off with his detachment. My sergeant, Papilette, with two troopers, followed the English at a distance, and returned in half an hour to say that, after some parley, and the flashing of lanterns upon them from the grille, they had been admitted into the Abbey.

So far, then, all had gone well. It was a cloudy night with a sprinkling of rain, which was in our favour, as there was the less chance of our presence being discovered. My vedettes I placed two hundred yards in every direction, to guard against a surprise, and also to prevent any peasant who might stumble upon us from carrying the news to the Abbey. Oudin and Papilette were to take turns of duty, while the others with their horses had snug quarters in a great wooden granary. Having walked round and seen that all was as it should be, I flung myself upon the bed which the innkeeper had set apart for me, and fell into a dreamless sleep.

No doubt you have heard my name mentioned as being the beau-ideal of a soldier, and that not only by friends and admirers like our fellow-townsfolk, but also by old officers of the great wars who have shared the fortunes of those famous campaigns with me. Truth and modesty compel me to say, however, that this is not so. There are some gifts which I lack — very few, no doubt — but, still, amid the vast armies of the Emperor there may have been some who were free from those blemishes which stood between me and perfection. Of bravery I say nothing. Those who have seen me in the field are best fitted to speak about that. I have often heard the soldiers discussing round the camp-fires as to who was the bravest man in the Grand Army. Some said Murat, and some said Lasalle, and some Ney; but for my own part, when they asked me, I merely shrugged my shoulders and smiled. It would have seemed mere conceit if I had answered that there was no man braver than Brigadier Gerard. At the same time, facts are facts, and a man knows best what his own feelings are. But there are other gifts besides bravery which are necessary for a soldier, and one of them is that he should be a light sleeper. Now, from my boyhood onwards, I have been hard to wake, and it was this which brought me to ruin upon that night.

It may have been about two o'clock in the

morning that I was suddenly conscious of a feeling of suffocation. I tried to call out, but there was something which prevented me from uttering a sound. I struggled to rise, but I could only flounder like a hamstrung horse. I was strapped at the ankles, strapped at the knees, and strapped again at the wrists. Only my eyes were free to move, and there at the foot of my couch, by the light of a Portuguese lamp, whom should I see but the Abbot and the innkeeper!

The latter's heavy, white face had appeared to me when I looked upon it the evening before to express nothing but stupidity and terror. Now, on the contrary, every feature bespoke brutality and ferocity. Never have I seen a more dreadful-looking villain. In his hand he held a long, dull-coloured knife. The Abbot, on the other hand, was as polished and as dignified as ever. His Capuchin gown had been thrown open, however, and I saw beneath it a black, frogged coat, such as I have seen among the English officers. As our eyes met he leaned over the wooden end of the bed and laughed silently until it creaked again.

'You will, I am sure, excuse my mirth, my dear Colonel Gerard,' said he. 'The fact is, that the expression upon your face when you grasped the situation was just a little funny. I have no doubt that you are an excellent soldier, but I hardly think that you are fit to measure wits with the Marshal Millefleurs, as your fellows have been good enough to call me. You appear to have given me credit for singularly little intelligence, which argues, if I may be allowed to say so, a want of acuteness upon your own part. Indeed, with the single exception of my thick-headed compatriot, the British dragoon, I have never met anyone who was less competent to carry out such a mission.'

You can imagine how I felt and how I looked, as I listened to this insolent harangue, which was all delivered in that flowery and condescending manner which had gained this rascal his nickname. I could say nothing, but they must have read my threat in my eyes, for the fellow who had played the part of the innkeeper whispered something to his companion.

'No, no, my dear Chenier, he will be infinitely more valuable alive,' said he. 'By the way, Colonel, it is just as well that you are a sound sleeper, for my friend here, who is a little rough in his ways, would certainly have cut your throat if you had raised any alarm. I should recommend you to keep in his good graces, for Sergeant Chenier, late of the 7th Imperial Light Infantry, is a much more dangerous person than Captain Alexis Morgan, of His Majesty's foot-guards.'

Chenier grinned and shook his knife at me, while I tried to look the loathing which I felt at the thought that a soldier of the Emperor could fall so low.

'It may amuse you to know,' said the Marshal, in that soft, suave voice of his, 'that both your expeditions were watched from the time that you left your respective camps. I think that you will allow that Chenier and I played our parts with some subtlety. We had made every arrangement for your reception at the Abbey, though we had hoped to receive the whole squadron instead of half. When the gates are secured behind them, our visitors will find themselves in a very charming little mediaeval quadrangle, with no possible exit, commanded by musketry fire from a hundred windows. They may choose to be shot down; or they may choose to surrender. Between ourselves, I have not the slightest doubt that they have been wise enough to do the latter. But since you are naturally interested in the matter, we thought that you would care to come with us and to see for yourself. I think I can promise you that you will find your titled friend waiting for you at the Abbey with a face as long as your own.'

The two villains began whispering together,

debating, as far as I could hear, which was the best way of avoiding my vedettes.

'I will make sure that it is all clear upon the other side of the barn,' said the Marshal at last. 'You will stay here, my good Chenier, and if the prisoner gives any trouble you will know what to do.'

So we were left together, this murderous renegade and I — he sitting at the end of the bed, sharpening his knife upon his boot in the light of the single smoky little oil-lamp. As to me, I only wonder now, as I look back upon it, that I did not go mad with vexation and self-reproach as I lay helplessly upon the couch, unable to utter a word or move a finger, with the knowledge that my fifty gallant lads were so close to me, and yet with no means of letting them know the straits to which I was reduced. It was no new thing for me to be a prisoner; but to be taken by these renegades, and to be led into their Abbey in the midst of their jeers, befooled and out-witted by their insolent leaders — that was indeed more than I could endure. The knife of the butcher beside me would cut less deeply than that.

I twitched softly at my wrists, and then at my ankles, but whichever of the two had secured me was no bungler at his work. I could not move either of them an inch. Then

I tried to work the handkerchief down over my mouth, but the ruffian beside me raised his knife with such a threatening snarl that I had to desist. I was lying still looking at his bull neck, and wondering whether it would ever be my good fortune to fit it for a cravat, when I heard returning steps coming down the inn passage and up the stair. What word would the villain bring back? If he found it impossible to kidnap me, he would probably murder me where I lay. For my own part, I was indifferent which it might be, and I looked at the doorway with the contempt and defiance which I longed to put into words. But you can imagine my feelings, my dear friends, when, instead of the tall figure and dark, sneering face of the Capuchin, my eyes fell upon the grey pelisse and huge moustaches of my good little sub-officer, Papilette!

The French soldier of those days had seen too much to be ever taken by surprise. His eyes had hardly rested upon my bound figure and the sinister face beside me before he had seen how the matter lay.

'Sacred name of a dog!' he growled, and out flashed his great sabre. Chenier sprang forward at him with his knife, and then, thinking better of it, he darted back and stabbed frantically at my heart. For my own part, I had hurled myself off the bed on the side opposite to him, and the blade grazed my side before ripping its way through blanket and sheet. An instant later I heard the thud of a heavy fall, and then almost simultaneously a second object struck the floor — something lighter but harder, which rolled under the bed. I will not horrify you with details, my friends. Suffice it that Papilette was one of the strongest swordsmen in the regiment, and that his sabre was heavy and sharp. It left a red blotch upon my wrists and my ankles, as it cut the thongs which bound me.

When I had thrown off my gag, the first use which I made of my lips was to kiss the sergeant's scarred cheeks. The next was to ask him if all was well with the command. Yes, they had had no alarms. Oudin had just relieved him, and he had come to report. Had he seen the Abbot? No, he had seen nothing of him. Then we must form a cordon and prevent his escape. I was hurrying out to give the orders, when I heard a slow and measured step enter the door below, and come creaking up the stairs.

Papilette understood it all in an instant. 'You are not to kill him,' I whispered, and thrust him into the shadow on one side of the door; I crouched on the other. Up he came, up and up, and every footfall seemed to be upon my heart. The brown skirt of his gown was not over the threshold before we were both on him, like two wolves on a buck. Down we crashed, the three of us, he fighting like a tiger, and with such amazing strength that he might have broken away from the two of us. Thrice he got to his feet, and thrice we had him over again, until Papilette made him feel that there was a point to his sabre. He had sense enough then to know that the game was up, and to lie still while I lashed him with the very cords which had been round my own limbs.

'There has been a fresh deal, my fine fellow,' said I, 'and you will find that I have some of the trumps in *my* hand this time.'

'Luck always comes to the aid of a fool,' he answered. 'Perhaps it is as well, otherwise the world would fall too completely into the power of the astute. So, you have killed Chenier, I see. He was an insubordinate dog, and always smelt abominably of garlic. Might I trouble you to lay me upon the bed? The floor of these Portuguese tabernas is hardly a fitting couch for anyone who has prejudices in favour of cleanliness.'

I could not but admire the coolness of the man, and the way in which he preserved the same insolent air of condescension in spite of this sudden turning of the tables. I dispatched

Papilette to summon a guard, whilst I stood over our prisoner with my drawn sword, never taking my eyes off him for an instant, for I must confess that I had conceived a great respect for his audacity and resource.

'I trust,' said he, 'that your men will treat me in a becoming manner.'

'You will get your deserts — you may depend upon that.'

'I ask nothing more. You may not be aware of my exalted birth, but I am so placed that I cannot name my father without treason, nor my mother without a scandal. I cannot *claim* Royal honours, but these things are so much more graceful when they are conceded without a claim. The thongs are cutting my skin. Might I beg you to loosen them?'

'You do not give me credit for much intelligence,' I remarked, repeating his own words.

'*Touché*,' he cried, like a pinked fencer. 'But here come your men, so it matters little whether you loosen them or not.'

I ordered the gown to be stripped from him and placed him under a strong guard. Then, as morning was already breaking, I had to consider what my next step was to be. The poor Bart and his Englishmen had fallen victims to the deep scheme which might, had we adopted all the crafty suggestions of our adviser, have ended in the capture of the whole instead of the half of our force. I must extricate them if it were still possible. Then there was the old lady, the Countess of La Ronda, to be thought of. As to the Abbey, since its garrison was on the alert it was hopeless to think of capturing that. All turned now upon the value which they placed upon their leader. The game depended upon my playing that one card. I will tell you how boldly and how skilfully I played it.

It was hardly light before my bugler blew the assembly, and out we trotted on to the plain. My prisoner was placed on horseback in the very centre of the troops. It chanced that there was a large tree just out of musket-shot from the main gate of the Abbey, and under this we halted. Had they opened the great doors in order to attack us, I should have charged home upon them; but, as I had expected, they stood upon the defensive, lining the long wall and pouring down a torrent of hootings and taunts and derisive laughter upon us. A few fired their muskets, but finding that we were out of reach they soon ceased to waste their powder. It was the strangest sight to see that mixture of uniforms, French, English, and Portuguese, cavalry, infantry, and artillery, all wagging their heads and shaking their fists at us.

My word, their hubbub soon died away when we opened our ranks, and showed whom we had got in the midst of us! There was silence for a few seconds, and then such a howl of rage and grief! I could see some of them dancing like mad-men upon the wall. He must have been a singular person, this prisoner of ours, to have gained the affection of such a gang.

I had brought a rope from the inn, and we slung it over the lower bough of the tree.

'You will permit me, monsieur, to undo your collar,' said Papilette, with mock politeness.

'If your hands are perfectly clean,' answered our prisoner, and set the whole half-squadron laughing.

There was another yell from the wall, followed by a profound hush as the noose was tightened round Marshal Millefleurs' neck. Then came a shriek from a bugle, the Abbey gates flew open, and three men rushed out waving white cloths in their hands. Ah, how my heart bounded with joy at the sight of them. And yet I would not advance an inch to meet them, so that all the eagerness might seem to be upon their side. I allowed my trumpeter, however, to wave a handkerchief in reply, upon which the three envoys came running towards us. The Marshal, still pinioned, and with the rope round his neck, sat his horse with a half smile, as one who is slightly bored and yet strives out of courtesy not to show it. If I were in such a situation I could not wish to carry myself better, and surely I can say no more than that.

They were a singular trio, these ambassadors. The one was a Portuguese caçadore in his dark uniform, the second a French chasseur in the lightest green, and the third a big English artilleryman in blue and gold. They saluted, all three, and the Frenchman did the talking.

'We have thirty-seven English dragoons in our hands,' said he. 'We give you our most solemn oath that they shall all hang from the Abbey wall within five minutes of the death of our Marshal.'

'Thirty-seven!' I cried. 'You have fifty-one.'

'Fourteen were cut down before they could be secured.'

'And the officer?'

'He would not surrender his sword save with his life. It was not our fault. We would have saved him if we could.'

Alas for my poor Bart! I had met him but twice, and yet he was a man very much after my heart. I have always had a regard for the English for the sake of that one friend. A braver man and a worse swordsman I have never met.

I did not, as you may think, take these rascals' word for anything. Papilette was dispatched with one of them, and returned to say that it was too true. I had now to think of the living.

'You will release the thirty-seven dragoons if I free your leader?'

'We will give you ten of them.'

'Up with him!' I cried.

'Twenty,' shouted the chasseur.

'No more words,' said I. 'Pull on the rope!'

'All of them,' cried the envoy, as the cord tightened round the Marshal's neck.

'With horses and arms?'

They could see that I was not a man to jest with.

'All complete,' said the chasseur, sulkily.

'And the Countess of La Ronda as well?' said I.

But here I met with firmer opposition. No threats of mine could induce them to give up the Countess. We tightened the cord. We moved the horse. We did all but leave the Marshal suspended. If once I broke his neck the dragoons were dead men. It was as precious to me as to them.

'Allow me to remark,' said the Marshal, blandly, 'that you are exposing me to a risk of a quinsy. Do you not think, since there is a difference of opinion upon this point, that it would be an excellent idea to consult the lady herself? We would neither of us, I am sure, wish to override her own inclinations.'

Nothing could be more satisfactory. You can imagine how quickly I grasped at so simple a solution. In ten minutes she was before us, a most stately dame, with her grey curls peeping out from under her mantilla. Her face was as yellow as though it reflected the countless doubloons of her treasury.

'This gentleman,' said the Marshal, 'is exceedingly anxious to convey you to a place where you will never see us more. It is for you to decide whether you would wish to go with him, or whether you prefer to remain with me.'

She was at his horse's side in an instant. 'My own Alexis,' she cried, 'nothing can ever part us.'

He looked at me with a sneer upon his handsome face.

'By the way, you made a small slip of the tongue, my dear Colonel,' said he. 'Except by courtesy, no such person exists as the Dowager Countess of La Ronda. The lady whom I have the honour to present to you is my very dear wife, Mrs Alexis Morgan — or shall I say Madame la Marèchale Millefleurs?'

It was at this moment that I came to the

conclusion that I was dealing with the cleverest, and also the most unscrupulous, man whom I had ever met. As I looked upon this unfortunate old woman my soul was filled with wonder and disgust. As for her, her eyes were raised to his face with such a look as a young recruit might give to the Emperor.

'So be it,' said I at last; 'give me the dragoons and let me go.'

They were brought out with their horses and weapons, and the rope was taken from the Marshal's neck.

'Good-bye, my dear Colonel,' said he. 'I am afraid that you will have rather a lame account to give of your mission, when you find your way back to Massena, though, from all I hear, he will probably be too busy to think of you. I am free to confess that you have extricated yourself from your difficulties with greater ability than I had given you credit for. I presume that there is nothing which I can do for you before you go?'

'There is one thing.'

'And that is?'

'To give fitting burial to this young officer and his men.'

'I pledge my word to it.'

'And there is one other.'

'Name it.'

'To give me five minutes in the open with a

sword in your hand and a horse between your legs.'

'Tut, tut!' said he. 'I should either have to cut short your promising career, or else to bid adieu to my own bonny bride. It is unreasonable to ask such a request of a man in the first joys of matrimony.'

I gathered my horsemen together and wheeled them into column.

'Au revoir,' I cried, shaking my sword at him. 'The next time you may not escape so easily.'

'Au revoir,' he answered. 'When you are weary of the Emperor, you will always find a commission waiting for you in the service of the Marshal Millefleurs.'

6

How the Brigadier Played for a Kingdom

It has sometimes struck me that some of you, when you have heard me tell these little adventures of mine, may have gone away with the impression that I was conceited. There could not be a greater mistake than this, for I have always observed that really fine soldiers are free from this failing. It is true that I have had to depict myself sometimes as brave, sometimes as full of resource, always as interesting; but, then, it really was so, and I had to take the facts as I found them. It would be an unworthy affectation if I were to pretend that my career has been anything but a fine one. The incident which I will tell you tonight, however, is one which you will understand that only a modest man would describe. After all, when one has attained such a position as mine, one can afford to speak of what an ordinary man might be tempted to conceal.

You must know, then, that after the Russian campaign the remains of our poor army were quartered along the western bank of the Elbe, where they might thaw their frozen blood and try, with the help of the good German beer, to put a little between their skin and their bones. There were some things which we could not hope to regain, for I daresay that three large commissariat fourgons would not have sufficed to carry the fingers and the toes which the army had shed during that retreat. Still, lean and crippled as we were, we had much to be thankful for when we thought of our poor comrades whom we had left behind, and of the snowfields — the horrible, horrible snowfields. To this day, my friends, I do not care to see red and white together. Even my red cap thrown down upon my white counterpane has given me dreams in which I have seen those monstrous plains, the reeling, tortured army, and the crimson smears which glared upon the snow behind them. You will coax no story out of me about that business, for the thought of it is enough to turn my wine to vinegar and my tobacco to straw.

Of the half-million who crossed the Elbe in the autumn of the year '12 about forty thousand infantry were left in the spring of '13. But they were terrible men, these forty thousand: men of iron, eaters of horses, and sleepers in the snow; filled, too, with rage and bitterness against the Russians. They would hold the Elbe until the great army of conscripts, which the Emperor was raising in France, should be ready to help them to cross it once more.

But the cavalry was in a deplorable condition. My own hussars were at Borna, and when I paraded them first, I burst into tears at the sight of them. My fine men and my beautiful horses — it broke my heart to see the state to which they were reduced. 'But, courage,' I thought, 'they have lost much, but their Colonel is still left to them.' I set to work, therefore, to repair their disasters, and had already constructed two good squadrons, when an order came that all colonels of cavalry should repair instantly to the depôts of the regiments in France to organize the recruits and the remounts for the coming campaign.

You will think, doubtless, that I was over-joyed at this chance of visiting home once more. I will not deny that it was a pleasure to me to know that I should see my mother again, and there were a few girls who would be very glad at the news; but there were others in the army who had a stronger claim. I would have given my place to any who had wives and children whom they might not see again. However, there is no arguing when the blue paper with the little red seal arrives, so within an hour I was off upon my great ride from the Elbe to the Vosges. At last I was to have a period of quiet. War lay behind my mare's tail and peace in front of her nostrils. So I thought, as the sound of the bugles died in the distance, and the long, white road curled away in front of me through plain and forest and mountain, with France somewhere beyond the blue haze which lay upon the horizon.

It is interesting, but it is also fatiguing, to ride in the rear of an army. In the harvest time our soldiers could do without supplies, for they had been trained to pluck the grain in the fields as they passed, and to grind it for themselves in their bivouacs. It was at that time of year, therefore, that those swift marches were performed which were the wonder and the despair of Europe. But now the starving men had to be made robust once more, and I was forced to draw into the ditch continually as the Coburg sheep and the Bavarian bullocks came streaming past with waggon loads of Berlin beer and good French cognac. Sometimes, too, I would hear the dry rattle of the drums and the shrill whistle of the fifes, and long columns of our good little infantry men would swing past me with the white dust lying thick upon their blue tunics. These were old soldiers drawn from the garrisons of our German fortresses, for it was not until May that the new conscripts began to arrive from France.

Well, I was rather tired of this eternal stopping and dodging, so that I was not sorry when I came to Altenburg to find that the road divided, and that I could take the southern and quieter branch. There were few wayfarers between there and Greiz, and the road wound through groves of oaks and beeches, which shot their branches across the path. You will think it strange that a Colonel of hussars should again and again pull up his horse in order to admire the beauty of the feathery branches and the little, green, new-budded leaves, but if you had spent six months among the fir trees of Russia you would be able to understand me.

There was something, however, which pleased me very much less than the beauty of the forests, and that was the words and looks of the folk who lived in the woodland villages. We had always been excellent friends with the Germans, and during the last six years they had never seemed to bear us any malice for having made a little free with their country. We had shown kindnesses to the men and received them from the women, so that good, comfortable Germany was a second home to all of us. But now there was something which I could not understand in the behaviour of the people. The travellers made no answer to my salute; the foresters turned their heads away to avoid seeing me; and in the villages the folk would gather into knots in the roadway and would scowl at me as I passed. Even women would do this, and it was something new for me in those days to see anything but a smile in a woman's eyes when they were turned upon me.

It was in the hamlet of Schmolin, just ten miles out of Altenburg, that the thing became most marked. I had stopped at the little inn there just to damp my moustache and to wash the dust out of poor Violette's throat. It was my way to give some little compliment, or possibly a kiss, to the maid who served me; but this one would have neither the one nor the other, but darted a glance at me like a bayonet-thrust. Then when I raised my glass to the folk who drank their beer by the door they turned their backs on me, save only one fellow, who cried, 'Here's a toast for you, boys! Here's to the letter T!' At that they all emptied their beer mugs and laughed; but it was not a laugh that had good-fellowship in it.

I was turning this over in my head and wondering what their boorish conduct could mean, when I saw, as I rode from the village, a great T new carved upon a tree. I had already seen more than one in my morning's ride, but I had given no thought to them until the words of the beer-drinker gave them an importance. It chanced that a respectable-looking person was riding past me at the moment, so I turned to him for information.

'Can you tell me, sir,' said I, 'what this letter T is?'

He looked at it and then at me in the most singular fashion. 'Young man,' said he, 'it is not the letter N.' Then before I could ask further he clapped his spurs into his horses ribs and rode, stomach to earth, upon his way.

At first his words had no particular significance in my mind, but as I trotted onwards Violette chanced to half turn her dainty head, and my eyes were caught by the gleam of the brazen N's at the end of the bridle-chain. It was the Emperor's mark. And those T's meant something which was opposite to it. Things had been happening in Germany, then, during our absence, and the giant sleeper had begun to stir. I thought of the mutinous faces that I had seen, and I felt that if I could only have looked into the hearts of these people I might have had some strange news to bring into France with me. It made me the more eager to get my remounts, and to see ten strong squadrons behind my kettle-drums once more.

While these thoughts were passing through my head I had been alternately walking and trotting, as a man should who has a long journey before, and a willing horse beneath, him. The woods were very open at this point, and beside the road there lay a great heap of fagots. As I passed there came a sharp sound from among them, and, glancing round, I saw a face looking out at me — a hot, red face, like that of a man who is beside himself with excitement and anxiety. A second glance told me that it was the very person with whom I had talked an hour before in the village.

'Come nearer!' he hissed. 'Nearer still! Now dismount and pretend to be mending the stirrup leather. Spies may be watching us, and it means death to me if I am seen helping you.'

'Death!' I whispered. 'From whom?'

'From the Tugendbund. From Lutzow's night-riders. You Frenchmen are living on a powder magazine, and the match has been struck that will fire it.'

'But this is all strange to me,' said I, still fumbling at the leathers of my horse. 'What is this Tugendbund?'

'It is the secret society which has planned

the great rising which is to drive you out of Germany, just as you have been driven out of Russia.'

'And these T's stand for it?'

'They are the signal. I should have told you all this in the village, but I dared not be seen speaking with you. I galloped through the woods to cut you off, and concealed both my horse and myself.'

'I am very much indebted to you,' said I, 'and the more so as you are the only German that I have met today from whom I have had common civility.'

'All that I possess I have gained through contracting for the French armies,' said he. 'Your Emperor has been a good friend to me. But I beg that you will ride on now, for we have talked long enough. Beware only of Lutzow's night-riders!'

'Banditti?' I asked.

'All that is best in Germany,' said he. 'But for God's sake ride forwards, for I have risked my life and exposed my good name in order to carry you this warning.'

Well, if I had been heavy with thought before, you can think how I felt after my strange talk with the man among the fagots. What came home to me even more than his words was his shivering, broken voice, his twitching face, and his eyes glancing swiftly to right and left, and opening in horror whenever a branch cracked upon a tree. It was clear that he was in the last extremity of terror, and it is possible that he had cause, for shortly after I had left him I heard a distant gunshot and a shouting from somewhere behind me. It may have been some sportsman halloaing to his dogs, but I never again heard of or saw the man who had given me my warning.

I kept a good look-out after this, riding swiftly where the country was open, and slowly where there might be an ambuscade. It was serious for me, since 500 good miles of German soil lay in front of me; but somehow I did not take it very much to heart, for the Germans had always seemed to me to be a kindly, gentle people, whose hands closed more readily round a pipe-stem than a sword-hilt — not out of want of valour, you understand, but because they are genial, open souls, who would rather be on good terms with all men. I did not know then that beneath that homely surface there lurks a devilry as fierce as, and far more persistent than, that of the Castilian or the Italian.

And it was not long before I had shown to me that there was something more serious abroad than rough words and hard looks. I had come to a spot where the road runs upwards through a wild tract of heath-land and vanishes into an oak wood. I may have been halfway up the hill when, looking forward, I saw something gleaming under the shadow of the tree-trunks, and a man came out with a coat which was so slashed and spangled with gold that he blazed like a fire in the sunlight. He appeared to be very drunk, for he reeled and staggered as he came towards me. One of his hands was held up to his ear and clutched a great red handkerchief, which was fixed to his neck.

I had reined up the mare and was looking at him with some disgust, for it seemed strange to me that one who wore so gorgeous a uniform should show himself in such a state in broad daylight. For his part, he looked hard in my direction and came slowly onwards, stopping from time to time and swaying about as he gazed at me. Suddenly, as I again advanced, he screamed out his thanks to Christ, and, lurching forwards, he fell with a crash upon the dusty road. His hands flew forward with the fall, and I saw that what I had taken for a red cloth was a monstrous wound, which had left a great gap in his neck, from which a dark blood-clot hung, like an epaulette upon his shoulder.

'My God!' I cried, as I sprang to his aid. 'And I thought that you were drunk!'

'Not drunk, but dying,' said he. 'But thank Heaven that I have seen a French officer while I have still strength to speak.'

I laid him among the heather and poured some brandy down his throat. All round us was the vast countryside, green and peaceful, with nothing living in sight save only the mutilated man beside me.

'Who has done this?' I asked, 'and what are you? You are French, and yet the uniform is strange to me.'

'It is that of the Emperor's new guard of honour. I am the Marquis of Château St Arnaud, and I am the ninth of my blood who has died in the service of France. I have been pursued and wounded by the night-riders of Lutzow, but I hid among the brushwood yonder, and waited in the hope that a Frenchman might pass. I could not be sure at first if you were friend or foe, but I felt that death was very near, and that I must take the chance.'

'Keep your heart up, comrade,' said I; 'I have seen a man with a worse wound who has lived to boast of it.'

'No, no,' he whispered; 'I am going fast.' He laid his hand upon mine as he spoke, and I saw that his fingernails were already blue. 'But I have papers here in my tunic which you must carry at once to the Prince of

Saxe-Felstein, at his Castle of Hof. He is still true to us, but the Princess is our deadly enemy. She is striving to make him declare against us. If he does so, it will determine all those who are wavering, for the King of Prussia is his uncle and the King of Bavaria his cousin. These papers will hold him to us if they can only reach him before he takes the last step. Place them in his hands tonight, and, perhaps, you will have saved all Germany for the Emperor. Had my horse not been shot, I might, wounded as I am — ' He choked, and the cold hand tightened into a grip, which left mine as bloodless as itself. Then, with a groan, his head jerked back, and it was all over with him.

Here was a fine start for my journey home. I was left with a commission of which I knew little, which would lead me to delay the pressing needs of my hussars, and which at the same time was of such importance that it was impossible for me to avoid it. I opened the Marquis's tunic, the brilliance of which had been devised by the Emperor in order to attract those young aristocrats from whom he hoped to raise these new regiments of his Guard. It was a small packet of papers which I drew out, tied up with silk, and addressed to the Prince of Saxe-Felstein. In the corner, in a sprawling, untidy hand, which I knew to be the Emperor's own, was written: 'Pressing and most important.' It was an order to me, those four words — an order as clear as if it had come straight from the firm lips with the cold grey eyes looking into mine. My troopers might wait for their horses, the dead Marquis might lie where I had laid him amongst the heather, but if the mare and her rider had a breath left in them the papers should reach the Prince that night.

I should not have feared to ride by the road through the wood, for I have learned in Spain that the safest time to pass through a guerilla country is after an outrage, and that the moment of danger is when all is peaceful. When I came to look upon my map, however, I saw that Hof lay further to the south of me, and that I might reach it more directly by keeping to the moors. Off I set, therefore, and had not gone fifty yards before two carbine shots rang out of the brushwood and a bullet hummed past me like a bee. It was clear that the night-riders were bolder in their ways than the brigands of Spain, and that my mission would have ended where it had begun if I had kept to the road.

It was a mad ride, that — a ride with a loose rein, girth-deep in heather and in gorse, plunging through bushes, flying down hill-sides, with my neck at the mercy of my dear little Violette. But she — she never slipped, she never faltered, as swift and as surefooted as if she knew that her rider carried the fate of all Germany beneath the buttons of his pelisse. And I — I had long borne the name of being the best horseman in the six brigades of light cavalry, but I never rode as I rode then. My friend the Bart had told me of how they hunt the fox in England, but the swiftest fox would have been captured by me that day. The wild pigeons which flew overhead did not take a straighter course than Violette and I below. As an officer, I have always been ready to sacrifice myself for my men, though the Emperor would not have thanked me for it, for he had many men, but only one — well, cavalry leaders of the first class are rare.

But here I had an object which was indeed worth a sacrifice, and I thought no more of my life than of the clods of earth that flew from my darling's heels.

We struck the road once more as the light was failing, and galloped into the little village of Lobenstein. But we had hardly got upon the cobblestones when off came one of the mare's shoes, and I had to lead her to the village smithy. His fire was low, and his day's work done, so that it would be an hour at the least before I could hope to push on to Hof.

Cursing at the delay, I strode into the village inn and ordered a cold chicken and some wine to be served for my dinner. It was but a few miles to Hof, and I had every hope that I might deliver my papers to the Prince on that very night, and be on my way for France next morning with despatches for the Emperor in my bosom. I will tell you now what befell me in the inn of Lobenstein.

The chicken had been served and the wine drawn, and I had turned upon both as a man may who has ridden such a ride, when I was aware of a murmur and a scuffling in the hall outside my door. At first I thought that it was some brawl between peasants in their cups, and I left them to settle their own affairs. But of a sudden there broke from among the low, sullen growl of the voices such a sound as would send Etienne Gerard leaping from his death-bed. It was the whimpering cry of a woman in pain. Down clattered my knife and my fork, and in an instant I was in the thick of the crowd which had gathered outside my door.

The heavy-cheeked landlord was there and his flaxen-haired wife, the two men from the stables, a chambermaid, and two or three villagers. All of them, women and men, were flushed and angry, while there in the centre of them, with pale cheeks and terror in her eyes, stood the loveliest woman that ever a soldier would wish to look upon. With her queenly head thrown back, and a touch of defiance mingled with her fear, she looked as she gazed round her like a creature of a different race from the vile, coarse-featured crew who surrounded her. I had not taken two steps from my door before she sprang to meet me, her hand resting upon my arm and her blue eyes sparkling with joy and triumph.

'A French soldier and gentleman!' she cried. 'Now at last I am safe.'

'Yes, madam, you are safe,' said I, and I could not resist taking her hand in mine in order that I might reassure her. 'You have only to command me,' I added, kissing the hand as a sign that I meant what I was saying.

'I am Polish,' she cried; 'the Countess Palotta is my name. They abuse me because I love the French. I do not know what they might have done to me had Heaven not sent you to my help.'

I kissed her hand again lest she should doubt my intentions. Then I turned upon the crew with such an expression as I know how to assume. In an instant the hall was empty.

'Countess,' said I, 'you are now under my protection. You are faint, and a glass of wine is necessary to restore you.' I offered her my arm and escorted her into my room, where she sat by my side at the table and took the refreshment which I offered her.

How she blossomed out in my presence, this woman, like a flower before the sun! She lit up the room with her beauty. She must have read my admiration in my eyes, and it seemed to me that I also could see something of the sort in her own. Ah! my friends, I was no ordinary-looking man when I was in my thirtieth year. In the whole light cavalry it would have been hard to find a finer pair of whiskers. Murat's may have been a shade longer, but the best judges are agreed that Murat's were a shade too long. And then I had a manner. Some women are to be approached in one way and some in another, just as a siege is an affair of fascines and gabions in hard weather and of trenches in soft. But the man who can mix daring with timidity, who can be outrageous with an air of humility, and presumptuous with a tone of deference, that is the man whom mothers have to fear. For myself, I felt that I was the guardian of this lonely lady, and knowing what a dangerous man I had to deal with, I kept strict watch upon myself. Still, even a guardian has his privileges, and I did not neglect them.

But her talk was as charming as her face. In

219

a few words she explained that she was travelling to Poland, and that her brother who had been her escort had fallen ill upon the way. She had more than once met with ill-treatment from the country folk because she could not conceal her good-will towards the French. Then turning from her own affairs she questioned me about the army, and so came round to myself and my own exploits. They were familiar to her, she said, for she knew several of Poniatowski's officers, and they had spoken of my doings. Yet she would be glad to hear them from my own lips. Never have I had so delightful a conversation. Most women make the mistake of talking rather too much about their own affairs, but this one listened to my tales just as you are listening now, ever asking for more and more and more. The hours slipped rapidly by, and it was with horror that I heard the village clock strike eleven, and so learned that for four hours I had forgotten the Emperor's business.

'Pardon me, my dear lady,' I cried, springing to my feet, 'but I must go on instantly to Hof.'

She rose also, and looked at me with a pale, reproachful face. 'And me?' she said. 'What is to become of me?'

'It is the Emperor's affair. I have already

stayed far too long. My duty calls me, and I must go.'

'You must go? And I must be abandoned alone to these savages? Oh, why did I ever meet you? Why did you ever teach me to rely upon your strength?' Her eyes glazed over, and in an instant she was sobbing upon my bosom.

Here was a trying moment for a guardian! Here was a time when he had to keep a watch upon a forward young officer. But I was equal to it. I smoothed her rich brown hair and whispered such consolations as I could think of in her ear, with one arm round her, it is true, but that was to hold her lest she should faint. She turned her tear-stained face to mine. 'Water,' she whispered. 'For God's sake, water!'

I saw that in another moment she would be senseless. I laid the drooping head upon the sofa, and then rushed furiously from the room, hunting from chamber to chamber for a carafe. It was some minutes before I could get one and hurry back with it. You can imagine my feelings to find the room empty and the lady gone.

Not only was she gone, but her cap and silver-mounted riding switch which had lain upon the table were gone also. I rushed out and roared for the landlord. He knew nothing of the matter, had never seen the woman before, and did not care if he never saw her again. Had the peasants at the door seen anyone ride away? No, they had seen nobody. I searched here and searched there, until at last I chanced to find myself in front of a mirror, where I stood with my eyes staring and my jaw as far dropped as the chin-strap of my shako would allow.

Four buttons of my pelisse were open, and it did not need me to put my hand up to know that my precious papers were gone. Oh! the depth of cunning that lurks in a woman's heart. She had robbed me, this creature, robbed me as she clung to my breast. Even while I smoothed her hair, and whispered kind words into her ear, her hands had been at work beneath my dolman. And here I was, at the very last step of my journey, without the power of carrying out this mission which had already deprived one good man of his life, and was likely to rob another one of his credit. What would the Emperor say when he heard that I had lost his despatches? Would the army believe it of Etienne Gerard? And when they heard that a woman's hand had coaxed them from me, what laughter there would be at mess-table and at camp-fire! I could have rolled upon the ground in my despair.

But one thing was certain — all this affair of the fracas in the hall and the persecution of the so-called Countess was a piece of acting from the beginning. This villainous innkeeper must be in the plot. From him I might learn who she was and where my papers had gone. I snatched my sabre from the table and rushed out in search of him. But the scoundrel had guessed what I would do, and had made his preparations for me. It was in the corner of the yard that I found him, a blunderbuss in his hands and a mastiff held upon a leash by his son. The two stable-hands, with pitchforks, stood upon either side, and the wife held a great lantern behind him, so as to guide his aim.

'Ride away, sir, ride away!' he cried, with a crackling voice. 'Your horse is at the door, and no one will meddle with you if you go your way; but if you come against us, you are alone against three brave men.'

I had only the dog to fear, for the two forks and the blunderbuss were shaking about like branches in a wind. Still, I considered that, though I might force an answer with my sword-point at the throat of this fat rascal, still I should have no means of knowing whether that answer was the truth. It would be a struggle, then, with much to lose and nothing certain to gain. I looked them up and down, therefore, in a way that set their foolish weapons shaking worse than ever, and then, throwing myself upon my mare, I galloped away with the shrill laughter of the landlady jarring upon my ears.

I had already formed my resolution. Although I had lost my papers, I could make a very good guess as to what their contents would be, and this I would say from my own lips to the Prince of Saxe-Felstein, as though the Emperor had commissioned me to convey it in that way. It was a bold stroke and a dangerous one, but if I went too far I could afterwards be disavowed. It was that or nothing, and when all Germany hung on the balance the game should not be lost if the nerve of one man could save it.

It was midnight when I rode into Hof, but every window was blazing, which was enough it itself, in that sleepy country, to tell the ferment of excitement in which the people were. There was hooting and jeering as I rode through the crowded streets, and once a stone sang past my head, but I kept upon my way, neither slowing nor quickening my pace, until I came to the palace. It was lit from base to battlement, and the dark shadows, coming and going against the yellow glare, spoke of the turmoil within. For my part, I handed my mare to a groom at the gate, and striding in I demanded, in such a voice as an ambassador should have, to see the Prince instantly, upon business which would brook no delay.

The hall was dark, but I was conscious as I entered of a buzz of innumerable voices, which hushed into silence as I loudly proclaimed my mission. Some great meeting was being held then — a meeting which, as my instincts told me, was to decide this very question of war and peace. It was possible that I might still be in time to turn the scale for the Emperor and for France. As to the major-domo, he looked blackly at me, and showing me into a small ante-chamber he left me. A minute later he returned to say that the Prince could not be disturbed at present, but that the Princess would take my message.

The Princess! What use was there in giving it to her? Had I not been warned that she was German in heart and soul, and that it was she who was turning her husband and her State against us?

'It is the Prince that I must see,' said I.

'Nay, it is the Princess,' said a voice at the door, and a woman swept into the chamber. 'Von Rosen, you had best stay with us. Now, sir, what is it that you have to say to either Prince or Princess of Saxe-Felstein?'

At the first sound of the voice I had sprung to my feet. At the first glance I had thrilled with anger. Not twice in a lifetime does one meet that noble figure, that queenly head, and those eyes as blue as the Garonne, and as chilling as her winter waters.

'Time presses, sir!' she cried, with an impatient tap of her foot. 'What have you to say to me?'

'What have I to say to you?' I cried. 'What can I say, save that you have taught me never to trust a woman more? You have ruined and dishonoured me for ever.'

She looked with arched brows at her attendant.

'Is this the raving of fever, or does it come from some less innocent cause?' said she. 'Perhaps a little blood-letting — '

'Ah, you can act!' I cried. 'You have shown me that already.'

'Do you mean that we have met before?'

'I mean that you have robbed me within the last two hours.'

'This is past all bearing,' she cried, with an admirable affectation of anger. 'You claim, as I understand, to be an ambassador, but there are limits to the privileges which such an office brings with it.'

'You brazen it admirably,' said I. 'Your Highness will not make a fool of me twice in one night.' I sprang forward and, stooping down, caught up the hem of her dress. 'You would have done well to change it after you had ridden so far and so fast,' said I.

It was like the dawn upon a snow-peak to see her ivory cheeks flush suddenly to crimson.

'Insolent!' she cried. 'Call the foresters and have him thrust from the palace'

'I will see the Prince first.'

'You will never see the Prince. Ah! Hold him, Von Rosen, hold him.'

She had forgotten the man with whom she had to deal — was it likely that I would wait until they could bring their rascals? She had shown me her cards too soon. Her game was to stand between me and her husband. Mine was to speak face to face with him at any cost. One spring took me out of the chamber. In another I had crossed the hall. An instant later I had burst into the great room from which the murmur of the meeting had come. At the far end I saw a figure upon a high chair under a daïs. Beneath him was a line of high dignitaries, and then on every side I saw vaguely the heads of a vast assembly. Into the centre of the room I strode, my sabre clanking, my shako under my arm.

'I am the messenger of the Emperor,' I shouted. 'I bear his message to His Highness the Prince of Saxe-Felstein.'

The man beneath the daïs raised his head,

and I saw that his face was thin and wan, and that his back was bowed as though some huge burden was balanced between his shoulders.

'Your name, sir?' he asked.

'Colonel Etienne Gerard, of the Third Hussars.'

Every face in the gathering was turned upon me, and I heard the rustle of the innumerable necks and saw countless eyes without meeting one friendly one amongst them. The woman had swept past me, and was whispering, with many shakes of her head and dartings of her hands, into the Prince's ear. For my own part I threw out my chest and curled my moustache, glancing round in my own debonair fashion at the assembly. They were men, all of them, professors from the college, a sprinkling of their students, soldiers, gentlemen, artisans, all very silent and serious. In one corner there sat a group of men in black, with riding-coats drawn over their shoulders. They leaned their heads to each other, whispering under their breath, and with every movement I caught the clank of their sabres or the clink of their spurs.

'The Emperor's private letter to me informs me that it is the Marquis Château St Arnaud who is bearing his despatches,' said the Prince.

228

'The Marquis has been foully murdered,' I answered, and a buzz rose up from the people as I spoke. Many heads were turned, I noticed, towards the dark men in the cloaks.

'Where are your papers?' asked the Prince.

'I have none.'

A fierce clamour rose instantly around me. 'He is a spy! He plays a part!' they cried. 'Hang him!' roared a deep voice from the corner, and a dozen others took up the shout. For my part, I drew out my handkerchief and nicked the dust from the fur of my pelisse. The Prince held out his thin hands, and the tumult died away.

'Where, then, are your credentials, and what is your message?'

'My uniform is my credential, and my message is for your private ear.'

He passed his hand over his forehead with the gesture of a weak man who is at his wits' end what to do. The Princess stood beside him with her hand upon his throne, and again whispered in his ear.

'We are here in council together, some of my trusty subjects and myself,' said he. 'I have no secrets from them, and whatever message the Emperor may send to me at such a time concerns their interests no less than mine.'

There was a hum of applause at this, and

every eye was turned once more upon me. My faith, it was an awkward position in which I found myself, for it is one thing to address eight hundred hussars, and another to speak to such an audience on such a subject. But I fixed my eyes upon the Prince, and tried to say just what I should have said if we had been alone, shouting it out, too, as though I had my regiment on parade.

'You have often expressed friendship for the Emperor,' I cried. 'It is now at last that this friendship is about to be tried. If you will stand firm, he will reward you as only he can reward. It is an easy thing for him to turn a Prince into a King and a province into a power. His eyes are fixed upon you, and though you can do little to harm him, you can ruin yourself. At this moment he is crossing the Rhine with two hundred thousand men. Every fortress in the country is in his hands. He will be upon you in a week, and if you have played him false, God help both you and your people. You think that he is weakened because a few of us got the chilblains last winter. Look there!' I cried, pointing to a great star which blazed through the window above the Prince's head. 'That is the Emperor's star. When it wanes, he will wane — but not before.'

You would have been proud of me, my

friends, if you could have seen and heard me, for I clashed my sabre as I spoke, and swung my dolman as though my regiment was picketed outside in the courtyard. They listened to me in silence, but the back of the Prince bowed more and more as though the burden which weighed upon it was greater than his strength. He looked round with haggard eyes.

'We have heard a Frenchman speak for France,' said he. 'Let us have a German speak for Germany.'

The folk glanced at each other, and whispered to their neighbours. My speech, as I think, had its effect, and no man wished to be the first to commit himself in the eyes of the Emperor. The Princess looked round her with blazing eyes, and her clear voice broke the silence.

'Is a woman to give this Frenchman his answer?' she cried. 'Is it possible, then, that among the night-riders of Lutzow there is none who can use his tongue as well as his sabre?'

Over went a table with a crash, and a young man had bounded upon one of the chairs. He had the face of one inspired — pale, eager, with wild hawk eyes, and tangled hair. His sword hung straight from his side, and his riding-boots were brown with mire.

'It is Korner!' the people cried. 'It is young Korner, the poet! Ah, he will sing, he will sing.'

And he sang! It was soft, at first, and dreamy, telling of old Germany, the mother of nations, of the rich, warm plains, and the grey cities, and the fame of dead heroes. But then verse after verse rang like a trumpet-call. It was of the Germany of now, the Germany which had been taken unawares and overthrown, but which was up again, and snapping the bonds upon her giant limbs. What was life that one should covet it? What was glorious death that one should shun it? The mother, the great mother, was calling. Her sigh was in the night wind. She was crying to her own children for help. Would they come? Would they come? Would they come?

Ah, that terrible song, the spirit face and the ringing voice! Where were I, and France, and the Emperor? They did not shout, these people — they howled. They were up on the chairs and the tables. They were raving, sobbing, the tears running down their faces. Korner had sprung from the chair, and his comrades were round him with their sabres in the air. A flush had come into the pale face of the Prince, and he rose from his throne.

'Colonel Gerard,' said he, 'you have heard

the answer which you are to carry to your Emperor. The die is cast, my children. Your Prince and you must stand or fall together.'

He bowed to show that all was over, and the people with a shout made for the door to carry the tidings into the town. For my own part, I had done all that a brave man might, and so I was not sorry to be carried out amid the stream. Why should I linger in the palace? I had had my answer and must carry it, such as it was. I wished neither to see Hof nor its people again until I entered it at the head of a vanguard. I turned from the throng, then, and walked silently and sadly in the direction in which they had led the mare.

It was dark down there by the stables, and I was peering round for the hostler, when suddenly my two arms were seized from behind. There were hands at my wrists and at my throat, and I felt the cold muzzle of a pistol under my ear.

'Keep your lips closed, you French dog,' whispered a fierce voice. 'We have him, captain.'

'Have you the bridle?'

'Here it is.'

'Sling it over his head.'

I felt the cold coil of leather tighten round my neck. An hostler with a stable lantern had come out and was gazing upon the scene. In its dim light I saw stern faces breaking everywhere through the gloom, with the black caps and dark cloaks of the night-riders.

'What would you do with him, captain?' cried a voice.

'Hang him at the palace gate.'

'An ambassador?'

'An ambassador without papers.'

'But the Prince?'

'Tut, man, do you not see that the Prince will then be committed to our side? He will be beyond all hope of forgiveness. At present he may swing round tomorrow as he has done before. He may eat his words, but a dead hussar is more than he can explain.'

'No, no, Von Strelitz, we cannot do it,' said another voice.

'Can we not? I shall show you that!' and there came a jerk on the bridle which nearly pulled me to the ground. At the same instant a sword flashed and the leather was cut through within two inches of my neck.

'By Heaven, Korner, this is rank mutiny,' cried the captain. 'You may hang yourself before you are through with it.'

'I have drawn my sword as a soldier and not as a brigand,' said the young poet. 'Blood may dim its blade, but never dishonour. Comrades, will you stand by and see this gentleman mishandled?'

A dozen sabres flew from their sheaths, and it was evident that my friends and my foes were about equally balanced. But the angry voices and the gleam of steel had brought the folk running from all parts.

'The Princess!' they cried. 'The Princess is coming!'

And even as they spoke I saw her in front of us, her sweet face framed in the darkness. I had cause to hate her, for she had cheated and befooled me, and yet it thrilled me then and thrills me now to think that my arms have embraced her, and that I have felt the scent of her hair in my nostrils. I know not whether she lies under her German earth, or whether she still lingers, a grey-haired woman in her Castle of Hof, but she lives ever, young and lovely, in the heart and memory of Etienne Gerard.

'For shame!' she cried, sweeping up to me, and tearing with her own hands the noose from my neck. 'You are fighting in God's own quarrel, and yet you would begin with such a devil's deed as this. This man is mine, and he who touches a hair of his head will answer for it to me.'

They were glad enough to slink off into the darkness before those scornful eyes. Then she turned once more to me.

'You can follow me, Colonel Gerard,' she

said. 'I have a word that I would speak to you.'

I walked behind her to the chamber into which I had originally been shown. She closed the door, and then looked at me with the archest twinkle in her eyes.

'Is it not confiding of me to trust myself with you?' said she. 'You will remember that it is the Princess of Saxe-Felstein and not the poor Countess Palotta of Poland.'

'Be the name what it might,' I answered, 'I helped a lady whom I believed to be in distress, and I have been robbed of my papers and almost of my honour as a reward.'

'Colonel Gerard,' said she, 'we have been playing a game, you and I, and the stake was a heavy one. You have shown by delivering a message which was never given to you that you would stand at nothing in the cause of your country. My heart is German and yours is French, and I also would go all lengths, even to deceit and to theft, if at this crisis I could help my suffering fatherland. You see how frank I am.'

'You tell me nothing that I have not seen.'

'But now that the game is played and won, why should we bear malice? I will say this, that if ever I were in such a plight as that which I pretended in the inn of Lobenstein, I

236

should never wish to meet a more gallant protector or a truer-hearted gentleman than Colonel Etienne Gerard. I had never thought that I could feel for a Frenchman as I felt for you when I slipped the papers from your breast.'

'But you took them, none the less.'

'They were necessary to me and to Germany. I knew the arguments which they contained and the effect which they would have upon the Prince. If they had reached him all would have been lost.'

'Why should your Highness descend to such expedients when a score of these brigands, who wished to hang me at your castle gate, would have done the work as well?'

'They are not brigands, but the best blood of Germany,' she cried, hotly. 'If you have been roughly used, you will remember the indignities to which every German has been subjected, from the Queen of Prussia downwards. As to why I did not have you waylaid upon the road, I may say that I had parties out on all sides, and that I was waiting at Lobenstein to hear of their success. When instead of their news you yourself arrived I was in despair, for there was only the one weak woman betwixt you and my husband. You see the straits to which I was driven before I used the weapon of my sex.'

'I confess that you have conquered me, your Highness, and it only remains for me to leave you in possession of the field.'

'But you will take your papers with you.' She held them out to me as she spoke. 'The Prince has crossed the Rubicon now, and nothing can bring him back. You can return these to the Emperor, and tell him that we refused to receive them. No one can accuse you then of having lost your despatches. Good-bye, Colonel Gerard, and the best I can wish you is that when you reach France you may remain there. In a year's time there will be no place for a Frenchman upon this side of the Rhine.'

And thus it was that I played the Princess of Saxe-Felstein with all Germany for a stake, and lost my game to her. I had much to think of as I walked my poor, tired Violette along the highway which leads westward from Hof. But amid all the thoughts there came back to me always the proud, beautiful face of the German woman, and the voice of the soldier-poet as he sang from the chair. And I understood then that there was something terrible in this strong, patient Germany — this mother root of nations — and I saw that such a land, so old and so beloved, never could be conquered. And as I rode I saw that the dawn was breaking, and that the great star at which I had pointed through the palace window was dim and pale in the western sky.

7

How the Brigadier won his Medal

The Duke of Tarentum, or Macdonald, as his old comrades prefer to call him, was, as I could perceive, in the vilest of tempers. His grim, Scotch face was like one of those grotesque door-knockers which one sees in the Faubourg St Germain. We heard afterwards that the Emperor had said in jest that he would have sent him against Wellington in the South, but that he was afraid to trust him within the sound of the pipes. Major Charpentier and I could plainly see that he was smouldering with anger.

'Brigadier Gerard of the Hussars,' said he, with the air of the corporal with the recruit.

I saluted.

'Major Charpentier of the Horse Grenadiers.'

My companion answered to his name.

'The Emperor has a mission for you.'

Without more ado he flung open the door and announced us.

I have seen Napoleon ten times on horseback to once on foot, and I think that he does wisely to show himself to the troops in this fashion, for he cuts a very good figure in the saddle. As we saw him now he was the shortest man out of six by a good hand's breadth, and yet I am no very big man myself, though I ride quite heavy enough for a hussar. It is evident, too, that his body is too long for his legs. With his big, round head, his curved shoulders, and his clean-shaven face, he is more like a Professor at the Sorbonne than the first soldier in France. Every man to his taste, but it seems to me that, if I could clap a pair of fine light cavalry whiskers, like my own, on to him, it would do him no harm. He has a firm mouth, however, and his eyes are remarkable. I have seen them once turned on me in anger, and I had rather ride at a square on a spent horse than face them again. I am not a man who is easily daunted, either.

He was standing at the side of the room, away from the window, looking up at a great map of the country which was hung upon the wall. Berthier stood beside him, trying to look wise, and just as we entered, Napoleon snatched his sword impatiently from him and pointed with it on the map. He was talking fast and low, but I heard him say, 'The valley of the Meuse,' and twice he repeated 'Berlin.' As we entered, his aide-de-camp advanced to us, but the Emperor stopped him and beckoned us to his side.

'You have not yet received the cross of honour, Brigadier Gerard?' he asked.

I replied that I had not, and was about to add that it was not for want of having deserved it, when he cut me short in his decided fashion.

'And you, Major?' he asked.

'No, sire.'

'Then you shall both have your opportunity now.'

He led us to the great map upon the wall and placed the tip of Berthier's sword on Rheims.

'I will be frank with you, gentlemen, as with two comrades. You have both been with me since Marengo, I believe?' He had a strangely pleasant smile, which used to light up his pale face with a kind of cold sunshine. 'Here at Rheims are our present headquarters on this the 14th of March. Very good. Here is Paris, distant by road a good twenty-five leagues. Blucher lies to the north, Schwarzenberg to the south.' He prodded at the map with the sword as he spoke.

'Now,' said he, 'the further into the country these people march, the more completely I shall crush them. They are about to advance upon Paris. Very good. Let them do so. My brother, the King of Spain, will be there with a hundred thousand men. It is to him that I send you. You will hand him this letter, a copy of which I confide to each of you. It is to tell him that I am coming at once, in two days' time, with every man and horse and gun to his relief. I must give them forty-eight hours to recover. Then straight to Paris! You understand me, gentlemen?'

Ah, if I could tell you the glow of pride which it gave me to be taken into the great man's confidence in this way. As he handed our letters to us I clicked my spurs and threw out my chest, smiling and nodding to let him know that I saw what he would be after. He smiled also, and rested his hand for a moment upon the cape of my dolman. I would have given half my arrears of pay if my mother could have seen me at that instant.

'I will show you your route,' said he, turning back to the map. 'Your orders are to ride together as far as Bazoches. You will then separate, the one making for Paris by Oulchy and Neuilly, and the other to the north by Braine, Soissons, and Senlis. Have you anything to say, Brigadier Gerard?'

I am a rough soldier, but I have words and ideas. I had begun to speak about glory and the peril of France when he cut me short.

'And you, Major Charpentier?'

'If we find our route unsafe, are we at

liberty to choose another?' said he.

'Soldiers do not choose, they obey.' He inclined his head to show that we were dismissed, and turned round to Berthier. I do not know what he said, but I heard them both laughing.

Well, as you may think, we lost little time in getting upon our way. In half an hour we were riding down the High Street of Rheims, and it struck twelve o'clock as we passed the Cathedral. I had my little grey mare, Violette, the one which Sebastiani had wished to buy after Dresden. It is the fastest horse in the six brigades of light cavalry, and was only beaten by the Duke of Rovigo's racer from England. As to Charpentier, he had the kind of horse which a horse grenadier or a cuirassier would be likely to ride: a back like a bedstead, you understand, and legs like the posts. He is a hulking fellow himself, so that they looked a singular pair. And yet in his insane conceit he ogled the girls as they waved their handkerchiefs to me from the windows, and he twirled his ugly red moustache up into his eyes, just as if it were to him that their attention was addressed.

When we came out of the town we passed through the French camp, and then across the battle-field of yesterday, which was still covered both by our own poor fellows and by the Russians. But of the two the camp was the sadder sight. Our army was thawing away. The Guards were all right, though the young guard was full of conscripts. The artillery and the heavy cavalry were also good if there were more of them, but the infantry privates with their under officers looked like schoolboys with their masters. And we had no reserves. When one considered that there were 80,000 Prussians to the north and 150,000 Russians and Austrians to the south, it might make even the bravest man grave.

For my own part, I confess that I shed a tear until the thought came that the Emperor was still with us, and that on that very morning he had placed his hand upon my dolman and had promised me a medal of honour. This set me singing, and I spurred Violette on, until Charpentier had to beg me to have mercy on his great, snorting, panting camel. The road was beaten into paste and rutted two feet deep by the artillery, so that he was right in saying that it was not the place for a gallop.

I have never been very friendly with this Charpentier; and now for twenty miles of the way I could not draw a word from him. He rode with his brows puckered and his chin upon his breast, like a man who is heavy with thought. More than once I asked him what was on his mind, thinking that, perhaps, with my quicker intelligence I might set the matter straight. His answer always was that it was his mission of which he was thinking, which surprised me, because, although I had never thought much of his intelligence, still it seemed to me to be impossible that anyone could be puzzled by so simple and soldierly a task.

Well, we came at last to Bazoches, where he was to take the southern road and I the northern. He half turned in his saddle before he left me, and he looked at me with a singular expression of inquiry in his face.

'What do you make of it, Brigadier?' he asked.

'Of what?'

'Of our mission.'

'Surely it is plain enough.'

'You think so? Why should the Emperor tell us his plans?'

'Because he recognized our intelligence.'

My companion laughed in a manner which I found annoying.

'May I ask what you intend to do if you find these villages full of Prussians?' he asked.

'I shall obey my orders.'

'But you will be killed.'

'Very possibly.'

He laughed again, and so offensively that I

clapped my hand to my sword. But before I could tell him what I thought of his stupidity and rudeness he had wheeled his horse, and was lumbering away down the other road. I saw his big fur cap vanish over the brow of the hill, and then I rode upon my way, wondering at his conduct. From time to time I put my hand to the breast of my tunic and felt the paper crackle beneath my fingers. Ah, my precious paper, which should be turned into the little silver medal for which I had yearned so long. All the way from Braine to Sermoise I was thinking of what my mother would say when she saw it.

I stopped to give Violette a meal at a wayside auberge on the side of a hill not far from Soissons — a place surrounded by old oaks, and with so many crows that one could scarce hear one's own voice. It was from the innkeeper that I learned that Marmont had fallen back two days before, and that the Prussians were over the Aisne. An hour later, in the fading light, I saw two of their vedettes upon the hill to the right, and then, as darkness gathered, the heavens to the north were all glimmering from the lights of a bivouac.

When I heard that Blucher had been there for two days, I was much surprised that the Emperor should not have known that the country through which he had ordered me to carry my precious letter was already occupied by the enemy. Still, I thought of the tone of his voice when he said to Charpentier that a soldier must not choose, but must obey. I should follow the route he had laid down for me as long as Violette could move a hoof or I a finger upon her bridle. All the way from Sermoise to Soissons, where the road dips up and down, curving among fir woods, I kept my pistol ready and my sword-belt braced, pushing on swiftly where the path was straight, and then coming slowly round the corners in the way we learned in Spain.

When I came to the farmhouse which lies to the right of the road just after you cross the wooden bridge over the Crise, near where the great statue of the Virgin stands, a woman cried to me from the field, saying that the Prussians were in Soissons. A small party of their lancers, she said, had come in that very afternoon, and a whole division was expected before midnight. I did not wait to hear the end of her tale, but clapped spurs into Violette, and in five minutes was galloping her into the town.

Three Uhlans were at the mouth of the main street, their horses tethered, and they gossiping together, each with a pipe as long as my sabre. I saw them well in the light of an open door, but of me they could have seen only the flash of Violette's grey side and the black flutter of my cloak. A moment later I flew through a stream of them rushing from an open gateway. Violette's shoulder sent one of them reeling, and I stabbed at another but missed him. Pang, pang, went two carbines, but I had flown round the curve of the street, and never so much as heard the hiss of the balls. Ah, we were great, both Violette and I. She lay down to it like a coursed hare, the fire flying from her hoofs. I stood in my stirrups and brandished my sword. Someone sprang for my bridle. I sliced him through the arm, and I heard him howling behind me. Two horsemen closed upon me. I cut one down and outpaced the other. A minute later I was clear of the town, and flying down a broad white road with the black poplars on either side. For a time I heard the rattle of hoofs behind me, but they died and died until I could not tell them from the throbbing of my own heart. Soon I pulled up and listened, but all was silent. They had given up the chase.

Well, the first thing that I did was to dismount and to lead my mare into a small wood through which a stream ran. There I watered her and rubbed her down, giving her two pieces of sugar soaked in cognac from my flask. She was spent from the sharp chase, but it was wonderful to see how she came round with a half-hour's rest. When my thighs closed upon her again, I could tell by the spring and the swing of her that it would not be her fault if I did not win my way safe to Paris.

I must have been well within the enemy's lines now, for I heard a number of them shouting one of their rough drinking songs out of a house by the roadside, and I went round by the fields to avoid it. At another time two men came out into the moonlight (for by this time it was a cloudless night) and shouted something in German, but I galloped on without heeding them, and they were afraid to fire, for their own hussars are dressed exactly as I was. It is best to take no notice at these times, and then they put you down as a deaf man.

It was a lovely moon, and every tree threw a black bar across the road. I could see the countryside just as if it were daytime, and very peaceful it looked, save that there was a great fire raging somewhere in the north. In the silence of the night-time, and with the knowledge that danger was in front and behind me, the sight of that great distant fire was very striking and awesome. But I am not easily clouded, for I have seen too many singular things, so I hummed a tune between my teeth and thought of little Lisette, whom I might see in Paris. My mind was full of her when, trotting round a corner, I came straight upon half-a-dozen German dragoons, who were sitting round a brushwood fire by the roadside.

I am an excellent soldier. I do not say this because I am prejudiced in my own favour, but because I really am so. I can weigh every chance in a moment, and decide with as much certainty as though I had brooded for a week. Now I saw like a flash that, come what might, I should be chased, and on a horse which had already done a long twelve leagues. But it was better to be chased onwards than to be chased back. On this moonlit night, with fresh horses behind me, I must take my risk in either case; but if I were to shake them off, I preferred that it should be near Senlis than near Soissons.

All this flashed on me as if by instinct, you understand. My eyes had hardly rested on the bearded faces under the brass helmets before my rowels had touched Violette, and she was off with a rattle like a pas-de-charge. Oh, the shouting and rushing and stamping from behind us! Three of them fired and three swung themselves on to their horses. A bullet rapped on the crupper of my saddle with a noise like a stick on a door. Violette sprang madly forward, and I thought she had been wounded, but it was only a graze above the near fore-fetlock. Ah, the dear little mare, how I loved her when I felt her settle down into that long, easy gallop of hers, her hoofs going like a Spanish girl's castanets. I could not hold myself. I turned on my saddle and shouted and raved, 'Vive l'Empereur!' I screamed and laughed at the gust of oaths that came back to me.

But it was not over yet. If she had been fresh she might have gained a mile in five. Now she could only hold her own with a very little over. There was one of them, a young boy of an officer, who was better mounted than the others. He drew ahead with every stride. Two hundred yards behind him were two troopers, but I saw every time that I glanced round that the distance between them was increasing. The other three who had waited to shoot were a long way in the rear.

The officer's mount was a bay — a fine horse, though not to be spoken of with Violette; yet it was a powerful brute, and it seemed to me that in a few miles its freshness might tell. I waited until the lad was a long way in front of his comrades, and then I eased my mare down a little — a very, very little, so that he might think he was really catching me. When he came within pistol-shot of me I drew and cocked my own pistol, and laid my chin upon my shoulder to see what he would do. He did not offer to fire, and I soon discerned the cause. The silly boy had taken his pistols from his holsters when he had camped for the night. He wagged his sword at me now and roared some threat or other. He did not seem to understand that he was at my mercy. I eased Violette down until there was not the length of a long lance between the grey tail and the bay muzzle.

'Rendez-vous!' he yelled.

'I must compliment monsieur upon his French,' said I, resting the barrel of my pistol upon my bridle-arm, which I have always found best when shooting from the saddle. I aimed at his face, and could see, even in the moonlight, how white he grew when he understood that it was all up with him. But even as my finger pressed the trigger I thought of his mother, and I put my ball through his horse's shoulder. I fear he hurt himself in the fall, for it was a fearful crash, but I had my letter to think of, so I stretched the mare into a gallop once more.

But they were not so easily shaken off, these brigands. The two troopers thought no more of their young officer than if he had been a recruit thrown in the riding-school.

They left him to the others and thundered on after me. I had pulled up on the brow of a hill, thinking that I had heard the last of them; but, my faith, I soon saw there was no time for loitering, so away we went, the mare tossing her head and I my shako, to show what we thought of two dragoons who tried to catch a hussar. But at this moment, even while I laughed at the thought, my heart stood still within me, for there at the end of the long white road was a black patch of cavalry waiting to receive me. To a young soldier it might have seemed the shadow of the trees, but to me it was a troop of hussars, and, turn where I could, death seemed to be waiting for me.

Well, I had the dragoons behind me and the hussars in front. Never since Moscow have I seemed to be in such peril. But for the honour of the brigade I had rather be cut down by a light cavalryman than by a heavy. I never drew bridle, therefore, or hesitated for an instant, but I let Violette have her head. I remember that I tried to pray as I rode, but I am a little out of practice at such things, and the only words I could remember were the prayer for fine weather which we used at the school on the evening before holidays. Even this seemed better than nothing, and I was pattering it out, when suddenly I heard

French voices in front of me. Ah, mon Dieu, but the joy went through my heart like a musket-ball. They were ours — our own dear little rascals from the corps of Marmont. Round whisked my two dragoons and galloped for their lives, with the moon gleaming on their brass helmets, while I trotted up to my friends with no undue haste, for I would have them understand that though a hussar may fly, it is not in his nature to fly very fast. Yet I fear that Violette's heaving flanks and foam-spattered muzzle gave the lie to my careless bearing.

Who should be at the head of the troop but old Bouvet, whom I saved at Leipzig! When he saw me his little pink eyes filled with tears, and, indeed, I could not but shed a few myself at the sight of his joy. I told him of my mission, but he laughed when I said that I must pass through Senlis.

'The enemy is there,' said he. 'You cannot go.'

'I prefer to go where the enemy is,' I answered.

'But why not go straight to Paris with your despatch? Why should you choose to pass through the one place where you are almost sure to be taken or killed?'

'A soldier does not choose — he obeys,' said I, just as I had heard Napoleon say it.

Old Bouvet laughed in his wheezy way, until I had to give my moustachios a twirl and look him up and down in a manner which brought him to reason.

'Well', said he, 'you had best come along with us, for we are all bound for Senlis. Our orders are to reconnoitre the place. A squadron of Poniatowski's Polish Lancers are in front of us. If you must ride through it, it is possible that we may be able to go with you.'

So away we went, jingling and clanking through the quiet night until we came up with the Poles — fine old soldiers all of them, though a trifle heavy for their horses. It was a treat to see them, for they could not have carried themselves better if they had belonged to my own brigade. We rode together, until in the early morning we saw the lights of Senlis. A peasant was coming along with a cart, and from him we learned how things were going there.

His information was certain, for his brother was the Mayor's coachman, and he had spoken with him late the night before. There was a single squadron of Cossacks — or a polk, as they call it in their frightful language — quartered upon the Mayor's house, which stands at the corner of the market-place, and is the largest building in the town. A whole division of Prussian infantry was encamped in the woods to the north, but only the Cossacks were in Senlis. Ah, what a chance to avenge ourselves upon these barbarians, whose cruelty to our poor countryfolk was the talk at every camp fire.

We were into the town like a torrent, hacked down the vedettes, rode over the guard, and were smashing in the doors of the Mayor's house before they understood that there was a Frenchman within twenty miles of them. We saw horrid heads at the windows — heads bearded to the temples, with tangled hair and sheepskin caps, and silly, gaping mouths. 'Hourra! Hourra!' they shrieked, and fired with their carbines, but our fellows were into the house and at their throats before they had wiped the sleep out of their eyes. It was dreadful to see how the Poles flung themselves upon them, like starving wolves upon a herd of fat bucks — for, as you know, the Poles have a blood feud against the Cossacks. The most were killed in the upper rooms, whither they had fled for shelter, and the blood was pouring down into the hall like rain from a roof. They are terrible soldiers, these Poles, though I think they are a trifle heavy for their horses. Man for man, they are as big as Kellerman's cuirassiers. Their equipment is, of course, much lighter, since they are without the cuirass, back-plate, and helmet.

Well, it was at this point that I made an error — a very serious error it must be admitted. Up to this moment I had carried out my mission in a manner which only my modesty prevents me from describing as remarkable. But now I did that which an official would condemn and a soldier excuse.

There is no doubt that the mare was spent, but still it is true that I might have galloped on through Senlis and reached the country, where I should have had no enemy between me and Paris. But what hussar can ride past a fight and never draw rein? It is to ask too much of him. Besides, I thought that if Violette had an hour of rest I might have three hours the better at the other end. Then on the top of it came those heads at the windows, with their sheepskin hats and their barbarous cries. I sprang from my saddle, threw Violette's bridle over a rail-post, and ran into the house with the rest. It is true that I was too late to be of service, and that I was nearly wounded by a lance-thrust from one of these dying savages. Still, it is a pity to miss even the smallest affair, for one never knows what opportunity for advancement may present itself. I have seen more soldierly work in outpost skirmishes and little gallop-and-hack affairs of the kind than in any of the

Emperor's big battles.

When the house was cleared I took a bucket of water out for Violette, and our peasant guide showed me where the good Mayor kept his fodder. My faith, but the little sweetheart was ready for it. Then I sponged down her legs, and leaving her still tethered I went back into the house to find a mouthful for myself, so that I should not need to halt again until I was in Paris.

And now I come to the part of my story which may seem singular to you, although I could tell you at least ten things every bit as queer which have happened to me in my lifetime. You can understand that, to a man who spends his life in scouting and vedette duties on the bloody ground which lies between two great armies, there are many chances of strange experiences. I'll tell you, however, exactly what occurred.

Old Bouvet was waiting in the passage when I entered, and he asked me whether we might not crack a bottle of wine together. 'My faith, we must not be long,' said he. 'There are ten thousand of Theilmann's Prussians in the woods up yonder.'

'Where is the wine?' I asked.

'Ah, you may trust two hussars to find where the wine is,' said he, and taking a candle in his hand, he led the way down the stone stairs into the kitchen.

When we got there we found another door, which opened on to a winding stair with the cellar at the bottom. The Cossacks had been there before us, as was easily seen by the broken bottles littered all over it. However, the Mayor was a *bon-vivant*, and I do not wish to have a better set of bins to pick from. Chambertin, Graves, Alicant, white wine and red, sparkling and still, they lay in pyramids peeping coyly out of sawdust. Old Bouvet stood with his candle looking here and peeping there, purring in his throat like a cat before a milk-pail. He had picked upon a Burgundy at last, and had his hand outstretched to the bottle when there came a roar of musketry from above us, a rush of feet, and such a yelping and screaming as I have never listened to. The Prussians were upon us!

Bouvet is a brave man: I will say that for him. He flashed out his sword and away he clattered up the stone steps, his spurs clinking as he ran. I followed him, but just as we came out into the kitchen passage a tremendous shout told us that the house had been recaptured.

'It is all over,' I cried, grasping at Bouvet's sleeve.

'There is one more to die,' he shouted, and

away he went like a madman up the second stair. In effect, I should have gone to my death also had I been in his place, for he had done very wrong in not throwing out his scouts to warn him if the Germans advanced upon him. For an instant I was about to rush up with him, and then I bethought myself that, after all, I had my own mission to think of, and that if I were taken the important letter of the Emperor would be sacrificed. I let Bouvet die alone, therefore, and I went down into the cellar again, closing the door behind me.

Well, it was not a very rosy prospect down there either. Bouvet had dropped the candle when the alarm came, and I, pawing about in the darkness, could find nothing but broken bottles. At last I came upon the candle, which had rolled under the curve of a cask, but, try as I would with my tinderbox, I could not light it. The reason was that the wick had been wet in a puddle of wine, so suspecting that this might be the case, I cut the end off with my sword. Then I found that it lighted easily enough. But what to do I could not imagine. The scoundrels upstairs were shouting themselves hoarse, several hundred of them from the sound, and it was clear that some of them would soon want to moisten their throats. There would be an end to a dashing soldier, and of the mission and of the medal. I thought of my mother and I thought of the Emperor. It made me weep to think that the one would lose so excellent a son and the other the best light cavalry officer he ever had since Lasalle's time. But presently I dashed the tears from my eyes. 'Courage!' I cried, striking myself upon the chest. 'Courage, my brave boy. Is it possible that one who has come safely from Moscow without so much as a frost-bite will die in a French wine-cellar?' At the thought I was up on my feet and clutching at the letter in my tunic, for the crackle of it gave me courage.

My first plan was to set fire to the house, in the hope of escaping in the confusion. My second to get into an empty wine-cask. I was looking round to see if I could find one, when suddenly, in the corner, I espied a little low door, painted of the same grey colour as the wall, so that it was only a man with quick sight who would have noticed it. I pushed against it, and at first I imagined that it was locked. Presently, however, it gave a little, and then I understood that it was held by the pressure of something on the other side. I put my feet against a hogshead of wine, and I gave such a push that the door flew open and I came down with a crash upon my back, the candle flying out of my hands, so that I found myself in darkness once more. I picked myself up and stared through the black archway into the gloom beyond.

There was a slight ray of light coming from some slit or grating. The dawn had broken outside, and I could dimly see the long, curving sides of several huge casks, which made me think that perhaps this was where the Mayor kept his reserves of wine while they were maturing. At any rate, it seemed to be a safer hiding-place than the outer cellar, so gathering up my candle, I was just closing the door behind me, when I suddenly saw something which filled me with amazement, and even, I confess, with the smallest little touch of fear.

I have said that at the further end of the cellar there was a dim grey fan of light striking downwards from somewhere near the roof. Well, as I peered through the darkness, I suddenly saw a great, tall man skip into this belt of daylight, and then out again into the darkness at the further end. My word, I gave such a start that my shako nearly broke its chin-strap! It was only a glance, but, none the less, I had time to see that the fellow had a hairy Cossack cap on his head, and that he was a great, long-legged, broad-shouldered brigand, with a sabre at his waist. My faith, even Etienne Gerard was a little staggered at being left alone with such a creature in the dark.

But only for a moment. 'Courage!' I thought. 'Am I not a hussar, a brigadier, too, at the age of thirty-one, and the chosen messenger of the Emperor?' After all, this skulker had more cause to be afraid of me than I of him. And then suddenly I understood that he was afraid — horribly afraid. I could read it from his quick step and his bent shoulders as he ran among the barrels, like a rat making for its hole. And, of course, it must have been he who had held the door against me, and not some packing-case or wine-cask as I had imagined. He was the pursued then, and I the pursuer. Aha, I felt my whiskers bristle as I advanced upon him through the darkness! He would find that he had no chicken to deal with, this robber from the North. For the moment I was magnificent.

At first I had feared to light my candle lest I should make a mark of myself, but now, after cracking my shin over a box, and catching my spurs in some canvas, I thought the bolder course the wiser. I lit it, therefore, and then I advanced with long strides, my sword in my hand. 'Come out, you rascal!' I cried. 'Nothing can save you. You will at last meet with your deserts.'

I held my candle high, and presently I caught a glimpse of the man's head staring at me over a barrel. He had a gold chevron on his black cap, and the expression of his face told me in an instant that he was an officer and a man of refinement.

'Monsieur,' he cried, in excellent French, 'I surrender myself on a promise of quarter. But if I do not have your promise, I will then sell my life as dearly as I can.'

'Sir,' said I, 'a Frenchman knows how to treat an unfortunate enemy. Your life is safe.' With that he handed his sword over the top of the barrel, and I bowed with the candle on my heart. 'Whom have I the honour of capturing?' I asked.

'I am the Count Boutkine, of the Emperor's own Don Cossacks,' said he. 'I came out with my troop to reconnoitre Senlis, and as we found no sign of your people we determined to spend the night here.'

'And would it be an indiscretion,' I asked, 'if I were to inquire how you came into the back cellar?'

'Nothing more simple,' said he. 'It was our intention to start at early dawn. Feeling chilled after dressing, I thought that a cup of wine would do me no harm, so I came down to see what I could find. As I was rummaging about, the house was suddenly carried by assault so rapidly that by the time I had climbed the stairs it was all over. It only remained for me to save myself, so I came down here and hid myself in the back cellar, where you have found me.'

I thought of how old Bouvet had behaved under the same conditions, and the tears sprang to my eyes as I contemplated the glory of France. Then I had to consider what I should do next. It was clear that this Russian Count, being in the back cellar while we were in the front one, had not heard the sounds which would have told him that the house was once again in the hands of his own allies. If he should once understand this the tables would be turned, and I should be his prisoner instead of the being mine. What was I to do? I was at my wits' end, when suddenly there came to me an idea so brilliant that I could not but be amazed at my own invention.

'Count Boutkine,' said I, 'I find myself in a most difficult position.'

'And why?' he asked.

'Because I have promised you your life.'

His jaw dropped a little.

'You would not withdraw your promise?' he cried.

'If the worst comes to the worst I can die in

your defence,' said I; 'but the difficulties are great.'

'What is it, then?' he asked.

'I will be frank with you,' said I. 'You must know that our fellows, and especially the Poles, are so incensed against the Cossacks that the mere sight of the uniform drives them mad. They precipitate themselves instantly upon the wearer and tear him limb from limb. Even their officers cannot restrain them.'

The Russian grew pale at my words and the way in which I said them.

'But this is terrible,' said he.

'Horrible!' said I. 'If we were to go up together at this moment I cannot promise how far I could protect you.'

'I am in your hands,' he cried. 'What would you suggest that we should do? Would it not be best that I should remain here?'

'That worst of all.'

'And why?'

'Because our fellows will ransack the house presently, and then you would be cut to pieces. No, no, I must go and break it to them. But even then, when once they see that accursed uniform, I do not know what may happen.'

'Should I then take the uniform off?'

'Excellent!' I cried. 'Hold, we have it! You

will take your uniform off and put on mine. That will make you sacred to every French soldier.'

'It is not the French I fear so much as the Poles.'

'But my uniform will be a safeguard against either.'

'How can I thank you?' he cried. 'But you — what are you to wear?'

'I will wear yours.'

'And perhaps fall a victim to your generosity?'

'It is my duty to take the risk,' I answered; 'but I have no fears. I will ascend in your uniform. A hundred swords will be turned upon me. 'Hold!' I will shout, 'I am the Brigadier Gerard!' Then they will see my face. They will know me. And I will tell them about you. Under the shield of these clothes you will be sacred.'

His fingers trembled with eagerness as he tore off his tunic. His boots and breeches were much like my own, so there was no need to change them, but I gave him my hussar jacket, my dolman, my shako, my sword-belt, and my sabre-tasche, while I took in exchange his high sheepskin cap with the gold chevron, his fur-trimmed coat, and his crooked sword. Be it well understood that in changing the tunics I did not forget to change

268

my thrice-precious letter also from my old one to my new.

'With your leave,' said I, 'I shall now bind you to a barrel.'

He made a great fuss over this, but I have learned in my soldiering never to throw away chances, and how could I tell that he might not, when my back was turned, see how the matter really stood, and break in upon my plans? He was leaning against a barrel at the time, so I ran six times round it with a rope, and then tied it with a big knot behind. If he wished to come upstairs he would, at least, have to carry a thousand litres of good French wine for a knapsack. I then shut the door of the back cellar behind me, so that he might not hear what was going forward, and tossing the candle away I ascended the kitchen stair.

There were only about twenty steps, and yet, while I came up them, I seemed to have time to think of everything that I had ever hoped to do. It was the same feeling that I had at Eylau when I lay with my broken leg and saw the horse artillery galloping down upon me. Of course, I knew that if I were taken I should be shot instantly as being disguised within the enemy's lines. Still, it was a glorious death — in the direct service of the Emperor — and I reflected that there could not be less than five lines, and perhaps seven, in the *Moniteur* about me. Palaret had eight lines, and I am sure that he had not so fine a career.

When I made my way out into the hall, with all the nonchalance in my face and manner that I could assume, the very first thing that I saw was Bouvet's dead body, with his legs drawn up and a broken sword in his hand. I could see by the black smudge that he had been shot at close quarters. I should have wished to salute as I went by, for he was a gallant man, but I feared lest I should be seen, and so I passed on.

The front of the hall was full of Prussian infantry, who were knocking loopholes in the wall, as though they expected that there might be yet another attack. Their officer, a little man, was running about giving directions. They were all too busy to take much notice of me, but another officer, who was standing by the door with a long pipe in his mouth, strode across and clapped me on the shoulder, pointing to the dead bodies of our poor hussars, and saying something which was meant for a jest, for his long beard opened and showed every fang in his head. I laughed heartily also, and said the only Russian words that I knew. I learned them from little Sophie, at Wilna, and they meant:

'If the night is fine we shall meet under the oak tree, but if it rains we shall meet in the byre.' It was all the same to this German, however, and I have no doubt that he gave me credit for saying something very witty indeed, for he roared laughing, and slapped me on my shoulder again. I nodded to him and marched out of the hall-door as coolly as if I were the commandant of the garrison.

There were a hundred horses tethered about outside, most of them belonging to the Poles and hussars. Good little Violette was waiting with the others, and she whinnied when she saw me coming towards her. But I would not mount her. No. I was much too cunning for that. On the contrary, I chose the most shaggy little Cossack horse that I could see, and I sprang upon it with as much assurance as though it had belonged to my father before me. It had a great bag of plunder slung over its neck, and this I laid upon Violette's back, and led her along beside me. Never have you seen such a picture of the Cossack returning from the foray. It was superb.

Well, the town was full of Prussians by this time. They lined the side-walks and pointed me out to each other, saying, as I could judge from their gestures, 'There goes one of those devils of Cossacks. They are the boys for foraging and plunder.'

One or two officers spoke to me with an air of authority, but I shook my head and smiled, and said, 'If the night is fine we shall meet under the oak tree, but if it rains we shall meet in the byre,' at which they shrugged their shoulders and gave the matter up. In this way I worked along until I was beyond the northern outskirt of the town. I could see in the roadway two lancer vedettes with their black and white pennons, and I knew that when I was once past these I should be a free man once more. I made my pony trot, therefore, Violette rubbing her nose against my knee all the time, and looking up at me to ask how she had deserved that this hairy doormat of a creature should be preferred to her. I was not more than a hundred yards from the Uhlans when, suddenly, you can imagine my feelings when I saw a real Cossack coming galloping along the road towards me.

Ah, my friend, you who read this, if you have any heart, you will feel for a man like me, who had gone through so many dangers and trials, only at this very last moment to be confronted with one which appeared to put an end to everything. I will confess that for a moment I lost heart, and was inclined to throw myself down in my despair, and to cry out that I had been betrayed. But, no; I was not beaten even now. I opened two buttons of my tunic so that I might get easily at the Emperor's message, for it was my fixed determination when all hope was gone to swallow the letter and then die sword in hand. Then I felt that my little, crooked sword was loose in its sheath, and I trotted on to where the vedettes were waiting. They seemed inclined to stop me, but I pointed to the other Cossack, who was still a couple of hundred yards off, and they, understanding that I merely wished to meet him, let me pass with a salute.

I dug my spurs into my pony then, for if I were only far enough from the lancers I thought I might manage the Cossack without much difficulty. He was an officer, a large, bearded man, with a gold chevron in his cap, just the same as mine. As I advanced he unconsciously aided me by pulling up his horse, so that I had a fine start of the vedettes. On I came for him, and I could see wonder changing to suspicion in his brown eyes as he looked at me and at my pony, and at my equipment. I do not know what it was that was wrong, but he saw something which was as it should not be. He shouted out a question, and then when I gave no answer he pulled out his sword. I was glad in my heart to see him do so, for I had always rather fight than cut down an unsuspecting enemy. Now I made at him full tilt, and, parrying his cut, I got my point in just under the fourth button of his tunic. Down he went, and the weight of him nearly took me off my horse before I could disengage. I never glanced at him to see if he were living or dead, for I sprang off my pony and on to Violette, with a shake of my bridle and a kiss of my hand to the two Uhlans behind me. They galloped after me, shouting, but Violette had had her rest, and was just as fresh as when she started. I took the first side road to the west and then the first to the south, which would take me away from the enemy's country. On we went and on, every stride taking me further from my foes and nearer to my friends. At last, when I reached the end of a long stretch of road, and looking back from it could see no sign of any pursuers, I understood that my troubles were over.

And it gave me a glow of happiness, as I rode, to think that I had done to the letter what the Emperor had ordered. What would he say when he saw me? What could he say which would do justice to the incredible way in which I had risen above every danger? He had ordered me to go through Sermoise, Soissons, and Senlis, little dreaming that they were all three occupied by the enemy. And yet I had done it. I had borne his letter in safety through each of these towns. Hussars, dragoons, lancers, Cossacks, and infantry — I had run the gauntlet of all of them, and had come out unharmed.

When I had got as far as Dammartin I caught a first glimpse of our own outposts. There was a troop of dragoons in a field, and of course I could see from the horsechair crests that they were French. I galloped towards them in order to ask them if all was safe between there and Paris, and as I rode I felt such a pride at having won my way back to my friends again, that I could not refrain from waving my sword in the air.

At this a young officer galloped out from among the dragoons, also brandishing his sword, and it warmed my heart to think that he should come riding with such ardour and enthusiasm to greet me. I made Violette caracole, and as we came together I brandished my sword more gallantly than ever, but you can imagine my feelings when he suddenly made a cut at me which would certainly have taken my head off if I had not fallen forward with my nose in Violette's mane. My faith, it whistled just over my cap like an east wind. Of course, it came from this accursed Cossack uniform which, in my excitement, I had forgotten all about, and this young dragoon had imagined that I was some Russian champion who was challenging the French cavalry. My word, he was a frightened man when he understood how near he had been to killing the celebrated Brigadier Gerard.

Well, the road was clear, and about three o'clock in the afternoon I was at St Denis, though it took me a long two hours to get from there to Paris, for the road was blocked with commissariat waggons and guns of the artillery reserve, which was going north to Marmont and Mortier. You cannot conceive the excitement which my appearance in such a costume made in Paris, and when I came to the Rue de Rivoli I should think I had a quarter of a mile of folk riding or running behind me. Word had got about from the dragoons (two of whom had come with me), and everybody knew about my adventures and how I had come by my uniform. It was a triumph — men shouting and women waving their handkerchiefs and blowing kisses from the windows.

Although I am a man singularly free from conceit, still I must confess that, on this one occasion, I could not restrain myself from showing that this reception gratified me. The Russian's coat had hung very loose upon me, but now I threw out my chest until it was as tight as a sausage-skin. And my little sweetheart of a mare tossed her mane and pawed with her front hoofs, frisking her tail about as though she said, 'We've done it together this time. It is to us that commissions should be intrusted.' When I kissed her between the nostrils as I dismounted at the gate of the Tuileries, there was as much shouting as if a bulletin had been read from the Grand Army.

I was hardly in costume to visit a King; but, after all, if one has a soldierly figure one can do without all that. I was shown up straight away to Joseph, whom I had often seen in Spain. He seemed as stout, as quiet, and as amiable as ever. Talleyrand was in the room with him, or I suppose I should call him the Duke of Benevento, but I confess that I like old names best. He read my letter when Joseph Buonaparte handed it to him, and then he looked at me with the strangest expression in those funny little, twinkling eyes of his.

'Were you the only messenger?' he asked.

'There was one other, sir,' said I. 'Major Charpentier, of the Horse Grenadiers.'

'He has not yet arrived,' said the King of Spain.

'If you had seen the legs of his horse, sire,

you would not wonder at it,' I remarked.

'There may be other reasons,' said Talleyrand, and he gave that singular smile of his.

Well, they paid me a compliment or two, though they might have said a good deal more and yet have said too little. I bowed myself out, and very glad I was to get away, for I hate a Court as much as I love a camp. Away I went to my old friend Chaubert, in the Rue Miromesnil, and there I got his hussar uniform, which fitted me very well. He and Lisette and I supped together in his rooms, and all my dangers were forgotten. In the morning I found Violette ready for another twenty-league stretch. It was my intention to return instantly to the Emperor's headquarters, for I was, as you may well imagine, impatient to hear his words of praise, and to receive my reward.

I need not say that I rode back by a safe route, for I had seen quite enough of Uhlans and Cossacks. I passed through Meaux and Château Thierry, and so in the evening I arrived at Rheims, where Napoleon was still lying. The bodies of our fellows and of St Prest's Russians had all been buried, and I could see changes in the camp also. The soldiers looked better cared for; some of the cavalry had received remounts, and everything was in excellent order. It was wonderful what a good general can effect in a couple of days.

When I came to the headquarters I was shown straight into the Emperor's room. He was drinking coffee at a writing-table, with a big plan drawn out on paper in front of him. Berthier and Macdonald were leaning, one over each shoulder, and he was talking so quickly that I don't believe that either of them could catch a half of what he was saying. But when his eyes fell upon me he dropped the pen on to the chart, and he sprang up with a look in his pale face which struck me cold.

'What the deuce are you doing here?' he shouted. When he was angry he had a voice like a peacock.

'I have the honour to report to you, sire,' said I, 'that I have delivered your despatch safely to the King of Spain.'

'What!' he yelled, and his two eyes transfixed me like bayonets. Oh, those dreadful eyes, shifting from grey to blue, like steel in the sunshine. I can see them now when I have a bad dream.

'What has become of Charpentier?' he asked.

'He is captured,' said Macdonald.

'By whom?'

'The Russians.'

'The Cossacks?'

'No, a single Cossack.'

'He gave himself up?'

'Without resistance.'

'He is an intelligent officer. You will see that the medal of honour is awarded to him.'

When I heard those words I had to rub my eyes to make sure that I was awake.

'As to you,' cried the Emperor, taking a step forward as if he would have struck me, 'you brain of a hare, what do you think that you were sent upon this mission for? Do you conceive that I would send a really important message by such a hand as yours, and through every village which the enemy holds? How you came through them passes my comprehension; but if your fellow-messenger had had but as little sense as you, my whole plan of campaign would have been ruined. Can you not see, coglione, that this message contained false news, and that it was intended to deceive the enemy whilst I put a very different scheme into execution?'

When I heard those cruel words and saw the angry, white face which glared at me, I had to hold the back of a chair, for my mind was failing me and my knees would hardly bear me up. But then I took courage as I reflected that I was an honourable gentleman, and that my whole life had been spent in toiling for this man and for my beloved country.

'Sire,' said I, and the tears would trickle down my cheeks whilst I spoke, 'when you are dealing with a man like me you would find it wiser to deal openly. Had I known that you had wished the despatch to fall into the hands of the enemy, I would have seen that it came there. As I believed that I was to guard it, I was prepared to sacrifice my life for it. I do not believe, sire, that any man in the world ever met with more toils and perils than I have done in trying to carry out what I thought was your will.'

I dashed the tears from my eyes as I spoke, and with such fire and spirit as I could command I gave him an account of it all, of my dash through Soissons, my brush with the dragoons, my adventure in Senlis, my rencontre with Count Boutkine in the cellar, my disguise, my meeting with the Cossack officer, my flight, and how at the last moment I was nearly cut down by a French dragoon. The Emperor, Berthier, and Macdonald listened with astonishment on their faces. When I had finished Napoleon stepped forward and he pinched me by the ear.

'There, there!' said he. 'Forget anything which I may have said. I would have done better to trust you. You may go.'

I turned to the door, and my hand was upon the handle, when the Emperor called upon me to stop.

'You will see,' said he, turning to the Duke of Tarentum, 'that Brigadier Gerard has the special medal of honour, for I believe that if he has the thickest head he has also the stoutest heart in my army.'

8

How the Brigadier Was Tempted by the Devil

The spring is at hand, my friends. I can see the little green spear-heads breaking out once more upon the chestnut trees, and the cafe tables have all been moved into the sunshine. It is more pleasant to sit there, and yet I do not wish to tell my little stories to the whole town. You have heard my doings as a lieutenant, as a squadron officer, as a colonel, as the chief of a brigade. But now I suddenly become something higher and more important. I become history.

If you have read of those closing years of the life of the Emperor which were spent in the Island of St Helena, you will remember that, again and again, he implored permission to send out one single letter which should be unopened by those who held him. Many times he made this request, and even went so far as to promise that he would provide for his own wants and cease to be an expense to the British Government if it were granted to him. But his guardians knew that he was a terrible man, this pale, fat gentleman in the straw hat, and they dared not grant him what he asked. Many have wondered who it was to whom he could have had anything so secret to say. Some have supposed that it was to his wife, and some that it was to his father-in-law; some that it was to the Emperor Alexander, and some to Marshal Soult. What will you think of me, my friends, when I tell you it was to me — to me, the Brigadier Gerard — that the Emperor wished to write? Yes, humble as you see me, with only my 100 francs a month of half-pay between me and hunger, it is none the less true that I was always in the Emperor's mind, and that he would have given his left hand for five minutes' talk with me. I will tell you tonight how this came about.

It was after the Battle of Fére-Champenoise where the conscripts in their blouses and their sabots made such a fine stand, that we, the more long-headed of us, began to understand that it was all over with us. Our reserve ammunition had been taken in the battle, and we were left with silent guns and empty caissons. Our cavalry, too, was in a deplorable condition, and my own brigade had been destroyed in the charge at Craonne. Then came the news that the enemy had taken Paris, that the citizens had mounted the white cockade; and finally, most terrible of all, that Marmont and his corps had gone over to the Bourbons. We looked at each other and asked how many more of our generals were going to turn against us. Already there were Jourdan, Marmont, Murat, Bernadotte, and Jomini — though nobody minded much about Jomini, for his pen was always sharper than his sword. We had been ready to fight Europe, but it looked now as though we were to fight Europe and half of France as well.

We had come to Fontainebleau by a long, forced march, and there we were assembled, the poor remnants of us, the corps of Ney, the corps of my cousin Gerard, and the corps of Macdonald: twenty-five thousand in all, with seven thousand of the guard. But we had our prestige, which was worth fifty thousand, and our Emperor, who was worth fifty thousand more. He was always among us, serene, smiling, confident, taking his snuff and playing with his little riding-whip. Never in the days of his greatest victories have I admired him as much as I did during the Campaign of France.

One evening I was with a few of my officers, drinking a glass of wine of Suresnes. I mention that it was wine of Suresnes just to show you that times were not very good with us. Suddenly I was disturbed by a message from Berthier that he wished to see me. When I speak of my old comrades-in-arms, I will, with your permission, leave out all the fine foreign titles which they had picked up during the wars. They are excellent for a Court, but you never heard them in the camp, for we could not afford to do away with our Ney, our Rapp, or our Soult — names which were as stirring to our ears as the blare of our trumpets blowing the reveille. It was Berthier, then, who sent to say that he wished to see me.

He had a suite of rooms at the end of the gallery of Francis the First, not very far from those of the Emperor. In the ante-chamber were waiting two men whom I knew well: Colonel Despienne, of the 57th of the line, and Captain Tremeau, of the Voltigeurs. They were both old soldiers — Tremeau had carried a musket in Egypt — and they were also both famous in the army for their courage and their skill with weapons. Tremeau had become a little stiff in the wrist, but Despienne was capable at his best of making me exert myself. He was a tiny fellow, about three inches short of the proper height for a man — he was exactly three inches shorter than myself — but both with the sabre and with the small-sword he had several times almost held his own against me when we used to exhibit at Verron's Hall of Arms in the Palais Royal. You may think that it made us sniff something in the wind when we found three such men called together into one room. You cannot see the lettuce and dressing without suspecting a salad.

'Name of a pipe!' said Tremeau, in his barrack-room fashion. 'Are we then expecting three champions of the Bourbons?'

To all of us the idea appeared not improbable. Certainly in the whole army we were the very three who might have been chosen to meet them.

'The Prince of Neufchâtel desires to speak with the Brigadier Gerard,' said a footman, appearing at the door.

In I went, leaving my two companions consumed with impatience behind me. It was a small room, but very gorgeously furnished. Berthier was seated opposite to me at a little table, with a pen in his hand and a note-book open before him. He was looking weary and slovenly — very different from that Berthier who used to give the fashion to the army, and who had so often set us poorer officers tearing our hair by trimming his pelisse with fur one campaign, and with grey astrakhan the next. On his clean-shaven, comely face there was an expression of trouble and he looked at me as I entered his chamber in a way which had in it something furtive and displeasing.

'Chief of Brigade Gerard!' said he.

'At your service, your Highness!' I answered.

'I must ask you, before I go further, to promise me, upon your honour as a gentleman and a soldier, that what is about to pass between us shall never be mentioned to any third person.'

My word, this was a fine beginning! I had no choice but to give the promise required.

'You must know, then, that it is all over with the Emperor,' said he, looking down at the table and speaking very slowly, as if he had a hard task in getting out the words. 'Jourdan at Rouen and Marmont at Paris have both mounted the white cockade, and it is rumoured that Talleyrand has talked Ney into doing the same. It is evident that further resistance is useless, and that it can only bring misery upon our country. I wish to ask you, therefore, whether you are prepared to join me in laying hands upon the Emperor's person, and bringing the war to a conclusion by delivering him over to the allies?'

I assure you that when I heard this infamous proposition put forward by the man who had been the earliest friend of the Emperor, and who had received greater favours from him than any of his followers, I could only stand and stare at him in amazement. For his part he tapped his pen-handle against his teeth, and looked at me with a slanting head.

'Well?' he asked.

'I am a little deaf on one side,' said I, coldly. 'There are some things which I cannot hear. I beg that you will permit me to return to my duties.'

'Nay, but you must not be headstrong,' rising up and laying his hand upon my shoulder. 'You are aware that the Senate has declared against Napoleon, and that the Emperor Alexander refuses to treat with him.'

'Sir,' I cried, with passion, 'I would have you know that I do not care the dregs of a wine-glass for the Senate or for the Emperor Alexander either.'

'Then for what do you care?'

'For my own honour and for the service of my glorious master, the Emperor Napoleon.'

'That is all very well,' said Berthier, peevishly, shrugging his shoulders. 'Facts are facts, and as men of the world, we must look them in the face. Are we to stand against the will of the nation? Are we to have civil war on the top of all our misfortunes? And, besides, we are thinning away. Every hour comes the news of fresh desertions. We have still time to make our peace, and, indeed, to earn the highest regard, by giving up the Emperor.'

I shook so with passion that my sabre clattered against my thigh.

'Sir,' I cried, 'I never thought to have seen the day when a Marshal of France would have so far degraded himself as to put forward such a proposal. I leave you to your own conscience; but as for me, until I have the Emperor's own order, there shall always be the sword of Etienne Gerard between his enemies and himself.'

I was so moved by my own words and by the fine position which I had taken up, that my voice broke, and I could hardly refrain from tears. I should have liked the whole army to have seen me as I stood with my head so proudly erect and my hand upon my heart proclaiming my devotion to the Emperor in his adversity. It was one of the supreme moments of my life.

'Very good,' said Berthier, ringing a bell for the lackey. 'You will show the Chief of Brigade Gerard into the salon.'

The footman led me into an inner room, where he desired me to be seated. For my own part, my only desire was to get away, and I could not understand why they should wish to detain me. When one has had no change of uniform during a whole winter's campaign, one does not feel at home in a palace.

I had been there about a quarter of an hour when the footman opened the door again, and in came Colonel Despienne. Good heavens, what a sight he was! His face was as white as a guardsman's gaiters, his eyes projecting, the veins swollen upon his forehead, and every hair of his moustache bristling like those of an angry cat. He was too angry to speak, and could only shake his hands at the ceiling and make a gurgling in his throat. 'Parricide! Viper!' those were the words that I could catch as he stamped up and down the room.

Of course it was evident to me that he had been subjected to the same infamous proposals as I had, and that he had received them in the same spirit. His lips were sealed to me, as mine were to him, by the promise which we had taken, but I contented myself with muttering 'Atrocious! Unspeakable!' — so that he might know that I was in agreement with him.

Well, we were still there, he striding furiously up and down, and I seated in the corner, when suddenly a most extraordinary uproar broke out in the room which we had just quitted. There was a snarling, worrying growl, like that of a fierce dog which has got his grip. Then came a crash and a voice calling for help. In we rushed, the two of us, and, my faith, we were none too soon.

Old Tremeau and Berthier were rolling together upon the floor, with the table upon the top of them. The Captain had one of his great, skinny yellow hands upon the Marshal's throat, and already his face was lead-coloured, and his eyes were starting from their sockets. As to Tremeau, he was beside himself, with foam upon the corners of his lips, and such a frantic expression upon him that I am convinced, had we not loosened his iron grip, finger by finger, that it would never have relaxed while the Marshal lived. His nails were white with the power of his grasp.

'I have been tempted by the devil!' he cried, as he staggered to his feet. 'Yes, I have been tempted by the devil!'

As to Berthier, he could only lean against the wall, and pant for a couple of minutes, putting his hands up to his throat and rolling his head about. Then, with an angry gesture, he turned to the heavy blue curtain which hung behind his chair.

The curtain was torn to one side and the Emperor stepped out into the room. We sprang to the salute, we three old soldiers, but it was all like a scene in a dream to us, and our eyes were as far out as Berthier's had been. Napoleon was dressed in his green-coated chasseur uniform, and he held his little, silver-headed switch in his hand. He looked at us each in turn, with a smile upon his face — that frightful smile in which neither eyes nor brow joined — and each in turn had, I believe, a pringling on his skin, for that was the effect which the Emperor's gaze had upon most of us. Then he walked across to Berthier and put his hand upon his shoulder.

'You must not quarrel with blows, my dear Prince,' said he; 'they are your title to nobility.' He spoke in that soft, caressing manner which he could assume. There was no one who could make the French tongue sound so pretty as the Emperor, and no one who could make it more harsh and terrible.

'I believe he would have killed me,' cried Berthier, still rolling his head about.

'Tut, tut! I should have come to your help had these officers not heard your cries. But I trust that you are not really hurt!' He spoke with earnestness, for he was in truth very fond of Berthier — more so than of any man, unless it were of poor Duroc.

Berthier laughed, though not with a very good grace.

'It is new for me to receive my injuries from French hands,' said he.

'And yet it was in the cause of France,' returned the Emperor. Then, turning to us, he took old Tremeau by the ear. 'Ah, old grumbler,' said he, 'you were one of my Egyptian grenadiers, were you not, and had your musket of honour at Marengo. I remember you very well, my good friend. So the old fires are not yet extinguished! They still burn up when you think that your Emperor is wronged. And you, Colonel Despienne, you would not even listen to the tempter. And you, Gerard, your faithful sword is ever to be between me and my enemies. Well, well, I have had some traitors about me, but now at last we are beginning to see who are the true men.'

You can fancy, my friends, the thrill of joy which it gave us when the greatest man in the whole world spoke to us in this fashion. Tremeau shook until I thought he would have fallen, and the tears ran down his gigantic moustache. If you had not seen it, you could never believe the influence which the Emperor had upon those coarse-grained, savage old veterans.

'Well, my faithful friends,' said he, 'if you will follow me into this room, I will explain to you the meaning of this little farce which we have been acting. I beg, Berthier, that you will remain in this chamber, and so make sure that no one interrupts us.'

It was new for us to be doing business, with

a Marshal of France as sentry at the door. However, we followed the Emperor as we were ordered, and he led us into the recess of the window, gathering us around him and sinking his voice as he addressed us.

'I have picked you out of the whole army,' said he, 'as being not only the most formidable but also the most faithful of my soldiers. I was convinced that you were all three men who would never waver in your fidelity to me. If I have ventured to put that fidelity to the proof, and to watch you while attempts were at my orders made upon your honour, it was only because, in the days when I have found the blackest treason amongst my own flesh and blood, it is necessary that I should be doubly circumspect. Suffice it that I am well convinced now that I can rely upon your valour.'

'To the death, sire!' cried Tremeau, and we both repeated it after him.

Napoleon drew us all yet a little closer to him, and sank his voice still lower.

'What I say to you now I have said to no one — not to my wife or my brothers; only to you. It is all up with us, my friends. We have come to our last rally. The game is finished, and we must make provision accordingly.'

My heart seemed to have changed to a nine-pounder ball as I listened to him. We had hoped against hope, but now when he, the man who was always serene and who always had reserves — when he, in that quiet, impassive voice of his, said that everything was over, we realized that the clouds had shut for ever, and the last gleam gone. Tremeau snarled and gripped at his sabre, Despienne ground his teeth, and for my own part I threw out my chest and clicked my heels to show the Emperor that there were some spirits which could rise to adversity.

'My papers and my fortune must be secured,' whispered the Emperor. 'The whole course of the future may depend upon my having them safe. They are our base for the next attempt — for I am very sure that these poor Bourbons would find that my footstool is too large to make a throne for them. Where am I to keep these precious things? My belongings will be searched — so will the houses of my supporters. They must be secured and concealed by men whom I can trust with that which is more precious to me than my life. Out of the whole of France, you are those whom I have chosen for this sacred trust.

'In the first place, I will tell you what these papers are. You shall not say that I have made you blind agents in the matter. They are the official proof of my divorce from Josephine, of my legal marriage to Marie Louise, and of the birth of my son and heir, the King of Rome. If we cannot prove each of these, the future claim of my family to the throne of France falls to the ground. Then there are securities to the value of forty millions of francs — an immense sum, my friends, but of no more value than this riding-switch when compared to the other papers of which I have spoken. I tell you these things that you may realize the enormous importance of the task which I am committing to your care. Listen, now, while I inform you where you are to get these papers, and what you are to do with them.

'They were handed over to my trusty friend, the Countess Walewski, at Paris, this morning. At five o'clock she starts for Fontainebleau in her blue berline. She should reach here between half-past nine and ten. The papers will be concealed in the berline, in a hiding-place which none know but herself. She has been warned that her carriage will be stopped outside the town by three mounted officers, and she will hand the packet over to your care. You are the younger man, Gerard, but you are of the senior grade. I confide to your care this amethyst ring, which you will show the lady as a token of your mission, and which you will leave with her as a receipt for her papers.

'Having received the packet, you will ride with it into the forest as far as the ruined dove-house — the Colombier. It is possible that I may meet you there — but if it seems to me to be dangerous, I will send my body-servant, Mustapha, whose directions you may take as being mine. There is no roof to the Colombier, and tonight will be a full moon. At the right of the entrance you will find three spades leaning against the wall. With these you will dig a hole three feet deep in the north-eastern corner — that is, in the corner to the left of the door, and nearest to Fontainebleau. Having buried the papers, you will replace the soil with great care, and you will then report to me at the palace.'

These were the Emperor's directions, but given with an accuracy and minuteness of detail such as no one but himself could put into an order. When he had finished, he made us swear to keep his secret as long as he lived, and as long as the papers should remain buried. Again and again he made us swear it before he dismissed us from his presence.

Colonel Despienne had quarters at the 'Sign of the Pheasant,' and it was there that we supped together. We were all three men who had been trained to take the strangest turns of fortune as part of our daily life and business, yet we were all flushed and moved by the extraordinary interview which we had had, and by the thought of the great adventure which lay before us. For my own part, it had been my fate three several times to take my orders from the lips of the Emperor himself, but neither the incident of the Ajaccio murderers nor the famous ride which I made to Paris appeared to offer such opportunities as this new and most intimate commission.

'If things go right with the Emperor,' said Despienne, 'we shall all live to be marshals yet.'

We drank with him to our future cocked hats and our bâtons.

It was agreed between us that we should make our way separately to our rendezvous, which was to be the first mile-stone upon the Paris road. In this way we should avoid the gossip which might get about if three men who were so well known were to be seen riding out together. My little Violette had cast a shoe that morning, and the farrier was at work upon her when I returned, so that my comrades were already there when I arrived at the trysting-place. I had taken with me not only my sabre, but also my new pair of English rifled pistols, with a mallet for knocking in the charges. They had cost me a hundred and fifty francs at Trouvel's, in the

Rue de Rivoli, but they would carry far further and straighter than the others. It was with one of them that I had saved old Bouvet's life at Leipzig.

The night was cloudless, and there was a brilliant moon behind us, so that we always had three black horsemen riding down the white road in front of us. The country is so thickly wooded, however, that we could not see very far. The great palace clock had already struck ten, but there was no sign of the Countess. We began to fear that something might have prevented her from starting.

And then suddenly we heard her in the distance. Very faint at first were the birr of wheels and the tat-tat-tat of the horses' feet. Then they grew louder and clearer and louder yet, until a pair of yellow lanterns swung round the curve, and in their light we saw the two big brown horses tearing along the high, blue carriage at the back of them. The postilion pulled them up panting and foaming within a few yards of us. In a moment we were at the window and had raised our hands in a salute to the beautiful pale face which looked out at us.

'We are the three officers of the Emperor, madame,' said I, in a low voice, leaning my face down to the open window. 'You have already been warned that we should wait upon you.'

The Countess had a very beautiful, cream-tinted complexion of a sort which I particularly admire, but she grew whiter and whiter as she looked up at me. Harsh lines deepened upon her face until she seemed, even as I looked at her, to turn from youth into age.

'It is evident to me,' she said, 'that you are three impostors.'

If she had struck me across the face with her delicate hand she could not have startled me more. It was not her words only, but the bitterness with which she hissed them out.

'Indeed, madame,' said I. 'You do us less than justice. These are the Colonel Despienne and Captain Tremeau. For myself, my name is Brigadier Gerard, and I have only to mention it to assure anyone who has heard of me that — '

'Oh, you villains!' she interrupted. 'You think that because I am only a woman I am very easily to be hoodwinked! You miserable impostors!'

I looked at Despienne, who had turned white with anger, and at Tremeau, who was tugging at his moustache.

'Madame,' said I, coldly, 'when the Emperor did us the honour to intrust us with this mission, he gave me this amethyst ring as a token. I had not thought that three honourable gentlemen would have needed such corroboration, but I can only confute your unworthy suspicions by placing it in your hands.'

She held it up in the light of the carriage lamp, and the most dreadful expression of grief and of horror contorted her face.

'It is his!' she screamed, and then, 'Oh, my God, what have I done? What have I done?'

I felt that something terrible had befallen. 'Quick, madame, quick!' I cried. 'Give us the papers!'

'I have already given them.'

'Given them! To whom?'

'To three officers.'

'When?'

'Within the half-hour.'

'Where are they?'

'God help me, I do not know. They stopped the berline, and I handed them over to them without hesitation, thinking that they had come from the Emperor.'

It was a thunder-clap. But those are the moments when I am at my finest.

'You remain here,' said I, to my comrades. 'If three horsemen pass you, stop them at any hazard. The lady will describe them to you. I will be with you presently.' One shake of the bridle, and I was flying into Fontainebleau as only Violette could have carried me. At the palace I flung myself off, rushed up the stairs, brushed aside the lackeys who would have stopped me, and pushed my way into the Emperor's own cabinet. He and Macdonald were busy with pencil and compasses over a chart. He looked up with an angry frown at my sudden entry, but his face changed colour when he saw that it was I.

'You can leave us, Marshal,' said he, and then, the instant the door was closed: 'What news about the papers?'

'They are gone!' said I, and in a few curt words I told him what had happened. His face was calm, but I saw the compasses quiver in his hand.

'You must recover them, Gerard!' he cried. 'The destinies of my dynasty are at stake. Not a moment is to be lost! To horse, sir, to horse!'

'Who are they, sire?'

'I cannot tell. I am surrounded with treason. But they will take them to Paris. To whom should they carry them but to the villain Talleyrand? Yes, yes, they are on the Paris road, and may yet be overtaken. With the three best mounts in my stables and — '

I did not wait to hear the end of the sentence. I was already clattering down the stairs. I am sure that five minutes had not passed before I was galloping Violette out of the town with the bridle of one of the Emperor's own Arab chargers in either hand. They wished me to take three, but I should have never dared to look my Violette in the face again. I feel that the spectacle must have been superb when I dashed up to my comrades and pulled the horses on to their haunches in the moonlight.

'No one has passed?'

'No one.'

'Then they are on the Paris road. Quick! Up and after them!'

They did not take long, those good soldiers. In a flash they were upon the Emperor's horses, and their own left masterless by the roadside. Then away we went upon our long chase, I in the centre, Despienne upon my right, and Tremeau a little behind, for he was the heavier man. Heavens, how we galloped! The twelve flying hoofs roared and roared along the hard, smooth road. Poplars and moon, black bars and silver streaks, for mile after mile our course lay along the same chequered track, with our shadows in front and our dust behind. We could hear the rasping of bolts and the creaking of shutters from the cottages as we thundered past them, but we were only three dark blurs upon the road by the time that the folk could look after us. It was just striking midnight as we raced into Corbail; but an hostler with a bucket in either hand was throwing his black shadow across the golden fan which was cast from the open door of the inn.

'Three riders!' I gasped. 'Have they passed?'

'I have just been watering their horses,' said he. 'I should think they — '

'On, on, my friends!' and away we flew, striking fire from the cobblestones of the little town. A gendarme tried to stop us, but his voice was drowned by our rattle and clatter. The houses slid past, and we were out on the country road again, with a clear twenty miles between ourselves and Paris. How could they escape us, with the finest horses in France behind them? Not one of the three had turned a hair, but Violette was always a head and shoulders to the front. She was going within herself too, and I knew by the spring of her that I had only to let her stretch herself, and the Emperor's horses would see the colour of her tail.

'There they are!' cried Despienne.

'We have them!' growled Tremeau.

'On, comrades, on!' I shouted, once more.

A long stretch of white road lay before us

in the moonlight. Far away down it we could see three cavaliers, lying low upon their horses' necks. Every instant they grew larger and clearer as we gained upon them. I could see quite plainly that the two upon either side were wrapped in mantles and rode upon chestnut horses, whilst the man between them was dressed in a chasseur uniform and mounted upon a grey. They were keeping abreast, but it was easy enough to see from the way in which he gathered his legs for each spring that the centre horse was far the fresher of the three. And the rider appeared to be the leader of the party, for we continually saw the glint of his face in the moonshine as he looked back to measure the distance between us. At first it was only a glimmer, then it was cut across with a moustache, and at last when we began to feel their dust in our throats I could give a name to my man.

'Halt, Colonel de Montluc!' I shouted. 'Halt, in the Emperor's name!'

I had known him for years as a daring officer and an unprincipled rascal. Indeed, there was a score between us, for he had shot my friend, Treville, at Warsaw, pulling his trigger, as some said, a good second before the drop of the handkerchief.

Well, the words were hardly out of my

mouth when his two comrades wheeled round and fired their pistols at us. I heard Despienne give a terrible cry, and at the same instant both Tremeau and I let drive at the same man. He fell forward with his hands swinging on each side of his horse's neck. His comrade spurred on to Tremeau, sabre in hand, and I heard the crash which comes when a strong cut is met by a stronger parry. For my own part I never turned my head, but I touched Violette with the spur for the first time and flew after the leader. That he should leave his comrades and fly was proof enough that I should leave mine and follow.

He had gained a couple of hundred paces, but the good little mare set that right before we could have passed two milestones. It was in vain that he spurred and thrashed like a gunner driver on a soft road. His hat flew off with his exertions, and his bald head gleamed in the moonshine. But do what he might, he still heard the rattle of the hoofs growing louder and louder behind him. I could not have been twenty yards from him, and the shadow head was touching the shadow haunch, when he turned with a curse in his saddle and emptied both his pistols, one after the other, into Violette.

I have been wounded myself so often that I have to stop and think before I can tell you the exact number of times. I have been hit by musket balls, by pistol bullets, and by bursting shells, besides being pierced by bayonet, lance, sabre, and finally by a brad-awl, which was the most painful of any. Yet out of all these injuries I have never known the same deadly sickness as came over me when I felt the poor, silent, patient creature, which I had come to love more than anything in the world except my mother and the Emperor, reel and stagger beneath me. I pulled my second pistol from my holster and fired point-blank between the fellow's broad shoulders. He slashed his horse across the flank with his whip, and for a moment I thought that I had missed him. But then on the green of his chasseur jacket I saw an ever-widening black smudge, and he began to sway in his saddle, very slightly at first, but more and more with every bound, until at last over he went, with his foot caught in the stirrup, and his shoulders thud-thud-thudding along the road, until the drag was too much for the tired horse, and I closed my hand upon the foam-spattered bridle-chain. As I pulled him up it eased the stirrup leather, and the spurred heel clinked loudly as it fell.

'Your papers!' I cried, springing from my saddle. 'This instant!'

But even as I said, it, the huddle of the green body and the fantastic sprawl of the limbs in the moonlight told me clearly enough that it was all over with him. My bullet had passed through his heart, and it was only his own iron will which had held him so long in the saddle. He had lived hard, this Montluc, and I will do him justice to say that he died hard also.

But it was the papers — always the papers — of which I thought. I opened his tunic and I felt in his shirt. Then I searched his holsters and his sabre-tasche. Finally I dragged off his boots, and undid his horse's girth so as to hunt under the saddle. There was not a nook or crevice which I did not ransack. It was useless. They were not upon him.

When this stunning blow came upon me I could have sat down by the roadside and wept. Fate seemed to be fighting against me, and that is an enemy from whom even a gallant hussar might not be ashamed to flinch. I stood with my arm over the neck of my poor wounded Violette, and I tried to think it all out, that I might act in the wisest way. I was aware that the Emperor had no great respect for my wits, and I longed to show him that he had done me an injustice. Montluc had not the papers. And yet Montluc had sacrificed his companions in order to make his escape. I could make nothing of that. On the other hand, it was clear that, if he had not got them, one or other of his comrades had. One of them was certainly dead. The other I had left fighting with Tremeau, and if he escaped from the old swordsman he had still to pass me. Clearly, my work lay behind me.

I hammered fresh charges into my pistols after I had turned this over in my head. Then I put them back in the holsters, and I examined my little mare, she jerking her head and cocking her ears the while, as if to tell me that an old soldier like herself did not make a fuss about a scratch or two. The first shot had merely grazed her off-shoulder, leaving a skin-mark, as if she had brushed a wall. The second was more serious. It had passed through the muscle of her neck, but already it had ceased to bleed. I reflected that if she weakened I could mount Montluc's grey, and meanwhile I led him along beside us, for he was a fine horse, worth fifteen hundred francs at the least, and it seemed to me that no one had a better right to him than I.

Well, I was all impatience now to get back to the others, and I had just given Violette her head, when suddenly I saw something glimmering in a field by the roadside. It was the brass-work upon the chasseur hat which had flown from Montluc's head; and at the sight of it a thought made me jump in the saddle. How could the hat have flown off? With its weight, would it not have simply dropped? And here it lay, fifteen paces from the roadway! Of course, he must have thrown it off when he had made sure that I would overtake him. And if he threw it off — I did not stop to reason any more, but sprang from the mare with my heart beating the *pas-de-charge*. Yes, it was all right this time. There, in the crown of the hat was stuffed a roll of papers in a parchment wrapper bound round with yellow ribbon. I pulled it out with the one hand and, holding the hat in the other, I danced for joy in the moonlight. The Emperor would see that he had not made a mistake when he put his affairs into the charge of Etienne Gerard.

I had a safe pocket on the inside of my tunic just over my heart, where I kept a few little things which were dear to me, and into this I thrust my precious roll. Then I sprang upon Violette, and was pushing forward to see what had become of Tremeau, when I saw a horseman riding across the field in the distance. At the same instant I heard the sound of hoofs approaching me, and there in the moonlight was the Emperor upon his white charger, dressed in his grey overcoat and his three-cornered hat, just as I had seen him so often upon the field of battle.

'Well!' he cried, in the sharp, sergeant-major way of his. 'Where are my papers?'

I spurred forward and presented them without a word. He broke the ribbon and ran his eyes rapidly over them. Then, as we sat our horses head to tail, he threw his left arm across me with his hand upon my shoulder. Yes, my friends, simple as you see me, I have been embraced by my great master.

'Gerard,' he cried, 'you are a marvel!'

I did not wish to contradict him, and it brought a flush of joy upon my cheeks to know that he had done me justice at last.

'Where is the thief, Gerard?' he asked.

'Dead, sire.'

'You killed him?'

'He wounded my horse, sire, and would have escaped had I not shot him.'

'Did you recognize him?'

'De Montluc is his name, sire — a Colonel of Chasseurs.'

'Tut,' said the Emperor. 'We have got the poor pawn, but the hand which plays the game is still out of our reach.' He sat in silent thought for a little, with his chin sunk upon his chest. 'Ah, Talleyrand, Talleyrand,' I heard him mutter, 'if I had been in your place and you in mine, you would have crushed a viper when you held it under your heel. For five years I have known you for what you are, and yet I have let you live to sting me. Never mind, my brave,' he continued, turning to me, 'there will come a day of reckoning for everybody, and when it arrives, I promise you that my friends will be remembered as well as my enemies.'

'Sire,' said I, for I had had time for thought as well as he, 'if your plans about these papers have been carried to the ears of your enemies, I trust you do not think that it was owing to any indiscretion upon the part of myself or of my comrades.'

'It would be hardly reasonable for me to do so,' he answered, 'seeing that this plot was hatched in Paris, and that you only had your orders a few hours ago.'

'Then how — ?'

'Enough,' he cried, sternly. 'You take an undue advantage of your position.'

That was always the way with the Emperor. He would chat with you as with a friend and a brother, and then when he had wiled you into forgetting the gulf which lay between you, he would suddenly, with a word or with a look, remind you that it was as impassable as ever. When I have fondled my old hound until he has been encouraged to paw my knees, and I have then thrust him down again, it has made me think of the Emperor and his ways.

He reined his horse round, and I followed him in silence and with a heavy heart. But when he spoke again his words were enough to drive all thought of myself out of my mind.

'I could not sleep until I knew how you had fared,' said he. 'I have paid a price for my papers. There are not so many of my old soldiers left that I can afford to lose two in one night.'

When he said 'two' it turned me cold.

'Colonel Despienne was shot, sire,' I stammered.

'And Captain Tremeau cut down. Had I been a few minutes earlier, I might have saved him. The other escaped across the fields.'

I remembered that I had seen a horseman a moment before I had met the Emperor. He had taken to the fields to avoid me, but if I had known, and Violette been unwounded, the old soldier would not have gone unavenged. I was thinking sadly of his sword-play, and wondering whether it was his stiffening wrist which had been fatal to him, when Napoleon spoke again.

'Yes, Brigadier,' said he, 'you are now the only man who will know where these papers are concealed.'

It must have been imagination, my friends,

but for an instant I may confess that it seemed to me that there was a tone in the Emperor's voice which was not altogether one of sorrow. But the dark thought had hardly time to form itself in my mind before he let me see that I was doing him an injustice.

'Yes, I have paid a price for my papers,' he said, and I heard them crackle as he put his hand up to his bosom. 'No man has ever had more faithful servants — no man since the beginning of the world.'

As he spoke we came upon the scene of the struggle. Colonel Despienne and the man whom we had shot lay together some distance down the road, while their horses grazed contentedly beneath the poplars. Captain Tremeau lay in front of us upon his back, with his arms and legs stretched out, and his sabre broken short off in his hand. His tunic was open, and a huge blood-clot hung like a dark handkerchief out of a slit in his white shirt. I could see the gleam of his clenched teeth from under his immense moustache.

The Emperor sprang from his horse and bent down over the dead man.

'He was with me since Rivoli,' said he, sadly. 'He was one of my old grumblers in Egypt.'

And the voice brought the man back from

the dead. I saw his eyelids shiver. He twitched his arm, and moved the sword-hilt a few inches. He was trying to raise it in salute. Then the mouth opened, and the hilt tinkled down on to the ground.

'May we all die as gallantly,' said the Emperor, as he rose, and from my heart I added 'Amen.'

There was a farm within fifty yards of where we were standing, and the farmer, roused from his sleep by the clatter of hoofs and the cracking of pistols, had rushed out to the roadside. We saw him now, dumb with fear and astonishment, staring open-eyed at the Emperor. It was to him that we committed the care of the four dead men and of the horses also. For my own part, I thought it best to leave Violette with him and to take De Montluc's grey with me, for he could not refuse to give me back my own mare, whilst there might be difficulties about the other. Besides, my little friend's wound had to be considered, and we had a long return ride before us.

The Emperor did not at first talk much upon the way. Perhaps the deaths of Despienne and Tremeau still weighed heavily upon his spirits. He was always a reserved man, and in those times, when every hour brought him the news of some success of his enemies or defection of his friends, one could not expect him to be a merry companion. Nevertheless, when I reflected that he was carrying in his bosom those papers which he valued so highly, and which only a few hours ago appeared to be for ever lost, and when I further thought that it was I, Etienne Gerard, who had placed them there, I felt that I had deserved some little consideration. The same idea may have occurred to him, for when we had at last left the Paris high road, and had entered the forest, he began of his own accord to tell me that which I should have most liked to have asked him.

'As to the papers,' said he, 'I have already told you that there is no one now, except you and me, who knows where they are to be concealed. My Mameluke carried the spades to the pigeon-house, but I have told him nothing. Our plans, however, for bringing the packet from Paris have been formed since Monday. There were three in the secret, a woman and two men. The woman I would trust with my life; which of the two men has betrayed us I do not know, but I think that I may promise to find out.'

We were riding in the shadow of the trees at the time, and I could hear him slapping his riding-whip against his boot, and taking pinch after pinch of snuff, as was his way when he was excited.

'You wonder, no doubt,' said he, after a pause, 'why these rascals did not stop the carriage at Paris instead of at the entrance to Fontainebleau.'

In truth, the objection had not occurred to me, but I did not wish to appear to have less wits than he gave me credit for, so I answered that it was indeed surprising.

'Had they done so they would have made a public scandal, and run a chance of missing their end. Short of taking the berline to pieces, they could not have discovered the hiding-place. He planned it well — he could always plan well — and he chose his agents well also. But mine were the better.'

It is not for me to repeat to you, my friends, all that was said to me by the Emperor as we walked our horses amid the black shadows and through the moon-silvered glades of the great forest. Every word of it is impressed upon my memory, and before I pass away it is likely that I will place it all upon paper, so that others may read it in the days to come. He spoke freely of his past, and something also of his future; of the devotion of Macdonald, of the treason of Marmont, of the little King of Rome, concerning whom he talked with as much tenderness as any bourgeois father of a single child; and, finally, of his father-in-law, the Emperor of Austria, who would, he thought, stand between his enemies and himself. For myself, I dared not say a word, remembering how I had already brought a rebuke upon myself; but I rode by his side, hardly able to believe that this was indeed the great Emperor, the man whose glance sent a thrill through me, who was now pouring out his thoughts to me in short, eager sentences, the words rattling and racing like the hoofs of a galloping squadron. It is possible that, after the word-splittings and diplomacy of a Court, it was a relief to him to speak his mind to a plain soldier like myself.

In this way the Emperor and I — even after years it sends a flush of pride into my cheeks to be able to put those words together — the Emperor and I walked our horses through the Forest of Fontainebleau, until we came at last to the Colombier. The three spades were propped against the wall upon the right-hand side of the ruined door, and at the sight of them the tears sprang to my eyes as I thought of the hands for which they were intended. The Emperor seized one and I another.

'Quick!' said he. 'The dawn will be upon us before we get back to the palace.'

We dug the hole, and placing the papers in one of my pistol holsters to screen them from the damp, we laid them at the bottom and covered them up. We then carefully removed all marks of the ground having been disturbed, and we placed a large stone upon the top. I dare say that since the Emperor was a young gunner, and helped to train his pieces against Toulon, he had not worked so hard with his hands. He was mopping his forehead with his silk handkerchief long before we had come to the end of our task.

The first grey cold light of morning was stealing through the tree trunks when we came out together from the old pigeon-house. The Emperor laid his hand upon my shoulder as I stood ready to help him to mount.

'We have left the papers there,' said he, solemnly, 'and I desire that you shall leave all thought of them there also. Let the recollection of them pass entirely from your mind, to be revived only when you receive a direct order under my own hand and seal. From this time onwards you forget all that has passed.'

'I forget it, sire,' said I.

We rode together to the edge of the town, where he desired that I should separate from him. I had saluted, and was turning my horse, when he called me back.

'It is easy to mistake the points of the compass in the forest,' said he. 'Would you not say that it was in the north-eastern corner that we buried them?'

'Buried what, sire?'

'The papers, of course,' he cried, impatiently.

'What papers, sire?'

'Name of a name! Why, the papers that you have recovered for me.'

'I am really at a loss to know what your Majesty is talking about.'

He flushed with anger for a moment, and then he burst out laughing.

'Very good, Brigadier!' he cried. 'I begin to believe that you are as good a diplomatist as you are a soldier, and I cannot say more than that.'

* * *

So that was my strange adventure in which I found myself the friend and confident agent of the Emperor. When he returned from Elba he refrained from digging up the papers until his position should be secure, and they still remained in the corner of the old pigeon-house after his exile to St Helena. It was at this time that he was desirous of getting them into the hands of his own supporters, and for that purpose he wrote me, as I afterwards learned, three letters, all of which were intercepted by his guardians. Finally, he offered to support himself and his own establishment — which he might very easily have done out of the gigantic sum which belonged to him — if they would only pass one of his letters unopened. This request was refused, and so, up to his death in '21, the papers still remained where I have told you. How they came to be dug up by Count Bertrand and myself, and who eventually obtained them, is a story which I would tell you, were it not that the end has not yet come.

Some day you will hear of those papers, and you will see how, after he has been so long in his grave, that great man can still set Europe shaking. When that day comes, you will think of Etienne Gerard, and you will tell your children that you have heard the story from the lips of the man who was the only one living of all who took part in that strange history — the man who was tempted by Marshal Berthier, who led that wild pursuit upon the Paris road, who was honoured by the embrace of the Emperor, and who rode with him by moonlight in the Forest of Fontainebleau. The buds are bursting and the birds are calling, my friends. You may find better things to do in the sunlight than listening to the stories of an old, broken soldier. And yet you may well treasure what I say, for the buds will have burst and the birds sung in many seasons before France will see such another ruler as he whose servants we were proud to be.

THE END

We do hope that you have enjoyed reading this large print book.

Did you know that all of our titles are available for purchase?

We publish a wide range of high quality large print books including:
Romances, Mysteries, Classics
General Fiction
Non Fiction and Westerns

Special interest titles available in large print are:
The Little Oxford Dictionary
Music Book
Song Book
Hymn Book
Service Book

Also available from us courtesy of Oxford University Press:
Young Readers' Dictionary
(large print edition)
Young Readers' Thesaurus
(large print edition)

For further information or a free brochure, please contact us at:
Ulverscroft Large Print Books Ltd.,
The Green, Bradgate Road, Anstey,
Leicester, LE7 7FU, England.
Tel: (00 44) 0116 236 4325
Fax: (00 44) 0116 234 0205

Other titles published by
The House of Ulverscroft:

**THE CASE BOOK OF
SHERLOCK HOLMES**

Sir Arthur Conan Doyle

These stories include *The Adventure of The Illustrious Client*: a young lady appears to be in danger when Holmes is handed a note from Sir James Damery informing him that Baron Gruner is engaged to be married — and Holmes suspects that Gruner murdered his last wife . . . Then we find that Holmes has retired to the Sussex Downs, in *The Adventure of The Lion's Mane*. Out walking, he spots Fitzroy McPherson, a keen athlete, who staggers into view and collapses. His last words are 'the lion's mane', and his back bears the marks of someone who has been flogged . . .

HIS LAST BOW

Sir Arthur Conan Doyle

In *The Adventure of Wisteria Lodge,* Holmes is visited by a perturbed, proper, English gentleman, John Scott Eccles. He's immediately followed by Inspector Baynes, who questions him regarding the murder of Aloysius Garcia at Wisteria Lodge the previous night . . . Consequently, in *The Tiger of San Pedro,* a country house owner is discovered to have been a feared and hated dictator. Whilst in *The Adventure of The Dying Detective,* a small ivory box is significant when Holmes lies gravely ill in bed, and dying . . .

THE VALLEY OF FEAR

Sir Arthur Conan Doyle

In *The Tragedy of Birlstone* ,Holmes receives a coded message, from Porlock, 'the weak link in a chain leading to the controlling brain of the underworld' — Professor Moriarty. Holmes and Watson decipher the message as indicating that a man named Douglas, residing at Birlstone, is in danger. Then, assisting Inspector MacDonald of Scotland Yard, Holmes learns that Mr Douglas of Birlstone Manor has been murdered — however, the body belongs to another man. Then we read, in *The Scowrers*, the intriguing account of the man whose body it should have been . . .

THE RETURN OF SHERLOCK HOLMES

Sir Arthur Conan Doyle

The Return of Sherlock Holmes relates several of Holmes' adventures where he confronts many an odious character . . . The eponymous blackmail artist in *The Adventure of Charles Augustus Milverton*, is requested to call at 221B Baker Street, where we find that Holmes has been hired by Lady Eva Blackwell to retrieve some compromising letters . . . And in *The Adventure of The Golden Pince-Nez*, Inspector Stanley Hopkins visits Holmes and tells him of the murder of Willoughby Smith, where the victim had not an enemy in the world and there seems to be no apparent motive. A perplexing case which defies solution . . .